FINDING FAITH

BLOW HOLE BOYS #2

TABATHA VARGO

FINDING FAITH

Finding Faith/Tabatha Vargo

Editing services provided by Cassie McCown/Gathering Leaves.

Cover Art by Regina Wamba/Mae I Design and Photography

ISBN-13: 978-1493576746

ISBN-10: 1493576747

Also by Tabatha Vargo

The Chubby Girl Chronicles

On the Plus Side

Hot and Heavy-Coming Soon!

The Blow Hole Boys

Playing Patience (Zeke)

Perfecting Patience 1.5 (Zeke)

Finding Faith (Finn)

Convincing Constance (Tiny)-Coming Soon!

Having Hope (Chet)-Coming Soon!

www.tabathavargo.blogspot.com

www.facebook.com/tabathadvargo

www.twitter.com/tabathavargo

For Matthew.

I love you.

Prologue

Faith... sometimes it's passionate and fleeting. One minute you're swimming in it, diving into the deepest recesses of the one you worship. You bathe in their heat as their healing presence swarms all around you and builds an almost unbreakable devotion.

You believe in them, trust and rely on them blindly, knowing that if you fall, their loyal hands will catch you. You're convicted, so strongly dedicated to them that the rest of your world falls to the background and there is only their grace.

And the next minute, your reverence has broken apart, exposing breath and bone. Bringing you down and leaving you faithless in all things that once held purpose and hope. Beliefs unbind and all you can do is hold on to the memories of when you felt savored and whole.

I was once faithless. Believing only in myself and the things that I could touch with my two hands, but then love took up residence in my heart and stole my soul. Something bloomed inside of me that lacked explanation and reason and I nourished it, believing with that love, all things were possible. I prospered, held strong with just a promise of desire's sweet breaths.

And then I was abandoned and there was nothing.

Passion and desire desert you and you find that Faith, however tainted and brief, has changed you, reshaped your DNA and made you someone you never thought you'd be. And then you look back at the one that held your devotion for so long, and you find she's not rapture in soft pink, but a demon with creamy skin and endless eyes—endless eyes that I swore would never capture me again.

PART ONE:
YOUNG LOVE

ONE
FAITH

"I blew him," Amanda said loudly.

A girl walking down the hallway looked over at us like we were disgusting. I waited until she was out of earshot to respond.

"What do you mean you 'blew' him? Is that like some sick slang for something sexually disturbing?" I asked, confused.

Amanda's laughter got the attention of everyone around us. The last bell had just rung and the hallways were packed with girls in uniform hustling to get home. Her face was red and tears of laughter ran from her eyes.

"Oh my God, Faith, you crack me up, girl." She wiped the smudged eyeliner from underneath her eyes and took a deep breath.

I had no idea what was so funny, but at that point, I was too embarrassed to ask. I assumed that whatever she was talking about was sexual, and knowing her, it was probably disgusting. I was clueless to stuff like that. Daddy said when the time was right my husband would show me everything I needed to know.

My parents always made sure to keep me in the dark about the opposite sex. I once saw a naked man briefly while I was flipping through the channels. My mom saw it, too, and three days later, my dad had the cable turned off.

Amanda's laughter stopped and her face cleared. "Wait, you really don't know what that means, do you?"

I didn't bother answering. Instead, I put my head down to hide my red cheeks and stuffed my hair behind my ear. I didn't think my face could get any hotter—that is until Amanda took the time to actually explain the ins and outs of oral sex.

I spent the next twenty minutes staring at her like she was the most repulsive person alive as she explained in detail how she'd spent her night with her new boyfriend Kevin. Almost everything I knew about sex, Amanda taught me as she told me about her different boyfriends and what they'd done on their dates.

"That's disgusting." I felt sick to my stomach just hearing about it.

"Actually, it's kind of nice." She shrugged. "I'm sorry I laughed at you. Sometimes I forget your situation."

She reached in and gave me big hug. She knew what my life was like. She'd once had to live the same life before her situation changed.

"Don't worry about it. Sometimes I forget you're finally free." I laughed.

"Free, my ass! Mom's being a total bitch about me using her car for anything. Speaking of, Saturday night movies... yes or no?" Amanda asked as she pulled out her English book and slammed her locker shut.

She ran her fingers through her long blond hair and adjusted her hot-pink purse strap on her shoulder. Her chunky heels clunked against the floor as she waited for my answer. She could always pull off fun clothes like that. Honestly, I had no idea why she was still friends with me.

We'd known each other since we played with baby dolls and wore lacey socks with our Mary Janes. Sadly, on occasion I still wore lacey socks. When we were younger, we were both sheltered and childish, but she grew up and was no longer under her dad's strict thumb since her parents had shocked the church and got a divorce.

Amanda was constantly getting in trouble at school because she loved nothing more than to break the dress code by throwing in a pair of skinny jeans with her button-up top, or better yet, she'd leave too many buttons open, showing entirely too much skin for Principal Lynn.

I adored her, though. She kept me feeling alive, even if she didn't know it.

"I don't know. Maybe." I shrugged.

"You never do anything with us," she whined.

"I know, but—"

"But nothing. Look, I get the whole strict dad thing. I mean, seriously, look who you're talking to here, but you can sneak out. It's kind of a rite of passage for girls our age. Come on, Faith, please. You only live once and, honey, you ain't living."

My dad once told me that Amanda was a bad influence. I didn't tell him, but that was one of the main reasons I spent so much time with her. I never stepped out of line and living vicariously through her made staying in line more tolerable.

"I can't. If I could I would, but I really can't. I have church Sunday morning and if I'm out too late on Saturday, I'll never get up on time."

She rolled her green eyes and exhaled loudly. It wasn't technically a lie. I *would* be tired if I stayed out too late, but she knew the real reason I wouldn't go and it had nothing to do with me and everything to do with my dad. She'd seen him beat me once when we were nine, but she never spoke of it. Maybe she thought I didn't get beatings anymore now that I was older. She couldn't have been more wrong.

"You go to the church, like, every day. I'm sure God will understand if you miss one day." She adjusted her strap again and blew a stray piece of hair from her eyes. "Just think about it, okay? It could be fun."

Going on a double date with Amanda, her new boyfriend Kevin, and his cousin Tony did sound fun. Everything sounded fun to me since I never did anything but go to school and church. So I did think about it. I thought about it all through dinner that afternoon and when I couldn't think about it anymore, I went for the kill.

"Daddy, is it okay if I go out to a movie with some friends this Saturday night?" I poked at my untouched mashed potatoes and avoided eye contact.

It wasn't an unfair request. Seventeen-year-olds went to the movies all the time, but I knew before I asked that he was going to say no. It never stopped me from trying. One day... one day he'd say yes and I'd have just one night of freedom. All I needed was one night.

"I don't think that's a good idea," He said after he used his cloth napkin to wipe his mouth.

I didn't bother mentioning it again. I'd learned long ago it was futile to argue with a man of God. No matter what I said, he'd have some way to associate my request with Jesus and whether or not he'd approve of my actions. That argument won every time.

Instead, I settled for homework on my older-than-dirt computer. I loved it and hated it. It got me what I needed, but only after taking forever to do so.

An hour later and I still hadn't gotten past my sign-on screen. I was about to throw the computer from the desk when my dad interrupted. "What would Jesus do, Faith?"

Honestly, I hadn't thought about what Jesus would do as I mumbled angry words and smacked at my computer. I had a paper due the following day and my ancient computer and dial-up Internet were making that extremely difficult.

"Sorry, Daddy," I mumbled.

He patted my back as he walked by with his Bible in hand. He'd spent his time after dinner preparing for that night's special sermon. It was more than difficult to focus on studying with him calling out the words of God as if he were already standing behind the pulpit.

"You almost done?" he asked a few minutes later. "Sister Francis asked that we arrive early for tonight. She needs your help preparing for Bible school."

I wasn't even close to being done. "All done." I smiled sweetly.

Daddy always said church came first. God waited for no man. It didn't matter that I had to sit up some nights past my bedtime just to finish a paper.

The church my dad preached at, Riverbank Baptist, was bigger than it used to be. Just a few years before, they'd added on extra rooms to the back, including a small kitchen for when we had big dinners. A simple redbrick building that was older than my grandfather stood tall in the middle of a large patch of grass. A tiny patch of rocks represented the parking lot. About seven cars fit in the space, which meant on rainy days, a lot of people braved muddy shoes for God.

I was raised in Riverbank Baptist. So much time was spent with our church family that I could no longer figure out who was actually a blood relative and who wasn't. All in all, it didn't really matter. Family was family as far as I was concerned.

I met Sister Francis, the Sunday school teacher and possibly my aunt, in the kid's room as soon as we arrived. As her assistant, I was in charge of having worksheets printed out and the snacks ready to go. It didn't take much time, but it was my job. I enjoyed being around all the lively kids. They had spunk and said some pretty bizarre things that made me laugh.

"Thank the Lord you're here. I didn't think I'd get everything done," Sister Francis said as she flittered around the room and prepared for our special Wednesday class.

Her black flats pounded into the old hardwood flooring as she moved around the room to prepare. The edges of her shoes stretched to accommodate her thick ankles. A tiny run in her nude stockings rippled up the back of her knee, allowing her fleshy pale skin to poke out.

As a bigger lady, she was out of breath from all the activity. Her face was flushed, but her graying miniature beehive was still holding strong. Sister Francis had always worn her hair in her signature beehive. I could remember being seven and trying to peek over her nest of hair to get a good look at my daddy as he preached his heart out in front of the congregation.

I spent thirty minutes preparing the room for the kids and then I left and followed the sounds of my father's booming voice as it bounced off the curved ceilings of the chapel. I found myself at the back of the church, staring up at the choir and my daddy, who was blue in the face and shaking his Bible at the crowd. He was a passionate man, but only when it came to God.

Wednesday nights weren't usually as packed as Sundays, but I still didn't want everyone turning and looking back at me. Without wanting to cause a scene, I quickly slid onto the pew in the very back.

Usually, no one sat that far back. On any other day, I'd be sitting on the first pew with my mother, but I'd taken longer in the kids' room than usual. Mainly because I had no desire to listen to my father preach.

The last pew should've been empty. But instead of having an entire row to myself, I slid right into a hard wall of heat. The smell of paint and freshly cut grass filled my nostrils as my cheek met the hot flesh of a man's upper arm.

As I quickly pushed back, my eyes met the jagged design of a black tattoo. It wrapped around the arm in question and worked its way under the white sleeve of his T-shirt. My fear of the unknown kicked in and I slid quickly to the edge of the pew.

It was then that I was met with caramel-colored hair and soft baby-blue eyes. They skimmed my chin and cheeks before colliding with my own. His lips tilted in a grin before he ran his fingers through his hair, turned his attention away from me, and crossed his arms over his chest.

He was leaning back in the pew with his long legs sprawled out in front of him. Chains hug from his right pocket and slid across the shiny wood as he gapped his legs to get comfortable. His jeans were rugged and worn, with holes allowing me to see peeks of the skin and hair around his knees.

My eyes roamed across his strong features. A thin stroke of soft sable hair lined his jaw before bleeding down onto his chin and around his mouth. He bit at his thick lips in boredom, which pulled at the tiny silver stud beneath his bottom lip. Soft evening light spilled in through the stained-glass window and gave his face a red hue. The light flickered off of a piercing in his brow.

I couldn't look away. I'd never before seen anyone like him up close. Every time someone like him even came near, Daddy would pull me to the side and shelter me from anything unbecoming.

Besides, going to an all-girl school meant I rarely saw boys unless they were at the supermarket or church.

He turned toward me again with a raised brow. I was staring and it was rude, but even then I couldn't peel my eyes away.

"I'm not." He grinned down at me.

A dimple deepened on his cheek and another flicker of silver showed inside his mouth when he spoke. Dear God, was he pierced everywhere? I felt my cheeks heat at the unholy thought.

"You're not what?" I whispered.

I don't think I could talk any louder if I tried. It was bred into me to be seen, not heard, especially in church where it mattered most.

His smile widened and I felt my blush rush down my neck. "I'm not the devil."

Swallowing the dry lump in my throat, I shook my head like I understood. "I know."

"Oh really? How can you be sure?" He turned toward me a little more and I saw another tiny tattoo on his other arm.

If only Daddy could see me interacting with such a polluted person.

"Because this is a holy place and sin's not welcomed here."

He laughed quietly to himself and shook his head at me like I was confused. His caramel-colored hair spilled into his humor-filled eyes. For the first time in my life, I had the desire to reach out and touch a stranger. My fingers itched to push the hair from his clear blue eyes. It was a crime for them to be covered.

"What's so funny?" I asked.

"You couldn't be more far off. I'm not the devil, but the fact that I'm sitting here says a lot about your logic. An angel should know the difference between holy and hellfire."

Again, my body lit up with a hot flush.

"I'm no angel."

He reached up and flicked a piece of my thick hair from my face. I pulled back, making him laugh softly to himself.

"If it looks like an angel and talks like an angel, then it must be an angel." He smiled.

Even through his piercings and dark, looming looks, his smile was sweet. I wasn't sure how he was able to do that. Maybe he *was* the devil. I'd been told in life that evil would be a charmer—a rattlesnake masquerading as a prince. I was beginning to think there was some truth in that saying.

I tried to wrap my mind around his words. If it looks like a sinner and talks like a sinner, then it must be a sinner. And one thing I knew about the stranger in front of me was that he was made for sin.

Without another word, he stood, the chain hanging from his pocket clanking and drawing the attention of the entire room. Daddy stopped preaching and his eyes were wide in anger and shock. I expected him to run down the aisle and snatch me up to get me away from the strange boy with the sinister beauty.

He looked down at me and smiled again as he slid against the pew in front of me to get out. The front of his coarse jeans slid across my plain skirt, lifting it and revealing my ankles and white tennis shoes. A cool breeze rushed up my legs and I got chills. I wasn't sure if it was the cool breeze or the boy. Either way, it felt nice.

Ladies in fancy hats watched in disgust as he pushed loudly on the church doors and let dusk and evening air into the room. The doors slammed behind him, blocking out the fresh air and leaving me feeling like I was about to suffocate.

TWO
FINN

Vandalism. That's what I was charged with for being in the wrong place at the wrong time. I had much better things to do with my free time than spray-paint the side of a church. I can't draw for shit. The last thing I'd do is try to paint anything. The designs on the wall of the church were way more advanced in the art department than I could ever be.

No matter how many times I told the judge this, no matter how many times I pled not guilty, he still slapped community service on my ass. The court ordered me to attend that same church for thirty days and help them in any way.

My first day there, a few of the church ladies stared at me like I was Satan himself. Big eyes took me in from underneath flowery hats and thick over-applied eyelashes. I'd never been stared at so much, and that said a lot since I was the front man in a band.

I'm sure the congregation wasn't used to piercings and my few tattoos. I could understand that. Everyone was different, including the holy rollers. Even though I probably looked scary as hell to them, there were still a few that treated me like their long-lost grandson and patted me on the head. I didn't hate that part as much as I should've.

I'd never had a grandma. Don't get me wrong, I'm sure I had one out in the world bouncing around, but I'd never met her. When I thought of having grandparents, I envisioned lots of baked goods and cheek pinches—the smell of mothballs and handmade blankets. Some kids would hate that shit. Cheek pinches or not, having some form of family should be appreciated. I'd appreciate it.

I spent that first day of community service painting over the old red brick that had been destroyed. Luckily, the space wasn't huge and the church planned on having a local artist paint over the beige square I'd painted as a cover.

Once I was done with that, I mowed the front of the church. Cutting grass wasn't anything new for me. My adoptive mom went nuts if the grass got too tall. She was deathly afraid of critters and she swore they lived in tall grass. After having my ass eaten alive while mowing, I had to agree with her.

I pushed the old lawnmower into a little red shed on the side of the church and cleaned up in the bathroom. After helping everywhere they needed me, I took a seat on the last pew and waited until I could leave. The pastor had to sign my community service paper, confirming that I stayed for the entire sermon. I knew it was pointless to get him to sign it so I could leave early. Asking a preacher to lie? Only I would think of something like that.

My eyes rolled back in my head as I tried to stay awake through the preacher's blabbing. The pew was hard against my ass and back and I was getting a kink in my neck from trying to lay my head back against the wood. I prayed silently that it would be over soon, but the preacher continued his rant about Peter. So much for prayer making things happen.

My lashes tickled my cheeks as my eyes fluttered closed once more. The sermon faded to the background and my breathing evened out. Sleep had slowly come to take me away, and I was well on my way when someone bumped into me.

My brain rattled and my teeth clicked. My body jarred to the side and my eyes popped open. The sweet scent of roses filled my senses as warmth invaded my side. As quickly as the warmth came, it went as the person who bumped into me hustled to move away.

Soft pink and luminous light surrounded me. It's all I saw. Her sweater, her cheeks, and her lips... they were all soft pink and pretty. The light haloed around her, giving her an angelic glow. The way she stared back at me made me want to laugh. Her big doe eyes were wide, a mixture of brown and hazel swirling back at me. Perfect white teeth showed as her pouty lips gapped open in what could only be interpreted as shock.

Chocolate waves hung loosely around her untouched face. She looked like an actual angel, or at least the way you'd picture one. Maybe they were real. Maybe I never saw them because they only hung out in churches. All she was missing was her wings. She was beautiful, but in a church-girl, skirt-too-long kind of way. Lucky for her, I wasn't into the wholesome, angelic girls.

The last girl I dated was far from wholesome. Of course, that only lasted a week, but still, I could smell virgin on this girl a mile away. I'd lost my virginal blood when I was fourteen and since then I hadn't really slowed down. I didn't sleep around so much; I just dated... a lot.

The pastor stopped preaching and his eyes focused in on us. The entire congregation turned to face us, but she was too busy staring at me like I was about to catch fire to even notice. I didn't mind having attention on me. I actually thrived on it, but I didn't want everyone in the church thinking I'd corrupted the chick next to me.

I could still feel the stares on my back when I made it outside. Damn nosey-ass holy rollers. I walked to the side of the church and lit a cigarette. I hadn't had one since earlier that day and I was having a nicotine fit. The moment I inhaled, my skin felt tingly and my blood slowed in my veins. Relaxation. It wasn't like smoking some of that mean green, but it would have to do until I was no longer on holy ground.

"That's bad for you, you know?" A soft voice slid across me and soothed me like a drag from my smoke.

I dropped the cigarette to the ground and smashed it into the freshly cut grass with my boot.

The angel from inside stood before me with her hands locked in front of her. All her hair was pulled to one side and spilled over her shoulder. I wanted to run my fingers through it and see if it was as soft as it looked.

"Everything that feels good is bad for you." I grinned down at her.

"I have to disagree." She smoothed out her skirt with her hands and stepped closer. "I've never seen you here before."

"Maybe that's because I've never been here before." I leaned against the wall, careful not to touch the newly painted section.

"Makes sense, but why are you here now?"

I didn't respond. Instead, I pointed to the big beige square. It looked dry already, but the smell of fresh paint was still strong.

"Oh." Her face dropped. "I've always loved the brick on this church." She looked away from me and ran her fingers across the jagged brick. "When

I'm older and I have my own home, I hope it has brick just like this. Please don't ruin it anymore," she asked sweetly.

I wouldn't defend my innocence anymore. It was pointless. No one believed me anyway. The day I was busted, my ex-girlfriend, Jenny, had kicked me out and I had to walk home since I'd blown a head gasket in my fixer-upper mustang while racing my boy Leroy like a dumbass.

It wasn't my fault I'd used the churchyard as a cut through or that I'd stepped into some paint that ruined my favorite shoes. Who would've known there were people inside the church that late and that they'd come out at exactly that moment to catch me beside the church, trying to wipe the paint from my shoes?

"It won't happen again," I said stiffly.

She nodded at me and then smiled.

"Faith?" the pastor asked from behind her.

I hadn't even noticed he was there. He was a big man, taller than me by an inch or two, and from the way he towered over her, I assumed he knew it. His black dress pants were perfectly creased and his tie was neatly tied. I'd never learned how to tie a tie in all my life, but the shit looked hard. Salt-and-pepper hair dotted the sides and back of his head, leaving a bald spot on the top that attracted the overhead light.

I looked back at the angel in front of me. Her name was Faith. It was a good name for her. I didn't know much about the meaning of faith, but something told me she was the epitome of the definition.

"Yes, Daddy?" She shrank in front of him.

And then it all made sense. The pastor's daughter—somehow she became ten times more appealing. I'm not sure what it was about untouchable girls, but it was human nature to want something you couldn't have. The odds of me bagging a preacher's daughter were slim to none, but I'd never cared much about odds.

She went into herself at the sight of him. I didn't think she could get any smaller, but I was wrong. He must've been a hell of a strict man. The poor girl probably didn't have much of a life. It was obvious she'd never seen a fashion magazine since she had no sense of style. The sad-looking skirt said it all. She was entirely too pretty to be dressed like an Amish chick.

"I think it's time you came back in," he said as he looked over at me and gave me fake smile.

His low voice spoke volumes. He didn't want his daughter anywhere near me. I thought it was funny. I started thinking that maybe if I flirted hard enough, he'd release me and tell my probation officer that I did everything I was supposed to.

She turned back to me and smiled. I couldn't help myself. I winked and gave her my grin I knew the girls liked.

"It was nice meeting you, Faith. I hope I get to see more of you."

If looks could kill, the funeral home down the road would be wiping my ass and gutting me. Her father wasn't happy with me and I was just fine by that. I wasn't a huge fan of his nonstop blabbing either.

The front door of the church slammed after he ushered her back in. I laughed softly to myself as I lit another cigarette and relaxed. Not much later, the people started leaving the church and going to their cars.

I didn't bother calling my mom to come and get me. I'd already caused her enough shit as it was. The least I could do was let her relax for the rest of the night. So after having the preacher sign my paper, I set off for home on foot.

I hadn't really had to walk anywhere since I'd bought my old Mustang when I was sixteen. Thankfully, my mom didn't ask where I'd gotten the money since it took me months of selling white gutter glitter to afford it. Selling cocaine at sixteen had gotten me quite a bit of shit, but nothing as good as my sixty-nine Mustang. It looked like shit but ran like a champ. At least it did until I got stupid and blew up the fucking thing racing it.

I was halfway down the road when my mom pulled over and picked me up.

"You didn't have to walk, Jimmy. I told you I'd be there."

I'd always loved it when she called me Jimmy. My name was James, but she'd taken it upon herself when I first came to her to give me a nickname. At twelve years old, it was a nice change, just like her home had been. Being moved from one foster home to another meant living in some pretty shady places. The moment I walked into her house, I felt like I was home.

She looked over at me with tired eyes. The new pain medicine she was on was really taking its toll on her. Right after I was sent to her, she started having awful pains in her legs and lower back. She went to a different doctor every month, but no one could ever tell her what was wrong. It was the fifth doctor that finally diagnosed her with multiple sclerosis.

Over the years, she'd gotten worse. Her vision was wearing down and there were some days when she had problems moving. I was there to help her out as much as I could. She hated the help, but she needed it.

It was almost as if we were perfect for each other. I was an unwanted foster child who was dumped in foster home after foster home, and she was a woman who was unable to have kids. No one wanted me. Once she was diagnosed with MS, she needed me. It worked.

I could still remember the first time I'd called her mom. I got in trouble at school and the principal called her in. I'd introduced her as my mom in his office that day and the look of pure happiness on her face filled me with joy. I knew in that moment that calling her Mom had effectively erased her memory of all the bad things I'd gotten mixed up in since I moved in with her. It stuck from that point on. She called me Jimmy and I called her mom. We worked. We understood each other.

"I know, but I knew you weren't feeling good when I left earlier. I have two feet and I could use the exercise." I playfully patted at my stomach.

"Yeah, you're such a fatty. Who wants a six pack when you can have eight?" She joked as she reached over and poked my stomach. "So how was the church thing?"

"It was okay—lots of praying and preaching. I painted over the graffiti and cut the grass. That's pretty much all they needed from me today. Luckily, I don't have to go back until Sunday."

"Good." She smiled as she worked the car into the driveway.

I helped her into the house and then waited until she was comfortable on the couch. Her black-and-gray streaked hair was pulled into a tight bun, giving a good view of her brown eyes and clear skin. Besides a few wrinkles and the dark circles that had developed under her eyes, you'd never know she was almost fifty.

I pulled a throw off the back of our scruffy plaid couch and laid it over her legs. Once she was all set up with her remote, I went into the kitchen and cooked a small dinner for the two of us. It was late, but I was starving.

We spent the rest of our night watching our favorite sitcoms in the living room. The chair I sat in had seen better days, but it kept me from falling to sleep since there was a spring digging into my back. Our house and furniture wasn't the best, but it was home and it was ours.

When I first came to live with Mom, Ms. Janet, she had a really nice place and I enjoyed living in such richness. There were fine furnishings and the room she'd given me was huge and covered in all things sports. All that changed after her husband, Mr. Charles, died. We moved into something small on the opposite side of town.

Mom hated the new place, but I didn't care either way. If anything, I was more comfortable in the bad parts of town. The kids around our new house didn't look down on me the way the others did. I got in more trouble in school since more trouble was readily available, but I was happier.

The following Sunday, after taking out the trash and digging out a flower bed for Sister Francis, I went to the single church bathroom to clean my hands and face. I swiped at my pants with my dirt-covered hand before grabbing the doorknob. After pushing the door open, I ran right into Faith. Except this time she was sitting on the floor with her face down and her fist clutched to her chest as if her life depended on it. Her long skirt was hiked up over her knees, exposing a long, shapely leg.

I'm not sure what I'd expected to be lurking under that god-awful skirt, but I surely hadn't expected a set of gorgeous legs. A perfectly shaped thigh worked its way up under her skirt. I couldn't help myself. My eyes followed its path and begged the skirt to go away.

She moved and the bathroom light shifted across her leg, allowing me to see they weren't as perfect as I'd originally thought. The creamy skin was slightly tarnished with thin scars and welts. One thing I knew about was welts. One of my foster dad's favorite things to do was pick the perfect switch on a tree and use it on me. I'd gone to sleep many nights with welts that looked like that asshole's belt, his perfect switch, or better yet, his shoe.

My eyes were stuck on her legs as I pushed the door farther. Tear-filled eyes looked up at me, and she gasped. She quickly adjusted her skirt and swiped at the wet paths on her cheeks.

"I'm sorry. I didn't know anyone was in here." I leaned over and snatched a tissue from the tissue box on the counter and handed it to her.

I bent down on my knees to look directly into her sad brown eyes, and it felt as if a large hand was squeezing my heart. I wasn't a naturally emotional guy, but pulling the wings off of a butterfly wasn't my thing and this girl was hiding wings, just a different kind.

"Are you okay?" I asked softly.

She attempted to smile, but it never reached her eyes.

"Yeah, I'm okay—just having a moment," she said with an uncomfortable smirk.

She reached up with her free hand and nervously tucked her hair behind her ear, while her other hand remained clutched to her chest. A brown strand of hair escaped, and without realizing what I was doing, I tucked it behind her ear and out of her face again. She jerked at my touch and my heart shifted in my chest. It was the strangest feeling.

"What happened?" I asked.

I had the strongest urge to protect her.

There was once a little girl named Emily who I shared a foster home with. She was so sweet and small. I was with her for three months and during those three months, I'd been her protector. Faith reminded me so much of a grown-up Emily.

She opened her mouth to talk, but before she could answer, her father was at the door. His eyes beat into her and again, she shrank in his presence.

"That's enough playing around, Faith. Sister Francis is looking for you."

His eyes skimmed my face in aggravation. I turned my attention back to Faith, who was standing and adjusting her skirt. The way we were sitting alone in the bathroom couldn't have looked good, but I didn't care. I knew we were being innocent and that's all that mattered to me.

"See you around," she said as she stepped around me and out of the bathroom.

The pastor looked at me again and I saw a flash of anger in his eyes. His lips tightened in disapproval before he stepped away, letting the bathroom door slam. The noise seemed to shake the whole church.

I wasn't sure what it was, but something was off with that man and his daughter. I couldn't put my finger on it, but I knew a screwed-up family when I saw one. No matter how perfect the preacher pretended to be, something about him rubbed me the wrong way.

THREE
FAITH

"Spare the rod, spoil the child." My dad quoted the Bible as he put his belt back on.

I was sure it was his favorite part of the Good Book since he said it to me every day. It was easy for him since every day he found a reason to take his belt to me.

I clutched the silver cross lying against my chest. I'd had it my entire life. My mom's mom gave it to me when I was six and I'd never taken it off. It was usually hidden beneath my clothing, and it made me feel safe.

I used to pretend when I was younger that I could hide my soul in the cross so no one could ever take it away from me. My dad spent my childhood instilling in me the dangers of having a tainted soul and having it ripped away by the devil. It was my biggest fear. So when I was afraid that I'd done wrong or that something was going to hurt me, I'd imagine I was pouring my soul into the cross and I'd be guarded by something holy and good. It was how I made it through—my survival mechanism.

Years later, knowing it was impossible to tuck your soul away inside a silver charm, I still held strong to my cross and it still warmed my palm every time I felt like things were too much, when I thought I'd just about met my limit on the things I could take.

Once my dad left the room, I reached down and ran my fingers over my thigh. The thick welts were already starting to form. My skin felt hot to the touch and sore, but getting whipped with Daddy's belt didn't hurt anymore—not like it used to anyway. Instead of crying because of the pain, I'd shed the occasional hidden tear because of how degraded I felt.

It started when I was six—he caught me in a lie about eating an extra piece of candy—and it continued over the years. I never lied again from that moment on. It was beaten into me and it remained there. Lying was a sin, and if I lied, I was a sinner and I was going to burn in hell.

I was seventeen and afraid of any and everything, but mostly afraid of getting a spanking from my daddy like some elementary school child. How sad was I? No other girls my age even had to think about it. They were out living their lives, leaning and growing the proper way—by experience.

My home life was anything but exciting, which was why I almost hated going home after school each day. I suppose it was also the reason I'd do stupid things like burst out in tears randomly in the church bathroom. It wasn't the first time I'd done it, but it was the first I'd been caught.

I couldn't believe I'd done it again. I swore to myself that I wouldn't, but I felt like I was disappearing. It was as if every time his belt met my skin, it was erasing me. When I felt that way, the only way I could feel alive was to pinch myself, or better yet, clutch my cross and cry my eyes out in the bathroom.

It didn't make any sense to me. Crying, feeling any emotion in general, hurt and felt good at the same time. It was like I couldn't help it. I rarely did it anywhere but my bedroom at night. Only then could I have silent tears on my cheeks without anyone knowing about them.

Everyone had a breakdown every now and again. At least that's what I'd tell myself. I already felt like I belonged nowhere, that I was different from everyone else. Telling myself everyone else did it, too, made me feel a lot better.

Deep down I knew I had a depression problem and I needed to talk to someone, but what would my mother and father think if I asked to go to a therapist? They'd have me at the altar and have the entire congregation praying over me. Healing was God's job. That's what my dad would say to me. So instead of asking for help and risking another beating or having myself embarrassed in front of everyone, I hid it.

I usually locked the door. I wasn't sure what had possessed me to *not* double-check the lock before I let myself go, but when the new boy walked in on me my humiliation was on the severe side. I doubted he knew what I was in there doing, but still it wasn't fun. It's not like normal people sit around and cry for no reason. I was probably the only person in the world who did something so stupid.

Not to mention, the last thing I wanted him to see were the ugly welts from that afternoon's "lesson" about obeying my mother.

I skipped the movies the following Saturday night, but somehow Amanda talked me into going off with her, Kevin, and his cousin after church on Sunday. I had school the following day, but after being busted in the bathroom, sobbing like an escaped mental patient, I thought sneaking out and getting a little freedom was becoming necessary.

It was the first time in my life that I'd done something so careless, but I was about to break. I was getting the belt regardless of what I did these days, so why not at least give him a good reason. I ran that thought through my mind as I waited for Amanda to quietly pull up outside.

When she finally came, I climbed out of my window like a juvenile delinquent. The windowsill dug into my stomach and pinched the soft skin beneath my belly button. My heart was already in my throat from fear, but the windowsill pressing into my chest didn't help matters.

I stretched my legs out more until finally I could feel the grass beneath my tippy toes. Pushing up with my palms, I slid the rest of the way to the ground. My beige sweater snagged on a piece of cracked wood on the window frame and it ripped a tiny hole.

I still couldn't believe what I was doing. I never thought in a million years that I'd actually sneak out with Amanda, but I needed to get away. Things were getting worse emotionally and I needed a break away from my life, or the lack thereof. Even if it was just going on a stupid drive for two hours with two strangers and my best friend... that was enough. I wasn't stuck in my house, or school, or church, and that alone felt amazing.

I slid my window down quietly and waited for any sounds from inside my house. My heart remained jammed in my throat as I imagined my mom or dad bursting into my room to catch me in the act of breaking the rules.

"Come on, Faith," Amanda whispered from behind me.

I ran behind her to a waiting car, my simple white tennis shoes sinking into the damp grass.

Without thinking twice, I jumped into the back seat. My mouth was dry and I could barely swallow. The fear of getting caught was so strong and I was getting about sick and tired of feeling afraid all the time.

My stomach rolled with nerves and I began to shake as if I were freezing. No one around me seemed to notice. Once the car pulled away from my curb, I was afraid I'd go into a full panic attack and have to be rushed to the emergency room. I was thankful when the tense feeling slowly started wear off.

It was dark out, so dark that I couldn't see the guy in the seat next to me. That alone was frightening in itself, but I trusted Amanda. She was trouble, but I knew she'd never do anything to put me in actual danger. At least I hoped she wouldn't.

"Feels good, doesn't it?" Amanda said over the headrest of the passenger's seat, her eyes wild and excited.

She didn't wait for my response. Instead, she flopped around in her seat and leaned over to kiss who I could only guess was Kevin.

Again, I looked over at the guy in the seat next to me. Occasionally, some light from outside would flash and I'd actually see him and not just his silhouette.

He was a big guy, much bigger than my dad, and in the darkness, I couldn't tell if he was kind of chunky or really muscled. It wasn't until Kevin pulled up to a red light in the middle of town that I was able to get a good look. His dark hair was buzzed short and his eyes were so dark they blended in with the car around him, which made him look somewhat ghostly. I was only mildly freaked out by his total silence.

He lifted his arm to roll down the window, allowing me to see the bulge in his bicep—most definitely not fat, definitely muscles. Knowing he could go all caveman on me and throw me over his shoulder like a sack of potatoes didn't make me feel any better about sneaking out with strangers.

He noticed me staring and turned his attention back to me.

"I'm Tony, but all my friends call me Tiny." His voice was deep, like an older man, even though his baby face said differently.

I was thinking he was no more than eighteen. It was funny that his friends called him Tiny since there was nothing on the boy that was even remotely small. I blushed at that thought and looked down at my hands.

"My name's Faith. It's nice to meet you." I sounded as small as I felt next him.

He laughed a little to himself and turned his head to look back out the window.

"Don't worry about him. He's big and scary, but he's just a big ol' teddy bear. Aren't you, Tiny? Can you believe he's only a sophomore? He just joined Kevin's band. He's plays the bass and you know he's got to be damn good for Finn and Kevin to let him join so young," Amanda called from the front seat.

I was in total shock. One, Amanda had never said anything about Kevin being in a band, and two, I couldn't believe someone so big and full of muscles like Tony was so young. Looks were deceiving.

"I guess he plays okay." Kevin joked from the front seat as he looked through the rearview mirror.

Amanda and Kevin laughed when Tony, or Tiny, flipped them off. They looked nice together. Both were blond and pretty. As a matter of fact, Kevin looked nothing like how I'd picture a guy in a band. His clothes were too clean, his face shaved, with no piercings or tattoos that I could see. That being said, I could see what Amanda saw in him. He had a cocky attitude that reminded me of the new boy at church. It was more appealing than I'd admit.

Tiny shook his head at their laughter and tossed something out the window. I wanted to scream "litterbug" at him, but something told me he wouldn't appreciate me preaching at him. I didn't want to do anything to upset the giant.

I turned my attention away from Tiny.

"Who's Finn?" I asked.

Amanda turned in her seat again. "He's the singer in Kevin's band, Ordinary Malice. Kevin and him have been friends since middle school. He's sexy as hell."

"Hey!" Kevin said loudly. "What the hell?"

"He's nowhere near as sexy as you are, baby." She leaned over and kissed him.

He took his eyes off of the road and kissed her back. From my vantage point, I could see their tongues mingling together, and my stomach rolled again. A passing car honked at us when we veered out of our lane. I was on the verge of a mini heart attack when she released him and he focused on driving again.

I didn't ask any more questions. I didn't need to. I'd already had enough of being out and was silently praying they'd take me home already.

Fifteen minutes later, we pulled into the driveway of a brick house. It wasn't in the best neighborhood either. The yard was nice, but the house itself was old. It stood out against all the other houses that had junk in their yards and dogs hooked to chains, barking their heads off.

All three opened their doors and started to get out.

"Wait, where are we?" I asked in a panic.

Amanda turned back toward me and smiled.

"Come on, it'll be fun. I promise. This is Finn's house. They're going to play some tonight. They're good. Sometimes they even play at local bars that'll let them in."

She jumped out the car and shut the door behind her. I wanted to scream for her to come back right that second and take me home, but she was already disappearing into the garage. I'd thought we'd just drive around a bit, enjoy being free, and then they'd take me straight back home—

an hour tops. I had no idea they had plans. Amanda didn't tell me on purpose because she knew I would've backed out.

I had two choices. I could go inside and fade into a corner until I could persuade Amanda to get the boys to take me home. I was already regretting this and all I wanted was to be safe in my bed. Or I could sit in the car and wait for them to come back, but in a neighborhood like this one, I was probably safer inside the garage with the sex-crazed teenagers and their wild rock instruments.

Deciding that either way I didn't want to be alone, I got out of the car and slowly made my way to the garage. The dogs in the yards around me were going nuts trying to get loose and eat me alive. I stopped beside an older sports car with a tire missing. There was a concrete block in its place and oil leaked from underneath it and ran down the driveway.

I stepped away from the car and closer to the garage. That's when music started playing inside. It was loud; the sharp guitar cut at my ears and bass vibrated my knees. The garage door rumbled with the drums, and the sounds of female laughter was drowned out once the singer started to sing in his deep voice.

A strange smell floated out of the garage and all around me. I coughed a little and used my hand to wave it away as I stepped into the deafening, smoke-filled space. People were piled up on an old leather couch, watching the band play. I spotted Amanda from across the room, sitting on the couch, staring at Kevin with stars in her eyes.

The group she sat with passed around what looked like a small unfiltered cigarette. The smoke that flowed from it smelled awful. They were obviously doing drugs. I felt a little sick to my stomach when I saw Amanda take a drag. She was a childhood friend—my only friend. How could I not know that she was so involved in this kind of lifestyle?

I took in the room around me at people I'd never seen before—people that didn't see me. And then my eyes collided with someone familiar. It was the new boy at church, the troublemaker who'd painted the side of the building. He stared back at me as he sang into the microphone. His dark, raspy voice filled the garage, and since he was looking at me, it was as if he was singing to me.

His soft blue eyes took me in and his brows pulled down in confusion. Obviously I didn't belong there—I knew and he knew it. A thick piece of caramel hair fell into his eyes and he ran his fingers through it, pushing it out of his face.

Seeing him made me panic. What if he told my dad I was there? I didn't want to be surrounded by so many things I didn't understand. I wasn't okay with anything that was going on, and I wanted to leave, but more than anything, I didn't want my church family to find out I was involved with that kind of people. What would my dad do? If I got the belt for practically nothing, what would sneaking out get me?

Quickly, I backed away from the garage door and disappeared outside again. As soon as the night air hit me, I could breathe better and the music wasn't so loud. The dogs around me went crazy barking again. I didn't know where to go or what to do. I only knew I needed to get out of there before anyone else saw me or something bad happened. There could be a drive-by or a drug bust any minute. I didn't need my father finding out I was anywhere near this side of town.

I figured I'd brave the ghetto and turned to walk back the way we came. It was crazy, the craziest thing I'd ever done. It trumped sneaking out on a whole other level, but I had to do it. I'd be sure to let Amanda know how unhappy I was with her at school the following day. Maybe my dad was right. Maybe Amanda *was* a bad influence.

I was down the street a ways when I heard someone call my name. When I turned around, the new boy at church, who I now knew was Finn, the lead singer of Kevin's band, was taking long strides my way.

"Hey. Wait up," he said.

I stopped. When he reached my side, he was out of breath. Leaning over, he rested his palm against his thigh and held up a finger, telling me to give him a minute.

"You know, if you didn't smoke, you wouldn't be so out of breath right now," I said.

He looked up at me with a grin. A set of dimples dug into his flushed cheeks. "Are you going to preach to me, too, sweet girl?" He stood tall again after catching his breath. "Like I haven't heard enough preaching at church. I don't know how you can take that shit day after day."

I didn't confess that I was sick of being preached to. I couldn't tell him that, especially since I was kind of preaching at him.

"Sorry." I sighed.

"Don't worry about it. What are you doing here?" he asked roughly.

He sounded upset. Not that I could blame him. I was pretty upset about being there, too. We both knew I didn't belong.

I tried to think of a good excuse, but there wasn't one. And as badly as I wanted to come up with some really great lie to get myself out of the trouble I knew was going to come, I couldn't lie. I had to spill the truth and hope he didn't rush to church on Wednesday and tell my dad all about it.

"I came with my friend Amanda. She's dating your friend Kevin. I didn't know we were coming here. I'm not even supposed to be gone. My parents think I'm asleep at home. Please don't tell them you saw me. Please," I blurted out.

He was obviously getting in trouble a lot. Not just anyone got community service, and he seemed comfortable in his situation. Really, he had no room to tell on a person, but knowing my luck, he would. Some people would love to tell the pastor at a very prestigious church that his daughter was being sinful and sneaking out past dark. Maybe he was one of those people.

His eyes filled with humor and he started to laugh. It was a hearty laugh that sounded from his insides. It didn't help that it also made his adorable dimples pop. I hadn't really thought about boys all that much, but Finn was making me notice things I never had before.

Like his arms—the way his muscles moved under his skin when he did something with his hands. My eyes had also strayed to his stomach, which I could see clearly through his snug T-shirt. The thin white shirt left nothing to the imagination since it stuck to the indentions of his abdominal muscles.

He bent over and wrapped his arm around his stomach as he continued to laugh. I'm not sure what annoyed me more—the fact that my thought processes had gone into sinful territory, or the fact that he was laughing at me in my face.

"What's so funny?" I asked.

"You think I'd tell on you." He ended his laughter with a deep chuckle.

"Well, I don't really know you. Who's to say what you'd do?" I said, offended.

He sobered, but his cocky smirk stayed in place.

"Yeah, I guess you're right. Well, don't worry about it. I'd never tell on someone. I'm no nark. I do think it's kind of funny that a person like you would sneak out, though. I had no idea you were such a bad girl, Faith. I bet you even have some sexy sneak-out clothes hidden under that ugly skirt, don't you?" He reached out and pulled at my shirt.

I swatted at his hand, stepped back swiftly, and covered my blush with my palm. One, because the plain cotton bra and panties I wore could never be called sexy, and two, because I'd specifically picked out my skirt because it was my prettiest. At least I thought it was. It was obvious it was just as boring and prudish as the rest. It stung my feelings just a little that he called it ugly, though.

"Damn, I didn't mean it's, like, ugly. It's just too long." He attempted to apologize and failed miserably. He sighed. "Okay, let's try this again. Look, I'm Finn. That's my place." He pointed back at the garage. "And I don't think it's a good idea for you to be walking around out here by yourself. This isn't the best neighborhood. How about you come on back inside and I'll tell everyone to chill with the smoke."

Honestly, at that point, all I wanted was to go home, but the idea of going back inside and getting Amanda to take me home did appeal to me. However, there was no way I was going to be the prissy pastor's daughter crashing their party.

"No, don't do that. I don't want those people in there thinking I'm a brat. I'll be fine. I'm just going to walk home. "

He lifted both his arms, then ran his hands across his face roughly. His shirt came up and I got a small peek of the skin just above his jeans. I turned my head quickly and looked away.

"Look, come back with me. I'll grab my mom's keys and take you home real quick. Deal?"

"No, I don't think—"

"Please, Faith, just let me do this." He cut me off. "I'll feel like shit if you're found on the side of the road in the morning."

The blue of his eyes seemed to glow in the darkness around us as he silently cut me with his expression. His aggravation was apparent. He had the ability to make me feel like a small child being chastised. As if I didn't get enough of that at home.

Dogs barked unmercifully, and in the distance, a car alarm began to ring out. I looked over to my right and three strange men stood on their front porch and stared over at Finn and me. One wore a creepy smile that made his gold tooth visible.

What had I been thinking? No way did I want to end up missing or murdered on the side of an abandoned road. Finn wasn't safe, but I didn't think he'd harm me physically.

"Fine. Thank you," I said as I stepped around him and started to walk back to his driveway. "Could you please tell Amanda you're taking me home?"

"Will do." He smiled sarcastically.

He was hard to feel out. Either he was being friendly or he was annoyed by me. I was pretty good with people, but I didn't like how off center he made me feel. Especially since the more I looked at him and the more he spoke to me, the nicer looking he got. He was more of a gentleman than he let on. The ladies at church would probably disagree, but only a nice guy would care about whether or not I made it out of this side of town alive.

I stood alone in his driveway for a minute while he ran inside to get his keys and let Amanda know what was happening. I hated leaving her there like that, but that was her scene, not mine. Actually, I didn't really have a scene, unless you included church. Church was definitely my scene. Not that it was my choice.

Inside the garage, I could hear his friends complaining that he was leaving. I couldn't hear his response, but I felt awful for taking him away from his little gathering. I could still smell the pungent odor of that stuff they were smoking. I assumed it was marijuana, which only made me want to go home even more.

"All ready to go?" Finn asked as he came out of the garage swinging his keys around his finger.

I followed him over to an older white Jeep Cherokee. He opened the door for me, which was also unexpected, and I got in. He ran around to the other side and got in before cranking up the engine. The atmosphere around us lightened the farther away from his neighborhood we got.

At first we were quiet, not really knowing what to say to each other. It wasn't like we had anything in common. We were from totally different worlds.

"Thanks for the ride," I finally said to break the ice.

He looked over at me and grinned. His light irises glistened from under dark lashes. I was really beginning to like his eyes and I was seriously starting to enjoy his knowing grins a little more than I should have.

"No worries. We don't want a pretty thing like you getting kidnapped." He looked back at the road as if he didn't just give me the biggest compliment.

I couldn't remember anyone ever calling me pretty before. It made me feel funny. I can't say that I hated it. Actually, I kind of loved it. I could remember my mom telling me I looked nice once, and memories of my dad calling me his princess when I was a toddler still lingered, but now that I was older and feeling pretty really mattered, no one ever said it.

He turned to face me again and I felt my cheeks catch fire. I looked out the window so he couldn't see. A soft, manly chuckle sounded from his side of the car, letting me know he didn't miss my embarrassing blushing. The rest of the ride was uncomfortable. Every now and again I'd give him directions, but other than that we stayed quiet.

"Please be extra quiet," I said as we pulled up to my house.

He chuckled again and I gave him the evil eye as he snuck the car up to my house and put it in park. He turned in his seat and silently watched me as I twiddled my fingers in my lap. When his eyes were on me, I felt breathless. It was if he had some sort of freaky spell over me.

I needed to get away from him and get some sleep. The night had taught me one valuable lesson: I had no business sneaking out of my house or hanging around people who were nothing like me.

I unbuckled my seatbelt and popped my door open. I was about to thank him for the ride when the porch light turned on. It was only then that I noticed the living room lights.

Time stopped when my father stepped out on the front porch in his pajamas and then, with quick, angry strides, made his way over to Finn and me.

"Oh shit," Finn said.

I didn't bother correcting his language since I'd secretly been thinking the same exact thing. One night out and I was already having impure thoughts.

My dad took one look at me and Finn and his face transformed into something angry and red. His eyes looked at risk of popping out and the vein in the side of his neck ticked. The way he looked at me made me feel dirty, as if I'd been out all night doing the many things that Amanda had disgustingly told me about.

"Faith, I want you to go inside so I can have a talk with our friend Finn." He spoke calmly, but I knew what calm meant. Calm meant there was a storm coming.

It wasn't right for Finn to get in trouble simply for being a gentleman and making sure I got home safely.

"Daddy, Finn was just—"

He held up his hand to stop me. "That's enough, Faith. Please go inside with your mother. I'll be in there to deal with you in just a moment."

Deal with me. I didn't even want to think about how he was going to deal with me. I clutched my cross in preparation for the night's lesson. It was going to be a bad one.

"Pastor Warren, this is my fault," Finn said boldly. "I wanted to surprise Sister Francis with some special flowers in her flower bed and I talked Faith into helping me. You know how much she loves Sister Francis. There was no way I could've gotten it done before church Wednesday if she didn't help me."

As soon as the lie left his mouth, I turned and looked at him like he was crazy. First of all, there were no flowers planted yet, and my dad would know that the minute he stopped by the church for paperwork the following day. Secondly, I was amazed at how quickly and easily he was able to lie. I'd never seen anything like it and I was secretly jealous of his fabulous talent. I could've saved myself from the belt a few times if I were capable of such a thing.

"Is that true, Faith?" my father asked.

I didn't want to lie to him, but I really didn't want to get in trouble and I really didn't want Finn to get in trouble either. Regardless of what we were doing, I was still out past a decent time when I wasn't supposed to be. I was still going to hear it, but somehow saying I was planting flowers for Sister Francis sounded so much better than I was at a party with a bunch of stoners and band boys.

I opened my mouth to speak, but the lie wouldn't come out. Instead, I shook my head yes and silently prayed for forgiveness.

I felt sick doing it. I hadn't lied to my father since I was a little girl. My throat felt tight and cold chills wracked my body, causing me to wrap my arms around myself.

"You should've asked first and you're still going to be on restriction for sneaking out past your bedtime," my dad said adamantly. "As for you, Finn, I don't want Faith falling into your sinner ways. I'd appreciate it if you stayed away from my daughter outside of church."

My dad grabbed my arm and pulled me toward the front door. His fingernails dug in, pinching the soft skin. I looked over my shoulder at Finn and caught him glaring at my dad's back. Before I stepped inside the front door, I looked back again as he pulled away.

I got the worst beating ever that night. For the first time, Daddy lost control and his belt hit other places on my body instead of just my legs.

When I went to bed, my back ached and my arms and legs stung. I barely made it into bed before the tears came. I never cried during the beating—I'd never give him that satisfaction—but I'd almost given in to the pain.

On top of the belt beating, I got a month's worth of restriction, which didn't matter much to me since I practically lived on restriction as it was. I finally fell asleep two hours later with stale tears on my cheeks and anxiety for what would happen the following day churning in my stomach. It was only going to get worse once my dad got to the church and saw there were no flowers in the flower bed.

FOUR
FINN

I fucking hated flowers. I spent the rest of my night working on that damn flower garden, and I'd spent my last ten bucks on those damn over-scented weeds. I'd never been more thankful that Wal-Mart stayed open twenty-four hours or that I could flirt my way into the lawn and garden department after hours.

By the time I got back to my house, I was covered in dirt and exhausted. Everyone was gone and so was all the beer, which pissed me off pretty good. Instead of sitting around bitching about it, I went straight to my bathroom, got a shower, and crashed.

The next day, I slept way into noon. I'd decided to skip senior year and go straight to work for Uncle Lester, my dealer. He didn't even have any nieces or nephews, but everyone called him uncle. The best thing about Uncle Lester was he dressed like a pimp from the seventies and had a porn star mustache. He worked it, though, and he was the man when it came to the ladies. He was a strange man, but he always made sure I had a full supply of wacky dust. It wasn't honest pay, but it was pay.

With a busted head gasket and a blown tire, I needed whatever work I could get to get my car back on the road. In my mind, the band was my meal ticket, but if the worst happened and my band did nothing, I'd end up taking care of my mom and working some shitty job somewhere. I was born and bred for struggle.

I fixed myself a bowl of cereal in one of mom's mixing bowls and sat on the couch, deep in thought. Faith. I couldn't seem to get her off my mind. I wasn't sure why I'd lied for her. Maybe it was because I'd seen her welts, and the thought of her getting more made me sick to my stomach. Or maybe it was because her dad seemed to piss me off all the time. It wasn't that he was doing anything, but it was his "I'm the pastor so I'm better than you" mentality. He wasn't better than me. Actually, I'd give the ounce of cush and the eight ball in my top drawer to say he was probably more crooked than I could ever dream of being.

I fixed my mom some lunch and made sure she had her pills. She was having an especially painful day, which meant she wouldn't want to be bothered. Instead of sitting around and babying her to death, I smoked a bowl in the garage and headed out to get lost around the town.

It was days like that when I wished I had an actual job. I'd talked about it with my mom before, but she swore she needed me home more than she needed help financially. I understood and even though the thought of having money that I'd made legally sounded great, I couldn't take the chance of not being there for her if she needed me.

Later that afternoon, the boys came over and we practiced for the rest of the night. We'd been invited to play at a new underground club called The Pit and we wanted to make sure we sounded kickass. It wouldn't pay to play a shitty show, and we always had the hope that someone important would see us and take us out of our fucked-up situations.

I sang my heart out as Kevin, the lead guitarist, crushed my garage with his rips. I'd known him since the first day of middle school. He was the first friend I'd had for more than a few months. That was one of the worst things about being in the system and getting moved around so much. I never made any lasting friendships. I'd spent my life being passed by strangers and it was nice to have some loyalty in my life.

Reynolds, who could play the hell out of a pair of drums, was hitting the beats hard. He hated to practice, but he always showed up on time and played his heart out even if he was all geeked out half the time. We all had our vices, but I think he was developing a serious problem. His sudden appearance of nosebleeds made it hard to look away from his cocaine addiction. I was no saint. I sold the stuff and on occasion I'd down a line, but nothing as extreme as Reynolds.

Then there was the newbie, Tony. I'd given him the name Tiny, mainly because for a kid his age, he was fucking huge. The kid could play some bass, though, and he kept to himself. I could appreciate that. He seemed genuine and had yet to fuck me over in any way. In my world, that was enough for me.

I was confident that Ordinary Malice was going to go far. We'd already started attracting attention from the locals and playing bars even though none of us were twenty-one. Singing and writing music was my passion. I loved it and I'd give anything to be able to walk away from all the bullshit and make an honest living doing it.

The next day, I got a phone call from Faith. My house phone never rang so it was a shock when it did. The only reason we still had one was just in case of an emergency. Mom and I shared her cell, although I had it more than she did.

"I saw the flowers," Faith said.

She was whispering into the phone. The poor girl had probably never let go in her entire life. It was no way to live. It made me wonder how wild she'd be in the sack. As quickly as the thought came, I pushed it to the back of my mind. She wasn't like the rest of the girls and had already somehow managed to earn a certain amount of respect from me.

"And?" It sounded rude, but I was curious where the conversation was going.

"And I wanted to say thank you. My dad can be a bit strict, and while I did get in trouble for being out, it would've been even worse if he'd caught me in a lie."

"Don't worry about it. I would've had to do it come Wednesday anyway. At least this way maybe I won't be out in the heat all day."

It really had sucked that I'd missed hanging out with my friends that night. Not to mention, my ex, Jenny, had been there and there was a good chance I was going to get laid, but it was worth it in the end, I guess. Faith already had it bad from what I could see. The least I could do was help the girl out.

"Do you always sneak out like that?" I couldn't help but ask.

I thought I was seeing things when she'd stepped into my garage that night. She obviously didn't belong there, and I wasn't all that thrilled to have her there. A girl like her could be a liability. The last thing I needed was my boys getting accused of some crazy shit because an inexperienced girl got herself all caught up in our craziness.

She was a nice girl and I felt bad for her. The contrast between her and the rest of the girls in the room was pretty hilarious, though. They were all covered in makeup with painted-on clothes that left nothing to the imagination, and Faith was clean and covered.

I hadn't meant to call her skirt ugly, but it was a crime for such a pretty girl to be so uptight. Not that she should walk around with her ass hanging out, but damn, she must burn up in all those clothes.

"That was my first time. I won't be doing that again," she said adamantly.

It was kind of cute. She was so childlike since her father had obviously sheltered her for her entire life. When I thought of all the things she was missing out on, it was kind of depressing. She was a teenager. It was her job to experience all the crazy shit possible. It's how you become a good adult. You live and you learn. She was going to be thirty and still clueless to what life had to offer.

"That's a shame," I said with a grin as I rested the phone between my shoulder and my face.

Flirting was in my nature and I never suppressed what came naturally to me.

"Why's that?" she asked.

"Well, I was going to see if you wanted to hang out one night."

It was a last-minute decision, a kill-two-birds-with-one-stone kind of thing. I could get her out with me and show her a good time while pissing off her dad so much that he'd want me nowhere near his daughter. Win-win.

"Why?" she asked, confused.

She had no idea how pretty she was. I'd seen that when I called her pretty in the car on the way to her house. Confidence was sexy, but so was a beautiful girl who had no idea how beautiful she was.

"Because you seem like a nice girl, and I already told you I thought you were pretty."

I didn't mention the fact that I was also trying to get under her dad's skin. I somehow didn't think that would fly over well with her.

"But we're so different," she said.

She couldn't have been more right.

"Opposites attract. Don't you find me attractive?" I asked.

I'd seen the way she looked at me when she didn't think I noticed. I'd seen girls look at me that way before and all of them had tried to get a piece of me at some point. Not that I was complaining or holding out, but still, I knew a girl who was attracted to me when I saw one.

She didn't answer. I'd bet money that she was all huddled up in those restricting clothes, hiding from her parents like a five-year-old. And I'd also bet that she was ten shades of red since all she seemed to do was blush.

"I'm going to take that as a yes. Besides, it would just be a friend thing. Listen, don't think about it. I'll see you at the church on Wednesday, and don't worry about the flowers. I'm just glad you didn't get into any more trouble."

I hung up the phone with a big goofy smile on my face and plans to make the preacher man crazy.

The following Wednesday, there wasn't any outside work that needed to be done around the church. Sister Francis loved her flower garden and a few ladies around the church had praised me for my gardening skills that I had no idea I possessed.

I got stuck in a back room, filing papers. It didn't sound like much of a job, but after thirty minutes of that crap, I was dying to get outside to work in the sun. The room was too small and smelled like old lady's perfume. Every couple of minutes, I'd feel like I couldn't breathe and my eyes would water from the sickly sweet smell.

An hour later, I was done filing and headed over to Sister Francis to see if there was anything she needed. I stepped into the kids' room and was caught off guard by Faith dancing around.

I stood in the doorway and watched from afar as she laughed and shook her hips with the kids to some kiddie music about Jesus. Her smile was real, her happiness genuine. It was beautiful to watch.

She raised her hands above her head and shook them around. Her skirt lifted, revealing tiny feet and ankles. It was about that time that my mind shifted and I started imagining what her knees looked like, her thighs, her flat stomach, and from that point, the thoughts only got worse. I was so caught up daydreaming about Faith naked that I hadn't even realized she'd stopped dancing and was talking to me.

"Finn? Is there anything I can do for you?" She had her hands on her hips and looked at me like I was nuts.

Maybe I was. I'd just caught myself fantasizing about the pastor's daughter. That could never end well.

"Finn?" she asked again loudly.

Little snickers sounded from the kids around us.

"Yeah. I was curious if Sister Francis needed me to do anything. I'm all done filing."

"Actually, I could use your help in here if you need something to do." She smiled.

She seemed to smile at me a lot more than she did before the whole flower incident.

"Okay. What can I do?" I asked.

I spent the rest of the time playing with the kids. I hadn't been around kids since my last foster home. Those foster parents had entirely too many kids, so me and four others who were younger than me slept in one room. It was obviously those people just wanted the state checks that came with us.

I kind of liked spending time with the kids. They were funny and asked a lot of questions. I found myself laughing with them quite a bit. And every now and again, when she didn't think I was looking, I'd see Faith smiling over at me. She really was beautiful, inside and out. I was pretty good at seeing through people, and when I looked at her, all I saw was goodness. She was selfless. I could tell by the way she treated the kids. There wasn't a bad bone in her body.

The next week was a blur of smoking bowls, making deals, singing, and hanging out at church with Faith. It got to a point where I'd get excited about going to church. I loved hanging out with her and the more she was around me, the more I got to see who she really was.

She was more than just the pastor's daughter. She was funny. She made me laugh so much most days that I'd go home with a sore stomach. She was sweet. Some days I'd sit to the side and watch as she took her time showing the kids how to spell a word or how to do something correctly. My initial assumption about Faith was right. She really was an angel.

Being around her was good. I barely smoked cigarettes anymore, since she said she hated the smell, and the only time I really hung out with my friends was when we had practice or a show. I'd make plans with them and then Faith would ask me to help her do something and I'd cancel with my friends.

I had a hard time telling her no about anything. So when the church had a bake sale coming and she asked me to help her bake some stuff, I was on board. I really wasn't much of a cook, but anything was better than filing or working in the churchyard.

"Do you have a girlfriend?" she asked as she mixed a bowl of cookie dough.

"Nah. I don't think dating is for me," I said as I buttered the baking pan.

"No girls? Seriously?" She looked at me like I had two heads.

"Oh no. There's girls, but not one that's steady."

Her face lit up as I expected, and I smiled to myself.

"So you're a player? Isn't that what they call boys like you?" She started picking at the cookie dough and rolling it into balls.

"I'm not a player. I'm honest with girls. I just don't do the whole girlfriend thing all that well."

"Oh come on, Finn, there had to be a girl that got through that hard exterior of yours once or twice." She smiled up at me as she continued to pick the raw cookie dough from her fingers.

I wanted to tell her that technically she had gotten through, but I didn't know how that would sound. We were friends—I'd never really been friends with a girl before—and we had an easy relationship. But I'd be lying if I said it wasn't slowly becoming uncomfortable. And if it was becoming uncomfortable, then maybe there was more there.

"Yeah, once or twice." I playfully winked at her to play it off.

She laughed and threw a wad of dough at my chest. It made a wet smacking noise and stuck to the front of my Guns N' Roses T-shirt.

"Oh no you didn't," I said in a girly voice as I wiggled my finger at her.

She laughed harder.

I picked the dough from my shirt and threw it back at her. Next thing I knew, we were running around the small kitchen at the back of the church and throwing flour and sugar all over each other. She held up her hands and screamed as I sprinkled sugar over the top of her head.

"Such a sweet girl like you should taste sweet, too." I laughed.

She turned in my arms and put her hands up to stop the sugar. I held the bag even higher out of her reach. She stood on her tiptoes and pressed her petite body against mine. Her sweet breath warmed the side of neck and she slid up and down my front as she tried to reach the sugar. She felt good against me and it was making me hard.

Everything stopped. The smile slipped from my face as I stared down at her. She continued to smile, flour dotted her cheeks, and sugar shimmered in her hair. Once her eyes met mine, she stopped reaching for the bag above my head. My arms fell slowly and I let my empty hand cup the side of her face, using my thumb to wipe some flour from her cheek.

Her smile slipped, too, as she looked up at me with wide brown eyes. Her eyelids fluttered closed as I caressed her cheek with my fingers. Little puffs of heated breath came from her mouth, pulling my attention to her soft pink lips. I ran a finger across her bottom lip, drawing a soft sigh from her.

I wasn't sure what was happening. I just knew I liked it, and by the glazed look in her eyes when she opened them, I could tell she liked it, too. I moved closer to her and she didn't move away. She felt amazing. I set the sugar bag on the counter beside me as I slipped my arms around her tiny waist. I'd never been nervous with a girl before, but Faith wasn't like any other girl I'd spent time with. She was better than them—so much better, as in she was too good for me.

She swallowed hard and licked her lips and I was gone from that point on. As if magnetized, I was being pulled into her for a kiss. Her lips and eyes begged for it. I slipped my fingers into her thick hair and pulled her face closer to mine.

My lips were barely touching hers when the door opened. We pulled apart quicker than I thought was possible and started awkwardly cleaning up the mess we'd caused. My heart was still beating funny even though we weren't close anymore.

"What the devil happened in here?" her dad asked from the door.

"We accidently spilled some," she said with her head down.

I instantly missed the playful girl from minutes before. I hated what happened to her in the presence of her dad, which only added to my hatred for him.

I couldn't believe what had almost happened. I couldn't believe how badly I wanted something as simple as a kiss from her. My thoughts were a mess. I didn't even respond to the pastor when he asked what happened. Instead, like some shy punk, I put my head down and kept cleaning.

"Well, let James clean it. There's someone here that wants to meet you." He held the door open and waited for her.

I hated the name James. The fact that he insisted on calling me that after I'd asked him to call me Finn enraged me, and I knew my anger stemmed from his treatment of Faith more than what he called me.

Faith smiled shyly up at me before she stepped away and out of the room. I didn't miss the smug smile on the pastor's face as he shut the door behind them and shut me out.

FIVE

FAITH

Finn. He was doing something to me. Since we'd started hanging out so much, I'd never felt so alive. I'd never secretly smiled to myself so much. Smiling wasn't something I did often, and since I'd met him I couldn't seem to stop. I felt like I was breathing a little easier, looking at the sun a little differently.

I wasn't out painting the town red or doing any drugs; I was just being around him, and it was amazing. He made me laugh until I cried and was probably the sweetest guy I'd ever had the privilege to meet, even though he'd never admit it. Not that I'd met a lot of guys, but there was just something about him—something special.

It was more than his baby-blue eyes that seemed to see right through me or his dimples that I was almost positive he reserved just for me. It was more than his looks, period. He made me feel different. Like I was just finding myself and living for the first time ever.

I couldn't believe he was about to kiss me in the church kitchen. I'd never been kissed before and, honestly, kissing had always kind of grossed me out, but the thought of feeling those full lips against mine made my stomach tighten in a way it never had before and gave me a breathless dizzy feeling. It was scary and exhilarating at the same time.

I was still feeling high off him when I came face to face with a family I'd never met before. I barely had time to collect my thoughts before my dad was introducing me to them. They'd just moved to town and were thinking of joining our church. My dad told me their names, but my ears were still foggy and I missed it. Still, I reached out my hand to the mother and smiled sweetly.

"And this is Stephen, their son. The Petersons were just telling me that Stephen's the same age as you, Faith. Isn't that nice?"

I looked over at Stephen. He was on the shorter side with cropped auburn hair and freckles across his cheeks and nose. When he smiled at me, his teeth were covered in metal, but still, he had a very nice smile. He was khaki covered like me, but instead of feeling comfortable with him, I instantly hated the dreariness of his whole look.

It was even becoming harder for *me* to put on my boring skirts in the morning. I knew in the back of my head that it had to do with Finn and his comfortable jeans and colorful band shirts, but I didn't care. He was showing me a thing or two about being comfortable in my own skin, and the prudish cover I'd been wearing my entire life had never felt more restricting.

"It's nice to meet you, Faith. That's such a beautiful name," he said boldly.

I felt my cheeks turn hot as I looked over at my father and waited for the angry look on his face that was always there when Finn said nice things to me... except, there was only a happy smile on his lips.

I didn't understand it. Daddy had never liked me being around boys, yet here he was introducing me to one and smiling happily as the boy complimented me.

“Thank you,” I whispered softly.

“That’s such a nice thing to say, Stephen. You know, since you’re new in town, maybe you and Faith should catch a movie or something. Maybe she can show you around town and get you familiar with the place before you start your new school on Monday. How’s that sound, kids?” my father said proudly.

My jaw almost hit the floor. My dad was definitely having a midlife something. Perhaps he was in the middle of a stroke and the side effects hadn’t starting showing, because my dad would never say such a thing. He’d never be okay with me going anywhere with anyone besides him and my mom. The idea of him allowing me to go on a date with a boy wasn’t something I’d ever thought would happen.

I looked back over at Stephen and he blushed brightly and smiled over at me.

“I think that sounds like fun. Do you want to go to a movie with me, Faith?” he asked.

I looked around at our parents, who were all full of smiles and crazy eyes. I needed to run to the bathroom and pinch myself. My occasional bathroom breakdowns had stopped, thanks to Finn, but I definitely needed a hard pinch or a nice slap across the face to fetch me back to reality.

I stood there with my mouth gapped open as everyone stared at me and waited for a response. Part of me wanted to say no. I didn't know this boy from Adam and he looked about as boring as I felt, but then again, what were the chances of my dad practically pushing me out the door and to the movies with some boy? I had to take what I could get, I guess. At least that way I'd have a moment to breathe some fresh air outside of school, home, and church.

I looked over at my dad and asked his permission with my eyes. He smiled down at me and shook his head yes.

"Okay," I squeaked.

The whole time all I could think about was Finn and how much I wished it were him I was going to the movies with. I really had to stop thinking about Finn so much. Yeah, it looked as if he was about to kiss me not ten minutes ago, but I had to face facts, and the fact was I wasn't even close to the kind of girl Finn would want. We were friends. I had to really stop thinking that sometimes when he looked at me there was more than friendship in his eyes.

After agreeing to my first date ever and watching as our parents made the arrangements, I stopped by the bathroom at church and splashed some cold water over my cheeks. They still felt warm from Finn's touch and the last thing I needed to do was go back in the kitchen with hot, embarrassed cheeks and make our friendship uncomfortable.

When I got back to the kitchen, Finn was leaning against the counter with his arms crossed. He hadn't heard me come in and he was facing the window with his eyes closed. The room was cleaned and all the cookies were in the oven. The smell of chocolate chip and sugar cookies filled the room. I would forever associate the smell with Finn, which made perfect sense since he was so sweet.

I smiled secretly at my thoughts. If I had ever told him I thought he was such a sweetie, he'd probably growl and do something ridiculously rude just to prove a point.

"Hey," I said as I walked up to him.

He opened his eyes and smiled at me. He looked genuinely happy to see me.

"Everything okay?" he asked.

"Yeah. My dad wanted to introduce me to a new family who's joining the church. And something kind of crazy happened."

He turned, rested his elbows on the counter, and cupped his cheeks with his hands. When he smiled, one of his dimples was hidden behind his palm and I wanted to pull it away so I could see them both.

"My dad set me up on a date."

His smile dropped instantly, and I thought for a minute that he'd ask me not to go. If he asked, whether I needed freedom or not, I'd skip the date. All he had to do was say the words, but instead, he started laughing. It felt like a slap in the face.

Why was it so funny that I could have a date?

"What?" I asked rudely.

"Nothing. It's just..." He couldn't finish his sentence he was laughing so hard.

"It's just what?" I asked again, louder.

He was really starting to make me mad.

"It's just go figure your dad would set you up with some church boy once I came around. Touché, big preacher man," he said to no one as he shook his head.

He wasn't making any sense.

"What do you mean?" I leaned against the counter and crossed my arms.

"Nothing. I think this is a great idea. I bet he's really nice and *clean*."

He was and I hated that he was. I hated even more that Finn thought I could only get a nice, clean boy. And even worse was that Finn was probably going to see him at Sunday's sermon and I could only imagine the jokes he was going to make just to be a smarty pants.

"There's nothing wrong with a nice, clean guy, Finn. Actually, I'd prefer them that way."

The moment the words left my lips, his face dropped. I wasn't sure if it was being around Finn or what, but I lied so easily and I hated it. I didn't prefer any kind of guy, but I knew I liked Finn, which was dumb on my part since it was totally obvious that he didn't feel the same.

He moved quickly and pinned me against the back wall. Kids' drawings stuck to my back and a picture of a cross covered in hard macaroni noodles dug into my arm. I sucked in a shocked breath.

"Opposed to a guy like me, huh?" He stuffed his hands in my hair and forced me to look up at him. Stormy bluish-gray eyes stared back at me from under dark lashes. "Are you going to hide behind pretty boys with clean thoughts all your life? Because I know you're not the saint your daddy thinks you are. I saw the hot look in your eyes when you thought I was going to kiss you. I know you secretly dream of dirty boys with filthy thoughts." His eyes dropped to my mouth briefly and I held my breath. "I'll tell you what... When you decide you can handle a real man, let me know."

He released me quickly and stepped away. Cold air replaced his heat and left chills in his wake.

No one had ever talked to me like that. I felt disgusted. Not because of his words or the fact that I could feel his arousal through his jeans when he was pressed against me, but because it was the most riveting thing that ever happened to me. It was a rush, but I felt my high spiraling down the farther away he got from me. He was right. Maybe I wasn't as holy as I'd tried to be my entire life.

We barely talked the rest of the time in the kitchen. He sat in the corner and cut his nails with a pocket knife while I pulled out the cookies when they were done. Once they cooled, we wrapped them in plastic wrap with little yellow bows tied around them. When that was done, we said our goodnights and my dad signed his paper for him to leave.

I watched him walk to his mom's car as I followed my mom and dad to ours. Once he was inside, he looked back at me with an angry expression. I wasn't sure what had happened, but then again, I was completely clueless when it came to guys.

The following Saturday night, I dressed in my white blouse and another dreaded khaki skirt. Once I was done getting dressed, my mom and dad sat in the living room with me as I waited for Stephen to pick me up. I actually felt nervous, and every time my dad turned the page of his newspaper, I jumped. He looked at me over his reading glasses like I was crazy before finally setting down his paper.

"Faith, I know I haven't really allowed you to do much, but if I kept you away from things, it was because I worried for your safety. It's a cruel world out there and believe it or not, there are people out there who would love nothing more than to taint such a precious girl like you. I feel good about Stephen. He's a nice boy and he comes from a nice God-fearing family."

I couldn't think of anything to say back. "I know, Daddy," I squeaked.

Headlights filled our front window and the butterflies in my stomach fought to escape. Within seconds, the doorbell rang and my parents met Stephen at the door and asked him to come in.

I sat quietly in the corner chair as my father talked Stephen to death. He talked until we barely had time to make it to the movie. It almost felt like he did it on purpose, like giving Stephen and me less time together would prevent us from doing anything sinful.

As I looked over at Stephen in the car on the way to the movie, I couldn't see him even thinking sinful thoughts, much less doing anything unbecoming. Finn, on the other hand, was a walking sin. The way he strutted into a room like he owned it with his sly grin and amazing dimples. He knew he was nice to look at. He was prideful and confident and it was like staring at the sun. I had to admit, I liked basking in his heat.

The movie Stephen took me to was G-rated. It was insulting. I was seventeen years old. I had no business going on a date to see a G-rated movie. It was definitely something Finn would never hear about. I could practically hear his laughter.

I took the box of popcorn from Stephen and he ushered me into the theater. The next two hours of my life I spent staring at the screen, but not really watching. Occasionally, Stephen would ask me a question and I'd nod. I was probably the most boring date ever, but then again, he was the most boring date ever so I guess we fit.

I found myself upset over the fact that I wasn't enjoying any of it. One night of freedom and there I was sitting at a kids' movie with some guy who barely talked to me, much less looked at me. There were parents and crying babies everywhere, so if I wanted to watch the movie, I wouldn't have been able to hear it anyway. It was a total waste of a night. I could've gotten more enjoyment out of reading.

I'd never been happier to see my house when we pulled up. Stephen wasted no time getting me home. He was the perfect guy for my dad. I should've been happy about that. The thought of actually having some form of life outside of church and school should've made my night, but all I could think about was Finn and how much fun we had, even at church. I could imagine how much fun he'd be on a date.

Stephen walked me to the front door at exactly nine o'clock. The automatic porch light came on and shined directly in my eyes.

"I had a good time," he said.

I was glad he did, but I couldn't say the same.

"Me too," I lied again.

Lying was becoming easier and easier. That was either a really bad thing or a really good thing.

"Could we do it again?" he asked.

I'd hoped he wouldn't ask, but I couldn't hurt his feelings. I didn't want to be mean and say no. Plus, what would my dad say? Instead, I smiled up at him sweetly and agreed.

"Sure."

His smile was brighter than my porch light as he leaned in. The thought of kissing him and getting my mouth stuck to his braces scared me. Thankfully, he softly pressed his lips to my cheek and pulled away.

"Goodnight, Faith."

"Goodnight, Stephen."

That night I went to bed with thoughts of Finn. His unrushed movements, as if the world moved on his time. His soft blue eyes that never missed anything and his cocky smile. These were the last things I saw before sleep took me away.

Six

Finn

There's a first time for everything. And I could say without blinking that it was the first time a girl had ever been stolen from me. Although, technically, she was never mine. That still didn't stop me from staring a hole in the back of Stephen's auburn head during church on Sunday and wishing he'd go back to wherever he came from.

I hadn't had a chance to be alone with Faith to find out how the date went, but with a guy like the freckled wonder, I'm sure it didn't go too far. Maybe a goodnight kiss?

Every now and again, Faith would turn her head to the side and I'd catch her looking at me from the front row. I liked it when she looked at me. It let me know she was thinking about me, which worked since I was thinking about her.

She was wearing blue. I'd only ever seen her in khaki and pink. I really liked her in blue. The way her brown waves looked against the soft color, the way the blue looked against her perfect skin—perfect skin that I would've gotten to know well if I'd been in Stephen's shoes.

With my attention back on the auburn head, I couldn't miss the fact that he kept looking over and smiling at Faith. She'd smile back, but the smiles never reached her eyes. She wasn't into him. She couldn't be into him. I mean, he was a short, redheaded boy with freckles and a mouth full of metal. Then again, I'm sure that didn't matter since her dad was letting her out of her cell as long as she was with him.

After five secret looks between the two, I couldn't take it anymore. It pissed me off every time it happened. I stood up and slipped out the back of the church. I leaned up against the brick and wished I had a smoke. I'd pretty much quit, but I'd give my left nut for bowl packed with some sticky green cush.

I leaned my head back against the brick and took in some fresh air. I wanted to be away from the church, the pastor, and all the craziness. I only had a few days left of community service, so I skipped. It was the only day I left without getting my paper signed. I was exhausted and I just wanted to go home and spend some time with my mom before the band came over to practice.

That afternoon, Uncle Lester stopped by for his money and hooked me up with his new stock. Even though I wanted to, I didn't sample it. The whole drug scene felt different to me—it felt wrong. I was considering giving it up altogether and getting a real job—something with benefits and drug tests, something with health insurance for my mom.

Reynolds gave me the okay on the powder and then bought half of it from me on the spot. I spent the rest of the night singing my ass off and goofing off with the boys. Amanda, Kevin's most recent girl and also Faith's friend, came with Kevin and watched from my couch. I thought about quizzing her on all things Faith but decided against looking like a total pussy boy.

The following Wednesday, I got to spend time with Faith. We got stuck in the back room, putting together posters for some car washing event the church was having. The church was big on raising money. Faith explained to me how the money was used to improve the church, but all I could think about was how sweet her mouth looked when she talked.

I watched across the table as she drew pretty angel wings on her words and dotted her I's with hearts. Chicks were always doing senseless shit like that, but when Faith did it, it was cute. She didn't do things to impress others—she did them because she wanted to go the extra step, because she enjoyed doing her best.

Every now and again, her hair would fall into her face and she'd push it back. She never wore it up. As much as I loved her hair, I'd love to push it back and look at her face clearly just once. I bet Stephen the perfect church boy got to see her face.

"So you never told me how the date went," I said as I picked up a black marker and started to write.

She looked up from her poster and a soft-pink blush covered her cheeks when she smiled. It left my stomach feeling funny. I didn't like it. Actually, I hated it.

"It was fun. We went to a movie," she said as she nervously tucked a piece of hair behind her ear.

She was so cute when she did that.

"That's it?"

"What do you mean that's it? What else were we supposed to do?" she asked, confused.

She really had no idea how the whole dating thing worked. Of course maybe I was the one that had it all wrong. Had that been me, we would've made out for at least an hour, followed by some hardcore sex, and then I would've taken her home as late as possible, if I even took her home at all.

I bet pretty boy took her home early and I bet he didn't even try to kiss her.

"Did he kiss you?"

I wasn't sure where the question came from. I wasn't one to blurt things out, but I'd thought about it so much since that day in the kitchen when she told me she had a date and I needed to know.

Her eyes widened with my question and the blush on her cheeks went from pink to red. Still, she didn't answer.

"Well, did he? I bet he didn't. He doesn't look like that type."

Her brows pinched a little and I thought maybe I'd made her angry, but then she spoke.

"No. He did."

Just like that my day when from okay to shitty. I envisioned myself ripping Stephens's braces from his teeth and forcing them down his throat. The little rat-nosed bastard wasn't good enough to breathe the same air as Faith, much less put his nasty fucking mouth on her.

"Oh." I cleared my throat.

It was the stupidest thing to say, but I felt like I was choking and it was the only sound I could get past the imaginary blockage in my throat. Plus, it was better than what I'd been thinking. I was pretty sure if Faith knew I wanted to beat the living shit out of Stephen her opinion of me wouldn't be good. Not that her opinion of me was any good to start off with.

"I mean, he kind of did," she said as she put her head down and continued to work on the poster.

"What do you mean kind of? Either he did or he didn't."

I should've been happy for her. She looked happy and I didn't miss the big smile she had on her face when she'd told Sister Francis she had another date with him the following weekend. I spent five minutes after that wishing I hadn't heard it.

"He kissed me on the cheek."

I couldn't help myself. I laughed. What a punk bitch. I'd kiss my grandma on the cheek—if I had a grandma—and yet he'd given his *date* a goodnight kiss on the cheek. There was no doubt about it; he was a puss.

"What's so funny?" she asked, offended.

With laughter still in my voice I said, "Nothing. I can't believe he kissed you on the cheek. He's a wild one, Faith. You better watch out for that boy."

This time she laughed. Her laughter was so nice. She didn't laugh nearly as much as she should've.

"It's not funny. He's just shy. Besides, maybe he'll give me real kiss on our next date." Her face dropped when she said those words.

I stopped laughing.

"What's wrong?" I asked.

She stood and looked down at me in panic. "Oh God, Finn. What if he tries to kiss me?"

Again, my stomach felt weak with that thought. I didn't want his lips anywhere near her. I'd thought once or twice about telling her she was too good for him, but then she'd smile and sound excited about their date, and I'd swallow those words. Faith's smile did things like that to me. I couldn't explain it. It didn't make any sense and I didn't understand it.

"Then kiss him if that's what you want." I swallowed hard.

Tiny hands were choking me. Not literally, but that's what it felt like.

"I've never kissed anyone before." Her cheeks lit up with embarrassment.

I knew that. It was one of the main reasons I thought about kissing her so much. The thought of sharing her first kiss with her made my heart beat funny. I wanted to share something that special with her. I wanted to brand myself in her memories that way. I wanted it more than anything I'd ever wanted before.

"You'll be fine. Kissing is something that comes naturally."

"But what if I'm bad at it? Oh my God, I can't do this." She ran her hands through her hair. Her anxiety showed clearly on her face.

I couldn't keep my gaze from falling to her pouty pink lips. She'd be an amazing kisser. The thought of pressing my lips to her soft, cushiony mouth gave me a physical reaction. Not the usual physical reaction I had with girls, but something deep inside—something that bound itself around my emotions and squeezed.

"That's impossible," I rasped.

"It's completely possible. Amanda says she's kissed a lot of guys who were bad kissers."

I cleared my throat so my voice wouldn't squeak with tightness.

"No. It's possible... just not for you."

"How do you know?"

No way could I answer that. What would she think if I told her that her lips were too sweet, her mouth too luscious? Kissing her could never be described as bad—never. I could say that in confidence without ever even getting close to her lips.

"I just know."

She wringed her hands and put her head down. Her breathing changed, and when she looked back up, she was biting the inside of her mouth nervously.

"Could you show me?"

Alarms went off in my head.

"Show you what?" I asked.

No way was she asking me what I thought she was asking me. I didn't know if I could handle that. Even a tiny bit of her would push me overboard.

"Could you show me how to kiss?"

She couldn't even look at me when she asked. Her fingers were turning purple she was squeezing them so tightly. She was so innocent, so perfect, and yet she was asking me for something. She needed something from *me*. Even it was something small, it made me feel important. I hadn't felt that way often in my life.

I stood and moved closer to her. My knees shook slightly, prompting me to lean against the table. I'd never felt like this before, all anxiety and nerves, but Faith did this to me every time I was around her, and I wasn't sure I could continue being selfless for long.

"You're joking, right?"

I secretly hoped she wasn't joking. Even if I had to pretend to be doing it for unselfish reasons, if I ever laid my lips to hers, it would be totally selfish and I was afraid I'd never let her go.

"Never mind. I get it. Why would you want to even pretend to kiss me?" Her cheeks were blazing.

"That's not what I meant. I mean are you sure? I'd be your first kiss kind of in a way. I know that's kind of a big deal to some chicks."

I needed her to understand what I was taking away from her—what I was taking away from Stephen if he'd even thought about. More than anything, I needed her permission just once more. I didn't want her to regret me later. That would kill me.

"Yes."

Her voice sounded different. It was thick with what I could only describe as passion. I didn't think she was capable of such an emotion, but when I took a better look at her, I could see that her cheeks were flushed and her eyes were lazy and glazed over.

I tucked a stray piece of chocolate hair behind her ear. Her big brown eyes collided with mine, and for a brief moment, I felt a hint of panic at her being able to see right through me. She was staring at my memories and my thought process, and it scared the shit out of me.

I licked at my lips and her eyes dipped to my mouth. She was so innocent. Had another girl looked at my mouth that way, I'd know they wanted me to kiss them. Not with Faith, though. She did it without realizing her eyes were saying, "Kiss me, Finn."

The soft scent of fresh powder and roses swarmed around me when I moved in closer. I wanted to kiss her. I deserved just that one innocent moment of showing her how to kiss—of being her first anything. I'd been a decent human being since the moment she bumped into my life. I'd earned a tiny kiss.

I moved in a bit more and her gaze was broken when her eyes fluttered closed. She lifted her chin and bit softly at her bottom lip. She was ready for it and she looked so damn sweet. It was like a kick to the face. I might have deserved a brief kiss, but she didn't do anything bad to deserve me.

I moved back and her eyebrows pinched in confusion before she opened her eyes and looked back at me. I took a deep breath and pressed my forehead to hers. She was all around me, pulling and pushing at every emotion I held deep within, but I couldn't do this to her. I couldn't take away such a special moment.

"Your first kiss should be special. I don't want to take that away from you."

Before stepping away completely, I took the opportunity to feel her skin once more. I used my thumb to caress her check and it felt as soft as it looked. Being this close to her was amazing. She was amazing, and some guy was going to be one lucky son of a bitch when she fell for him. Hopefully it wouldn't be that punk Stephen. She deserved a real man.

I closed my eyes and swallowed hard. Stepping away from her was the smartest and dumbest thing I'd ever done, but she was worth it.

And then her lips brushed mine and it was as if fireworks went off in my stomach. I opened my eyes and was met with her closed lids. Her long dark lashes fluttered and her eyes opened briefly, searing me deep before she closed them again and sighed against my mouth.

I lost it. I pulled her closer to me and wrapped my arm around her waist. Deepening the kiss, I lost my other hand in her long, wavy hair. I didn't want to push her so I kept my lips sealed, but even without all the hot tongue action, it was probably the best kiss I'd ever had.

I lost track of time. I lost all rational thought, but I gained so much in that moment. I gained insight into something that was real. Not just a quickie in some chick's bed, no sloppy wet kisses that would lead to more, just a moment that was genuine. She was branding herself on my memory, and I knew no matter where the world took me, my first kiss from an angel would never leave me.

I wasn't sure who started it. Probably me since she was innocent, but my tongue met hers and the taste of her invaded my mouth. She was sweet—so damn sweet. I pressed against her more and I felt her fingers dig desperately into my arms. A tiny noise slipped from her mouth and ran down my spine before dissolving into a hot sensation in my thighs and pelvis.

Her soft breath bathed my cheek. She was kissing me just as hard as I was kissing her. Tongue and teeth collided in something more passionate than I'd ever known. And then it was over and I was left trying to catch my breath.

She'd broken the kiss, her warm breath cooling against my moist lips. I took a deeper breath and the taste of her rolled over my tongue, making me want more. Opening my eyes, I found her standing there looking back at me in expectation. She looked almost unaffected by the kiss, but then I noticed her dilated pupils and the tiny shiver that quaked through her. She smiled innocently at me.

"What do you think?" she asked.

Her voice sounded forced and heavy.

I couldn't tell her what I really thought—I wouldn't even if I could. Instead, I took a deep, refreshing breath, grinned down at her, and stepped away.

"I... I think you'll be fine."

Me, on the other hand, I wasn't too sure about anymore.

SEVEN

FAITH

Wow. I'd finally had a taste of what I'd been missing and I wasn't sure I'd ever be the same again. I couldn't even believe I'd been so open about wanting to kiss Finn. Maybe having an excuse to do so made it easier, but once my lips were on his and he kissed me back, I was changed. When he stepped away from me and went back to work on his poster, I knew I was a different girl.

I'd only been kissed once in my life, but I was positive no other kiss would top that one. I may never be more than a friend to Finn, and I may live a boring life until I'm married to someone equally boring, but at least I had that moment. It was almost as if Finn's kiss had given me the courage to face the uneventful life that was laid before me.

Things got weird then. Finn stayed quiet while I made posters for the car wash. At one point my dad came in and asked if Finn could come in on an off day and help with cleaning the rock patch out front for a new parking lot the church was getting. He agreed, which meant I'd be going to church on a Thursday after school instead of doing homework. It was strange actually being excited about going there.

The following day I went to the church with my dad. I lied again and said there was stuff I needed to do in the kids' room. In reality, I sat at the window and watched as Finn helped shovel the rocks into a big container the church rented.

Every now and again, he'd use his shirt to wipe the sweat from his face and I'd get a view of his stomach. He was so beautiful—sculpted by the hand of God. There could be no other reason for such perfection. He might be a full-blown sinner, but his eyes were made of heaven and when he looked at me, there was warmth that I'd never known.

I'd been so lost in my thoughts that I didn't even realize when Finn disappeared. I stood on tiptoes and angled my head in different directions trying to see where he went, but he was nowhere to be found.

"Do you always stalk people from the church windows?" he whispered from behind me.

I spun around so quickly that I lost my balance and he had to catch me. His body felt hot against mine and his drenched T-shirt stuck to the front of my simple white blouse.

"I… I wasn't," I stuttered

"Uh-huh. So you always sit at the windows for an hour, staring out?" he slid his arm down my side and I felt it in my knees.

"I wasn't," I said clearly.

"Okay, if you say so, but let me ask you something. Do you like looking at me, Faith?"

His eyes slipped to my mouth and I sucked in an excited breath. I silently begged that he would kiss me again. I ached to feel his mouth on my mine. I liked the way he was looking at me and the way he felt so close against my body.

I was going to go straight to hell when I took my last breath. What kind of person sat in a church room and fantasized about a man? I had to admit it to myself; I was definitely fantasizing about Finn.

"I wa—" I started.

He ran his thumb across my lips, stopping my words. His eyes penetrated mine as he took slow, deep breaths. He moved his other hand, adjusting it on my ribs.

"Don't say you weren't. You were. I saw you. And you know what? I liked it. I liked it almost as much as I like looking at you."

I swallowed the moan that rose in my throat.

"You like looking at me?" The words barely came out.

His fingers spread into my hair, making my scalp tingle.

"Very much. As happy as I am that I won't have to come back to this church in a couple of weeks, I'm sad that I won't be able to look at you anymore. You make coming here tolerable."

His words were too much, too sweet, and I couldn't help but close my eyes and melt into him once his hand started massaging the back of my hairline. He was giving me something I hadn't known I needed. I'd never needed to be close to someone else. I'd never needed pretty words. I'd accepted my future of being stuck with a man of God who was passionate as a stick. But Finn had me rethinking that future. Maybe I wasn't as wholesome and good as Daddy said I was. Maybe I was more sinner than I realized and maybe I liked being that way.

He pressed his lips to the corner of my mouth and I waited for him to press them against my lips again, but the kiss never came. Slowly I opened my eyes to find him staring back at me with a confused look on his face. He shook his head a bit and then stepped away. My body felt too heavy and I almost dropped from the extra weight on my knees.

"What is it?" I rasped.

My voice sounded different. Not young and inexperienced, but heavy with lust and greed. I wanted him to kiss me. I wanted it badly.

"This is wrong," he simply stated.

He looked so unaffected by me that it stung a little. However, he was right. What we were doing was wrong and I was glad he had enough self-control to pull away from me since I didn't think I could ever pull away from him.

I put my head down so he couldn't see my disappointment, tucked my hair behind my ear, and cleared my throat.

"You're right. I'm sorry."

I had the sudden urge to cry. I was sick of being denied the things I wanted in my life. I was sick of always wondering what something was like. I'd had a taste of Finn and all it did was make the urge worse.

Why was this happening to me? I'd been good my entire life. I lived the way Daddy taught me was the right way. I went to church and said my prayers every chance I got. How was I able to allow such sinful impulses to take over me? The devil was working overtime on me, and I had the feeling that if I didn't stop myself soon, I'd do something that I couldn't undo and taint my soul.

Just thinking of my soul, I clutched at my cross and took slow, deep breaths.

"Don't be sorry. This was my fault. I'm the sinner, remember?" He smiled, but it didn't reach his eyes. "I'm going back outside. I just came in for a break. I'll see you around, okay?"

I nodded my answer and said nothing as he stepped away and left the room.

The following day, Friday, I went to the church again with Daddy and again, I sat at the window and watched Finn work. It was sad how mixed up in him I was. Perhaps it had something to do with that life-altering kiss—my first kiss. Maybe it was because he was so different than everything around me and a nice change of pace. Either way, I couldn't stop myself.

This time, I only looked when his back was to me. I didn't want to take the chance of him catching me staring again. It was hotter than the day before, and he and the other guy who was working on clearing out the rocks were drenched in sweat.

His shirt stuck to his body and begged to be taken off. I wanted to see what was under there. I wanted to see if there were more tattoos and piercings. I wanted it more than a cold glass of iced tea on a hot day. And then, as if hearing my thoughts, he reached down and pulled his shirt up and over his head.

If I'd thought that his body looked shapely under his clothing, I really had no idea what I was thinking. With his shirt gone, I could see every ripple; every move his body made was emphasized in the muscles that moved beneath his skin. There was a tattoo on his right shoulder blade that I couldn't make out, and when he turned toward where I stood, I didn't hide this time.

My eyes were glued to him. From his hard chest, down over his ribs and abdominal muscles, and past the light dusting of dark hair beneath his belly button. He took my breath away and I felt funny. My breasts felt heavy and sensitive. There was a deep tingling sensation that ran from my stomach into the lower parts of my body and past my thighs.

When I looked back up, he was staring back at me with an angry expression. He picked up his shirt and pulled it roughly over his head. Spearing his shovel into the dirt so it stood on his own, he walked toward the church.

Quickly, I moved away from the window and spun around. When I did, I ran into my dad. He towered over me with knowing eyes.

"'But I say to you that everyone who looks at a woman with lustful intent has already committed adultery with her in his heart.' Matthew 5:28. I think these days that goes for men as well. Don't let me catch you lusting after that boy again, Faith," he said with tight lips. "Thankfully, he won't be here much longer. Now come on. Stephen's here and wants to talk to you."

My cheeks flamed with embarrassment. Daddy never talked about sex or lust. Hearing him say the word made me feel sick to my stomach. I nodded my understanding and followed behind him. We barely made it to the door to leave when Stephen walked in.

His brassy auburn hair looked redder in the sunlight and the sun glinted off of his braces when he smiled at me. He really was a nice guy, but I couldn't, no matter how hard I tried to make myself, like him.

"Everyone okay in here?" he asked my dad with a smile.

"Yes, sir, just coming to get our girl," my dad said as he clapped me roughly on the back before he stepped away and left the room.

"Sorry. I hope I wasn't interrupting your work, but my mother said you were here today and since I didn't get your number on our last date, I thought I'd stop by and ask you if you wanted to grab a bite to eat since it's dinner time."

His smile was too friendly—his eyes not filled with any emotion whatsoever. I wondered to myself if my eyes looked the same to Finn when he first met me. Did they still look like that?

I didn't want to go. Honestly, I would've enjoyed sitting home and laying my hand on the hot stove more than I would going out with him again, but I knew I had to. I couldn't lie and say I had plans because my dad would mess that up. I had no choice but to go and pretend to enjoy myself.

"Sure." My face felt stiff when I smiled.

We turned toward the door to leave, and Finn was standing in the doorway.

"Hey. Where you guys headed?" he asked as he dried his hands on some paper towels from the bathroom.

"We were just going to grab some dinner," Stephen said with a friendly smile.

An odd expression flashed across Finn's face before it cleared quickly and he sent me his signature grin. The expression came and went so fast that it was as if I'd seen things.

"Well, have fun." His smile was false. Something was definitely off. "Don't do anything I would do."

His eyes locked with mine as if he were begging me for something. In my imagination, I heard him say, *Please don't go with him. Go with me. Be with me.* I almost pulled him to the side and asked him if he was okay.

"All ready?" Stephen asked as he slipped his hand in mine.

The gesture made me blush and my cheeks felt hot. Finn looked Stephen up and down and briefly, anger flashed in his eyes. What the heck was his problem anyway?

I smiled at Finn as Stephen led me past him out the door of the kids' room. Finn reached out and grabbed my other hand, prompting me to turn back and look at him. There was a crushed look in his eyes before he quickly dropped it back to my side. Stephen saw nothing, but when I passed my dad's office, he was standing at the door and his expression told me had hadn't missed Finn's little display.

EIGHT

FINN

I couldn't take it anymore. I had days left at the church and the way that Faith was eye-fucking me from the window was making me insane. She couldn't know she was doing it, which made it ten times worse. She wanted me and she didn't even understand she did.

All sex stuff aside, the crazy part was I was pretty sure I was falling for her. I couldn't even believe I was thinking that, but I was. I could tell by the way I felt when I was around her. I'd never felt that way before and I wasn't sure I liked it too much. My mind had never been so absorbed with one girl. She was all I could think about. It was making writing songs for the band hell. Everything came out sounding like an eighties love ballad.

So after catching her staring at my junk from the window, I wasted no time. I left my shovel there and made my way through the church with a mission. I was going to kiss her senseless and I was going to ask her on a proper date. The boys would find it hilarious and it was completely out of character for me, but fuck it.

Not to mention, the pastor would probably have a heart attack, but if I had to, I'd talk her into sneaking out with me. I wanted to spend time with her outside of the church, time away from all interruptions so I could take my time and peel back all her layers—find out what made her tick, what she liked and hated.

Finding out what was under those god-awful skirts was the least of my worries when it came to Faith. Don't get me wrong, sex with her was running all through my mind, but more than anything and for the first time ever, I really just wanted to spend time with her.

When I got to the door and saw her there with Stephen, I felt anger that I hadn't known before. I'd been in fights for less. I contemplated going in and beating the shit out of the dude, but technically he wasn't doing anything wrong.

I knew inside that he was the better man, but I didn't care. I wanted her to be mine and I was greedy and suddenly needy. Weeks of being around someone untouchable knowing they'd welcome your touch is a bitch.

As soon as I was done at the church, and after checking on my mom, I met up with some friends and smoked until my eyes burned. When I was done smoking, I took shot for shot with my buddy, Leroy, until I couldn't feel my face. I was on a downward spiral, but I didn't want to feel anything.

I woke up the next morning in my bed with my clothes still on. I had no idea how I'd gotten there or how long I'd been there, but my head felt like someone smashed it with a hammer. My eyes were sealed shut and I had to pry them apart. The sun broke in through my curtains and drilled my sensitive eyes and straight through to the back of my head. At least that's how it felt.

It took me longer than usual to get out of the bed, and when I did, I took my precious time peeling off my clothes. My shirt smelled like women's perfume and there was lipstick on my face. I threw my clothes on the floor next to my door and got a hot shower.

When I finally appeared in the kitchen, my mom looked at me and shook her head.

"Feeling better?" she asked with attitude.

"I feel like shit. What time did I get home last night?"

"You mean what time did I have to come pick you up? Hmm, I'd say it was about four this morning. The cop was super friendly about the whole thing since you started crying and acting crazy." She turned off the stove and shoveled some eggs onto a plate before setting it in front of me. "Eat. You'll feel better."

"Cops? I don't remember any cops, and I don't cry so that's bullshit," I said defensively.

"Watch your language and don't you get snippy with me, Jimmy." She pointed at me with the spatula.

I felt like shit for being mean to her.

"I'm sorry, Mom. I'm sorry about last night, too. I don't know what got into me." I took a bite of my eggs and my stomach turned.

"It's okay. You've done worse, but don't do that again. I was worried sick about you. Apparently, the cops were called by Leroy's neighbor because of the noise, and you refused to leave. They were about to take you in when Leroy called and told me to come get you. By the time I got there, you were in tears—something about losing faith and God punishing you."

She sat down at the table beside me and reached out for my hand. I squeezed her small fingers to assure her I was okay.

"I know you've been through a lot in your life, Jimmy, and if you ever need to talk, you know I'm always here for you. You can tell me anything and I'll never judge." Her eyes watered up and I had to look away.

"Thanks, Mom." I leaned up and kissed her on the cheek. "I love you and I'll always be grateful to you for taking me in." Emotion closed my throat.

"I'll always be grateful for you. I'm not sure I could've made it through without you."

She patted my hand and then got up and left the room. I could tell by her small limp that she was in pain. I felt awful for her having to get out of bed and deal with my drunken ass. It was a dumb thing for me to do and she deserved better out of me.

Later that afternoon, while I was out getting some stuff for my mom, I passed the church. Faith was sitting on the front steps alone, so I pulled in and parked in a dry patch of grass. I sat in the Jeep, watching as she wrote in a notebook. She had no idea she was being watched. She was so hypnotic—the slide of her soft hair against her shoulder as she pushed it from her face. The movement of her hand as she wrote slowly. She was beautiful.

She looked up when I shut my door and started toward her. Her smile was welcoming and bright. I couldn't help but smile back.

"Hey. What are you doing?" I asked as I sat beside her. "Writing naughty things about me in your diary?"

She looked me in the eye, her brown orbs sucking me in and capturing me.

"What if I am?" she asked.

I was more than shocked. Even though she blushed sweetly, I couldn't believe she'd said something so blunt and flirty. I liked it. I liked it a lot.

"Are you?" If she was, I wanted to read it.

She grinned at me as she closed the book. "Maybe."

I could play like that with her all day. Not only was it adorable as hell, it was turning me on. I'd never been turned on by something so innocent.

"Can I read it?"

A guy could hope.

"I'm not going to let you read my journal."

"Why not? My name's in it."

She laughed. "And that's exactly why you're not reading it. What are you doing here today anyway? It's Saturday." She quickly changed the subject.

"I was just driving by and saw you sitting out here all by your lonesome. I thought I'd stop by and say hi. Maybe find out how your date went last night," I said, even though I didn't want to know.

As a matter of fact, it was the last thing I wanted to know about. If she told me he kissed her, there was no telling what I'd do.

"It was fun. We went and had dinner at the restaurant next to the tracks downtown, and then he took me home."

It was official. Stephen was a dumbass.

"Did you get to try out your new kissing skills?" The hair on my arms stood on end as I waited for her to answer.

Her cheeks went pink, begging me to touch her face. I curled my fingers up in my palm and kept my hands to myself.

"No. Just another kiss on the cheek," she said with a frown. "I'm starting to think he doesn't like me very much."

"That's impossible. He likes you, trust me."

Why was I helping him? I needed to shut my big mouth.

"How do you know?" she asked.

"Because I just know."

She turned toward me and her eyes took me in. She bit at her bottom lip nervously and tucked a strand of her hair behind ear. I wanted to kiss her again. Stupid Stephen had the chance and he wasn't taking it. Damn him.

"Finn, what was yesterday about?"

"What do you mean?"

I knew what she meant. I had no business grabbing her hand that way, but I hadn't wanted her to go with him. I wanted her to stay and go out with me.

"Never mind." She turned away and picked at a weed growing between the brick of the steps.

I watched her for a bit before deciding to answer her question.

"I didn't want you to go. That's why I grabbed your hand."

Her eyes moved over my face as she tried to figure me out. She opened her mouth to say something, but Stephen chose that time to come out of the church.

"Hi, James," he said with a grin.

If he wasn't such a preacher's boy, I'd think it was a knowing grin.

"Hey. What're you doing here?"

"I was just stopping by to pick up Faith, but I had to speak to her father real quick. Is everything okay?" he asked as he saw the tension between the two of us.

I was probably tenser because he called me James. Not to mention that he was practically rubbing it in that he was taking her out and best friends with the big preacher man. As far as I was concerned, he could suck my dick. I was getting about sick of him and his little brownnosing ass.

Faith looked away like she felt guilty. There was no need to feel guilty. We weren't together so she wasn't doing anything wrong. It still sucked, though.

I stood and wiped dirt from the back of my jeans. "Well, you kids have fun at dinner."

"Oh, we're not going to dinner tonight—just the movies."

He reached down for Faith's hand and pulled her into the standing position. She smiled at him and tucked her hair behind her ear.

"That sounds exciting," I said sarcastically. "Have fun."

I walked away. I was getting mad and the last thing I wanted to do was punch the kid in his nose in the churchyard.

Once I was in the Jeep, I looked over and watched as they walked to what looked like his parents' car. He opened her door for her and she slipped inside. I revved my engine and pulled out of my parking space. When I made it to the main road, I peeled tires pulling out into traffic.

I was being childish. I knew that. I should've been used to being the unwanted one. I'd been the unwanted one for most of my life and it wasn't fair.

I didn't ask to be born to someone who didn't want kids, just like I didn't ask to fall for the preacher's daughter. Things happened that way and there's nothing you can do to control it. All you can do is ride the ride and pray you don't crash.

I never did take my mom her stuff from the store. I'm sure she was pissed about that. I wouldn't have known, though, since I'd left the cell with her and she had no way to reach me. I was hitting a low place—a place I hadn't been to since I was taken into my mom's home. It was like reliving the foster homes and the families who never wanted me over and over again. Having Faith walk away from me was nothing like being tossed on your ass and back into the system. If anything, it was worse. I wasn't used to feeling that way about a girl. Everything about my situation with Faith was different.

I should've gone home and talked to my mom. I should've done the right thing, but instead, I found myself at a friend's house, drinking away my sorrows ... again. Once I drank away all in inhibitions, I did something crazy. I drove to the movie theater and waited for Faith to come out.

NINE
FAITH

My dad seemed to be pushing Stephen and me together even more. I think it was because he caught Finn and me together so much lately. That and the secret touches Finn made sure to get in whenever we were together. Either way, I assumed my dad thought Stephen and me being together would make me forget about Finn.

It was exhausting and it was starting to get on my nerves. Especially since I couldn't stop thinking about Finn. It made me somehow feel dirty being on a date with one guy while thinking of another. I didn't even enjoy the fact that I was being allowed out. I'd gotten to the point where I'd rather sit home and do nothing than go out with Stephen, but I didn't want to be rude. I wasn't one to hurt someone's feelings on purpose.

One thing I knew for sure was something was happening between Finn and me. I wasn't sure what it was, but it lingered in the air between us when we were together. I didn't want to think too much into it and get hurt. It was more than obvious to me that I was falling for Finn. I might have already fallen, except I had no idea what it felt like to be in love with someone. I just knew that everything about him made me smile and every time I was with him, life felt tolerable—better even.

I rode in the passenger's side of Stephen's mom's car, thinking about whether or not I was in love with Finn. Was it even possible to love someone in a month? What would I do once he didn't come to the church to work anymore? Would I just forget about him? Could I? I knew I didn't want to. I wanted him. Even if I didn't understand what it meant to want someone, I wanted him.

I contemplated pulling out my hair when Stephen bought us movie tickets to yet another G-rated movie. In the back of my mind, I begged for something dirty and R-rated. I thought about asking Stephen to take me to a bad movie just so I could at least get a laugh from of his appalled facial expression. Geez, he was such a stick in the mud. More than ever, I longed for Finn's flirty ways and bad-boy looks.

An hour into the movie, I got up to go to the bathroom. I didn't really need to go, but a girl can only look at so many cartoon characters before her eyes start to blur. I stepped into the bathroom and looked at myself in the mirror. Something was different. I was different.

I washed my hands, dried them, and then ran my fingers through my hair to get it to lie down. When I'd killed enough time, I opened the door to leave the bathroom. I gasped when I found Finn standing there in the doorway, looking back at me. He pushed through and pulled me into the large stall in the back of the room.

Part of me was nervous, and the other part was so happy that something exciting was happening. Leave it to Finn to make things feel more alive. My hand felt small in his. The warmth from his fingers dissolved into mine and worked its way up my arm.

Once we were in the stall, he locked the door behind us and pushed me up against it. It didn't hurt and I was disgusted by the fact that I liked it. I enjoyed him taking over me—I enjoyed being manhandled. It was refreshing after dealing with Stephen and his shy, passive ways.

He placed a hand against the door on each side of my head, trapping me between them. Stormy blue eyes took me in—anger in his brows. Reaching up, I gripped his arm and took a deep breath. His eyes left mine and dipped down to my mouth. The anger on his face melted away and his face softened.

"I didn't mean to scare you," he slurred.

"What are you doing here?" I whispered.

Removing his hand from the door, he caressed my cheek with his thumb. I closed my eyes and enjoyed the feel of him.

"I needed to see you."

He wasn't talking right—his eyes not focusing well. There was a strange smell to him that stung my nose and made my eyes water. I could only assume it was alcohol.

"Have you been drinking?" I asked as I pressed against his chest to make him back up.

"That's right. Push me away. Do you know I've been pushed away my entire life? There was always someone giving me away like I was nothing."

He was talking out of his head and I was getting a little nervous.

"What are you talking about, Finn?" I reached down for the lock on the door just in case he wasn't the guy I thought he was and he pulled something crazy.

"My mom calls me Jimmy Finn. She's the only person who calls me that. I think that's funny since she's the only person who's ever wanted me. Foster home after foster home and the one woman who gives me a new name keeps me."

He was finally starting to make sense.

"You're adopted?" I asked.

He nodded his head with sad eyes. I'd once heard that kids were treated badly in foster homes. Amanda told me a story about a kid who'd been accidently killed by the parents and they never reported it so they could keep collecting money from the state.

I reached up and pushed his hair from his forehead. He closed his eyes and pressed his face into my palm. It was such a sweet thing for him to do. I ran my thumb across his cheek over and over again, enjoying the feel of his soft facial hair.

"I didn't know that about you," I said.

He opened his eyes and looked down at me. His blue irises glowed under the florescent lights of the red-and-black tiled bathroom.

"There's a lot that you don't know about me."

I opened my mouth to say something, but the bathroom door cracked open, stopping me.

"Faith?" Stephen called into the room.

No way would someone like him come into the ladies restroom. Instead, I could hear him standing outside the door. The noise from the theater lobby spilled into the bathroom and echoed off of the walls.

I moved to open the door, but Finn stopped me and held his finger against his lips, telling me to be quiet.

Stephen called my name into the bathroom once more before the door shut and the room became quiet again.

"Finn, I can't stay in here. I have to go back."

"Stay." He swallowed hard and his eyes glistened.

I'd never seen him this way. He looked vulnerable and it broke my heart. From what I knew of him over the past few weeks we spent together in church, he wasn't afraid of anything or anyone, but something was scaring him, and I suddenly had the urge to comfort him—to make him smile and bring life into his eyes.

"What's wrong, Finn? You can tell me whatever it is." I ran my fingers through his tousled hair.

Closing his eyes, he let out a quiet gasp, as if my fingers were the best thing he'd ever know. When he opened his baby blues again, they collided with mine and then something unexpected happened. A single tear wobbled on his lashes before escaping and rushing down his cheek.

I cupped his cheek and caught his tear with my thumb. "Sweetie, please tell me what's wrong? Did something happen?"

Again, he closed his eyes as if he were feeling pleasure before opening them again and showing his pain.

"Say it again," he said roughly, as if tears were clogging his throat.

"Say what?"

"Call me sweetie."

The expression on his face pulled at my heart. I wanted more than anything to make it go away.

"You're scaring me, Finn. Whatever it is that's bothering you, just tell me. Let me try to make it better."

He surprised me as he leaned over and rested his head against my shoulder. His breath was hot against my neck and I couldn't stop the chills that rushed through my body. I was hot and cold all over and the strange pulling sensation in my stomach left me feeling dizzy.

Sliding his arms around my waist, he molded himself to me. I had to admit, it felt amazing to be held that way. I pressed the back of my head into the door and cupped the back of his head in comfort.

"I'm sorry I'm scaring you. I'd never do anything to hurt you. I swear I'd never do anything to hurt you, ever. I'll be okay if you promise to stay. Don't go with Stephen. Please stay."

I melted all over. Finn, the most careless person I knew, was holding me in a manner I wasn't familiar with and begging me to stay with him as if he cared. I wanted to. I wanted to stay there with him, locked in the theater bathroom. Just the two of us in peace and quiet while the world outside moved on without us, but then I remembered that Stephen was out searching for me. He'd probably already called my dad, freaking out.

"Finn, I can't. He's outside waiting on me. I can't do that to him."

He looked up at me. His eyes still weren't focusing and briefly I thought maybe the only reason he was acting like this was because he was drinking.

"Him? Don't do this to me. Please, Faith, stay." He pulled away and leaned against the wall. I hadn't noticed before how badly he was slurring and leaning.

I'd never seen a drunk person before, other than on TV, but I was positive he was drunk.

"How did you get here?" I asked.

He peeked up through his hair, then laid his flushed face against the tile wall. "I drove."

"You drove drunk?"

I couldn't believe he'd just said that. Who would do such an idiotic thing?

He chuckled to himself and then finally smiled. His cheeks lifted and his beautiful dimples showed themselves. Even unsteady on his feet, with unfocused, glazed-over eyes, he was still gorgeous.

"Baby, I've done a lot worse." His grin became sinister.

"How are you supposed to get home?"

No way was I letting him drive home. He'd once made sure I made it home safely, and even if I had to call his mother, I'd make sure he made it home okay, as well.

"I'm driving. Why are we talking about this? Let's talk about something more fun. Like, can I kiss you again?"

I wanted him to. Lord knows I did, but I couldn't do that. Not when he was drunk and probably had no idea what he was saying. He'd wake up tomorrow and regret it. That's if he even remembered it. I never wanted to be something someone regretted.

"I'm calling your mother. I'm not letting you drive home like this." I turned to open the door and leave.

He caught my hand and slowly intertwined our fingers. He pulled me into his chest and used his other hand to push my hair from my face.

"I have her car. Will you drive me home, Faith? I need you."

Those three words did me in. I didn't want to say no to him. He needed me and I'd be there for him the way he had been for me. Even if he didn't know he was helping me, he was. He brought color to my life and I'd always be grateful for that.

"Give me your keys." I reached out my hand and waited as he dug through his jeans pocket.

I'd only ever driven a car once. My dad let me drive home from the grocery store and I'd hated it. I wasn't very good at it and every time a car came up behind me, I freaked out, but I had to do what I had to do.

We snuck out of the movie theater, careful not to run into Stephen or ever worse, my dad. I'm sure he'd been called by now. I was already thinking of things to say to my father when he freaked out on me. Not to mention poor Stephen. I felt awful for doing this to him, but he'd never understand. He was like a younger version of my father. They had no idea what it meant to be alive.

Finn leaned against me through the parking lot to his mother's Jeep. I opened the passenger's side and helped him get in. Once I was inside, I felt like I was too high off of the ground. It was much different than being in my dad's Taurus. I rolled down my window and slowly pulled out of the parking space.

I was more nervous about the fact that Finn watched me like a hawk from the darkness of his side of the car while I drove than I was about driving. I tried to remember how to get to Finn's house, but I'd only been there once and I had to keep asking him which way.

Nothing looked familiar to me and I kept waiting for his neighborhood to come up, but there was nothing but woods. I was starting to worry that Finn was drunker than I thought. I continued to drive as thoughts kept coming to me. Like, how was I going to get home? I thought about all the trouble I was going to be in when I finally did get home and how badly I was going to get it.

"Take a left here," Finn said from the darkness.

I took a left onto a dark road and continued to drive until finally I came to a clearing. There were woods behind me and in front of me was the ocean. The smell of saltwater engulfed the car as the waves rushed toward the shore that was practically in front of us. A long dock stretched out over the water and in the distance, I could see boats with lights on them. The Cooper River Bridge was the backdrop. It was lit up with light-blue lights as cars drove across it and into the black star-filled sky.

"It's beautiful," I said in awe.

I'd never seen a place more beautiful in my life. Not that I'd been many places.

I turned when I felt Finn's fingers in my hair. He was sitting beside me and pulling softly at my fingers on the steering wheel.

"Then it's perfect for you," he whispered in my ear.

My body went up in flames. I was burning and it felt so wonderful.

He captured my face in his hands and turned me to face him. Even in the darkness, I could see his light eyes as they skimmed my face and then landed on my lips.

"Can I please kiss you again?" He ran his thumb across my bottom lip as he asked.

I nodded my answer and closed my eyes. His soft lips landed on mine and I absorbed everything I could. The feel of his breath, the taste of him, and the way his tongue moved softly over my lip. I didn't want to miss a single second. Tiny noises traveled from his lips and rushed down my body, landing in the bottom of my spine.

When he broke the kiss, he pressed his forehead against mine and we both took a much needed breath.

"I have a tiny problem," he said as his lips brushed mine.

"What?"

I sounded like a different person. My voice was deeper, like that of an experienced woman. One kiss—that's all it took—and I was blooming under his heat like a ripened flower.

"I never thought I'd say this, but I think I might be falling in love with you."

He opened his eyes and looked deep into mine as he waited for my reaction. He was drunk.

Only a drunk man could think he was in love with me. Me? The boring pastor's daughter who never went anywhere or did anything exciting, but then again, wasn't I here alone with him in the middle of nowhere? Hadn't I run out on a date without telling anyone?

"That's the alcohol talking," I stated.

He blinked at me and then shook his head. "No. That's my heart talking. I've never felt this way about anyone before. I'm sorry if that freaks you out."

In that moment, everything changed. I was his and I didn't care who said I couldn't be. I didn't care about anything else. I just wanted to be with him and soak up every moment that was offered to us.

I slid my arms around his neck and he smiled down at me.

"I'm not freaked out, but I guess I have a problem, too," I said.

He leaned down and pressed his smiling lips against mine. "And what's that? Anything I can help with?"

"Maybe. It seems my heart wants to talk, too."

"Oh really? And what does your heart have to say?"

I sat quietly and tilted my head as if I were listening to something. "I'm falling for you, too."

The moment the words left my lips, his face lit up. The car no longer felt like a dark and scary place. It was light and peaceful. As if someone had just lifted tons off of our shoulders.

He leaned in and kissed me again. This time pushing a little farther and drawing noises from me. My body rebelled against everything my father had ever taught me, and I didn't care. If God didn't want me to have that moment, then I wouldn't have been there. My heart wouldn't have been so full of love for Finn.

"We need to slow down," he said against my lips.

"Why? Did I do something wrong?"

"God, no. You're doing everything just right."

I went back in and kissed him harder. I wasn't sure what was happening to me, but I couldn't get enough of him. I pressed my body against his in ways that didn't make any sense to me and silently cursed my restrictive skirt for not allowing me to move my legs they way they begged to move. I didn't understand any of it. I just knew it felt nice and I wanted to keep doing it. He chuckled against my lips and pulled away.

"I don't want to push you into anything. When you're ready, and if you decide you want me that way, I'll be here. I'll wait." He grinned.

I paused at the look in his eyes. I'd only known Finn for a few weeks, yet somehow he had wrapped himself around me so tightly—metaphorically and literally.

"You'd wait for me?"

The concept seemed foreign. I was nothing—a pastel blob on the face of the earth. Meanwhile, he was bright—a star that illuminated my existence. I was drawn to him and I didn't know if I'd ever want to pull myself away.

His thumb caressed my cheek and lips. He looked down at them as if he wanted to kiss me again and then licked his.

"I'd wait forever for you."

And just like that, we were together. I was his and he was mine. I didn't think twice about Stephen or my dad, and when Finn asked me to spend the night with him in his mom's Jeep, I did just that. I fell asleep in his arms with the sounds of the waves as our background noise and his fingers in my hair.

TEN

FINN

When I woke up, my arms were wrapped around Faith and her face was buried in my chest. I was blanketed in her warmth and covered in her long, flowing hair. I ran my hand up her back and a tiny noise sounded from her moist lips.

I looked down at her flushed cheeks and smiled. Her mouth was open and she snored softly when she breathed in. It was best moment of my life. I'd slept better lying on the bench seat in the back of my mom's Jeep than I had anywhere else in my life, and I'd slept in a lot of places.

I watched her sleep until the sun was fully shining into the windows. The seagulls outside seemed to get louder the brighter the sun grew. My leg was falling asleep, but I didn't move. I didn't want to wake her. The moment was too sweet to ruin.

When she finally woke, she leaned back and looked up at me with a sleepy smile. Her long hair lay across my arm. The soft scent of roses and fresh powder filled my senses as I bent my head down and gave her a tiny kiss.

"Good morning, beautiful," I said as I let my thumb explore her creamy cheek.

I couldn't stop touching her. It was as if I needed reassurance that she was really there with me. It wasn't that I wasn't used to girls being with me; it was that I wasn't used to girls like Faith. She was perfection, far too perfect for a screw-up like me, and I knew in my heart that I didn't deserve her, but I couldn't help myself.

I couldn't even think about the fact that my head was pounding. I had a tiny hangover and I felt a little embarrassed about my behavior the night before, but screw it. A drunk man tells no tales, and I'd been up front and honest with Faith, which was exactly what she deserved. At least I got it off my chest and at least she didn't turn me away like she probably should have.

Her cheeks flushed sweetly. "Good morning. You're the first person to ever call me beautiful. It feels weird when you say it."

"Then I guess I'll say it over and over again until it's not weird anymore," I said as I fingered a strand of her soft waves. "You're beautiful, Faith."

She smiled sweetly and then leaned up and kissed me. I kissed her back with all that I was and tried to stay in control of myself. Not only was it morning and my morning wood hurt like a bitch against my jeans, but she was pressing against me in ways that she couldn't know were making me crazy. I wanted her, more than I'd ever wanted a girl, but I also wanted to make sure she was ready.

She brought out a side of me that I hadn't known existed before. I wasn't usually a patient man, but she made me patient. She was slowly transforming me into a better person, a person worthy of her.

I gasped when I felt cool fingertips against my stomach. She fingered the creases of my abs slowly, as if she were memorizing me. Even though it was killing me, I restrained myself and allowed her the freedom to roam my body.

"You're so hard," she said as she pressed her palms to my chest.

I couldn't help myself. "In more ways than one." I grinned down at her.

Before she could figure out what I was saying, I kissed her again and chuckled against her mouth. Time slipped away as we made out in the back of my mom's Jeep like normal teenagers. The waves crashed against the shore outside and the birds flew above us in the warming breeze.

I felt something cold against my chest. I stopped kissing her and leaned back to find her necklace had escaped her shirt and was lying against me. She'd always worn the silver cross around her neck as far as I knew, and there had been many times when I'd see her pull it out of her shirt and hold it in her palm as if it soothed her.

I picked it up to inspect it. "Where did you get this?" I asked.

She looked down and pulled the small cross from my fingers. It disappeared in her tiny fist as she wrapped her hand around it. "My grandmother gave it to me when I was little."

"Do you ever take it off?"

"Never." She shook her head. "It saved me when I was little, so I never take it off."

She looked up at me. Her deep-brown eyes swirled with some profound emotion I wanted to know more about.

"What do you mean it saved you? Did something happen to you?"

I knew I was pressing her, but I was worried there was something going on in her life that she wasn't telling me about. I wanted to know everything when it came to Faith.

"When I was little, my dad used to tell me that if I was bad, the devil would come and steal my soul. For years, I worried that my soul was never safe. So whenever I felt like I'd done something bad, or when bad things would go on around me, I used to pretend that I could hide my soul inside my cross and keep it safe. I panic when I even think about taking it off. It's engraved in my head that I have to keep my soul safe."

When she looked up, a tiny tear clung to her cheek. I kissed it away before kissing her. When I pulled back, she smiled down at me.

"I'd never let anyone take your soul. It's too precious... You're too precious."

This time, she kissed me and I let her, but just when my body relaxed into her, she suddenly pulled away from me, leaving my lips burning and my breath stuck. She stared up at me in confusion and then as if released from a spell, she jumped up, her eyes wide with fear and her breathing deep and fast, as if she were in a panic.

"Oh my God, my dad's going to kill me." She gripped her cross with one hand and pawed at the door to open it with the other.

A salty breeze wafted into the car when she finally pushed it open. I followed behind her and my shoes sank into the thick sand beneath our feet.

"Don't freak out. This is my fault. I'll tell him it's my fault." I tried to calm her.

"No, this is my fault. I knew better than to leave the movies, but I did it anyway. Please, Finn, just take me home. I might as well face the firing squad. It might be a while before we get to see each other again, though."

Panic seized me. I hadn't thought about the consequences of my actions the night before. I never really thought about consequences ever, but not thinking was biting me in the ass. Because I'd practically forced her to the leave the movies the night before, I'd made it ten times more difficult to be able to see her. Of course once her dad knew she was with me, he was going to forbid her to see me again. I had to remember that I wasn't dealing with the girls from around my way, whose parents didn't give a shit about them.

I wouldn't let it happen. For the last few weeks of my life, I'd been able to see Faith, and if it were up to me, that would continue.

"Nah. If I want to see you bad enough, I'll just come to you. I'm kind of a pro at sneaking in windows." I grinned.

She gave me an adorable eye roll and threw her hands in the air in frustration. "That doesn't make me feel better, Finn."

I couldn't help myself. I laughed and pulled her to me. She melted in my arms.

"Don't worry about this, okay? I'll make it better."

And I would somehow. No matter what I had to do, I'd make it better. At least that's what I thought, but thirty minutes later, when we pulled on to her street, I knew things were about to get worse. Two police cruisers were in her driveway waiting for us. Her hand tightened in mine and I felt the moisture of her nervous palms. She was afraid and I hated it. I wanted to take away her fear.

"Just follow my lead," I said as I pulled in behind a cop car and put the Jeep in park.

She nodded her agreement, popped open the passenger's side door, and then climbed out. The front door to her house snapped open loudly, and her mother and father came barreling out of the house, followed by two police officers. The screened door was practically ripped from its hinges.

"You!" The preacher pointed his finger at me. "You kidnapped my daughter!"

I stood my ground, but suddenly Faith was standing between me and her father as he growled at me.

"Daddy, this wasn't Finn's fault. It was mine."

"I didn't kidnap her. She drove me home. I was drinking, sir, and..."

"I don't want to hear your excuses. You stay away from my daughter, do you understand me?"

"Daddy, please just calm down for a—"

She was quieted with the back of his hand. The sound of his hand landing against her cheek echoed all around me. Long brown hair shifted in front of me as she skidded to the side, landing hard against the Jeep before falling to the ground.

I didn't even realize I was moving until I felt my shoulder connect with his stomach. I slammed him on the ground as hard as I could and punched him in the face twice. He put his arms up to block, and I lifted my fist to hit him again. I would've kept punching except I felt tiny fingers dig into my arms as Faith pulled me away.

"Stop, Finn, please stop!" she was yelling.

Her mother was screaming nonsense, drawing attention to our little drama in their front yard. Strong fingers replaced Faith's as a cop pulled me from the pastor. I was thrown against the side of my Jeep and handcuffed immediately. I stopped fighting once the cop shifted my body and threw me into the back of his car. Faith stood there staring back at me with dirty tears running down her cheeks.

Neighbors had started coming out of their houses and were openly staring. I looked down at the pastor, who was still lying on the ground. His silvery hair shined in the sunlight as he turned his head to the side and spit a mouthful of blood onto the dirt at his side.

His wife helped him up from the ground and then he sat and talked to the police. I couldn't hear anything they were saying, and I couldn't keep my eyes from Faith. She still hadn't stopped crying, and I felt like shit for not being fast enough to stop her dad from hitting her and then for being so crazy with rage that I'd kicked her dad's ass.

There was no doubt in my mind that I was going to jail and my poor mom was going to have a hell of a day. I felt like shit. We'd only been together for a few hours, and already I'd made Faith cry and ruined my mom's day. I was a selfish asshole. I'd put what I wanted ahead of others and what they deserved.

I was shocked when one of the officers came over, opened the door, and pulled me out. Spinning me around to face the car, he unlocked my handcuffs.

"Well, son, it looks like it's your lucky day. Pastor Warren here has decided to not press charges."

I turned to face the pastor. His cheek was turning purple and there was a trickle of blood on his lip. He walked up to me and the officer and placed his hand on the officer's shoulder.

"Thank you, Ronald. We look forward to seeing you and the wife at church soon." He smiled.

When he turned to face me, his smile wasn't real. He was putting on a show for the police, and it only made me despise him more.

"James, I'd appreciate it if you stayed away from Faith. Your community service is done, so that means my family and I shouldn't be seeing much of you anymore. All is welcomed in the house of the Lord, so if you decide you'd like to come to church on Sunday's, then please, by all means, come, but make sure you're nowhere near Faith when you do."

My eyes collided with Faith's as his words sank in, but honestly, I'd known all along it was going to be difficult to see her.

He couldn't have known it at the time, but he'd issued a challenge and I'd accepted wholeheartedly. He wasn't going to keep me from what I wanted, and I wanted Faith. End of subject.

I nodded and turned to go back to my Jeep. I had to keep in control if I didn't want my mom having to spend money we didn't have to bail my stupid ass out of jail. I shut the door behind me, cranked up the Jeep, and then sat there and stared at Faith through the dusty windshield.

She held up her hand as if to say good-bye, with sadness in her eyes. I could see it in her face that she thought I was done. She thought I was just going to walk away from her so easily—let them win. Well, she had a lot of things to learn about me. I wasn't going to give up. When it came to her, I was just getting started.

ELEVEN

FAITH

That night I went to bed with a bruised cheek and more welts on my legs than I'd ever had. One of them actually bled to the point that I had to cover it with a bandage. It wasn't pretty, and for the first time in a long time, I cried because of the pain.

I was slowly coming to realize that my dad had something wrong with him. No person should feel enjoyment over beating another person, and what I saw in his face as he took his belt to me after the police left was joy. It had been a bad one. So bad in fact that my mother, who usually stayed out of it, stepped in and told him to stop.

Honor thy mother and father, and I did, but that didn't mean I wasn't allowed to hate them. I'd never used the word hate before. I had no idea I was capable of the emotion, but I was. I hated my father for what he'd done to me. I hated my mother for sitting by and watching it for so many years.

I rolled onto my side and stared out at the moonlight that drifted in past my white lace curtains. My mind hadn't stopped going since I'd stepped foot in my yard earlier that morning, but finally, I could feel myself getting tired. I'd never begged for sleep so much in my life. I wanted it all to go away for a few blissful hours until it was time to get up and run to school.

My eyes were heavy and slowly closing. Sleep was just beyond my reach and I was grabbing at it in full force. I was almost there when a shadow crept across my room. With wide eyes, I sat up and screamed, but a hand over my mouth stopped any noise from getting out.

My body tensed up and I went into full freak-out mode. I bucked in my bed in an attempt to get away, scratching at the hand with my nails and thrashing so hard that my mattress springs popped loudly. If I was being murdered or kidnapped, I wasn't going down without a good fight.

"Faith, it's me," Finn whispered.

I gave up my fight and took a minute to let my panic subside. My eyes adjusted to the darkness around me, once again allowing me to see his silhouette in the moonlight. I was so happy to see him, but at the same time, all I could think about was my dad coming in and catching him. He'd let Finn off once. I seriously doubted he'd let him off twice. The last thing I wanted was for Finn to get arrested. I wasn't sure what breaking and entering would get you, but I knew it was more than community service.

Once he removed his hand from my mouth, I sat up and threw my arms around his neck.

"What are you doing here?" I whispered into his shoulder.

Leaning back, he captured my face in his hands. "I wanted to make sure you were okay. I'm sorry about what happened today."

I wanted to see his face. I needed to see his smile and know that he was really there with me. Reaching over, I turned on my small bedside lamp so I could see more of him. Once the light was on his face, the smile he wore dropped. He softly fingered the bruised side of my face with heartbreak in his eyes.

I pressed my sore cheek into his palm. "I'm okay." I smiled.

"I should've moved faster. I shouldn't have let him touch you," he rasped.

"Stop." I pressed my finger to his lips. "That wasn't your fault. I'm just sorry you had to see that." I used a finger to move a strand of hair from his eyes. "No more depressing talk. How did you get in here?" I asked.

His frown was replaced with his signature cocky grin. "I told you sneaking in and out of windows was super easy for me."

I got up and made sure my bedroom door was locked, and then I opened my window wider so Finn could have a quick escape in case my dad came to my door. Once I was done with that, I turned back toward my bed and caught him staring at me.

"What?" I asked.

He stood and came to me. I loved it when he played with my hair so I was happy when he buried his fingers in the strands around my face. His smile darkened as his eyes dipped down and over my body.

"I've only ever seen you in long skirts. Your legs are so long and beautiful—sexy."

My face lit up with heat as I looked down at myself. I'd forgotten what I was wearing. My white cami and plaid boxers left little to the imagination. I felt even more embarrassed knowing that I had no bra or panties on underneath. I'd never been so naked around another person in my life.

"I should change," I said as I started to step away.

He caught me around the waist and I felt the heat of his fingers through the thin cotton covering my stomach.

"Don't. I like seeing you like this. Not because you're showing more skin, but because you look comfortable. You're so beautiful and you're clueless to it."

I didn't fight him when he slowly walked me back to my bed and pulled me onto his lap.

"What have we gotten ourselves into, huh?" He smiled and shook his head.

I ran my finger across his dimples and leaned in to kiss him. It was nice being able to do that. I never thought I'd be the kind of girl who would just out of nowhere kiss a guy, but I was comfortable with Finn.

He kissed me back like he was breathing me in, and when he ran his palm across my stomach, I didn't stop him. He'd told me before that he wouldn't rush me—that he'd wait for me, and I trusted that.

I tilted my head to the side and breathed deep to keep myself from making embarrassing noises when his lips moved from my mouth and to my neck. I'd never felt something so wonderful. He was teaching me new ways to live, and I was sucking up his lessons like they were my survival.

I could remember the many lectures I'd gotten over the years about being easily led by lust and sexual desires. I'd readily accepted that what my dad said was correct without knowing or understanding anything that had to do with the words lust and sex. But Finn was showing me how right my dad had been. Lust and desire could make you do some crazy things. So when Finn very slowly laid me back onto my bed, I didn't stop him.

I didn't care about anything else but his lips and hands—the feel of his breath on my skin and the deep noises he made, which made the hairs on my arms stand on end. I heard myself actually whine when he pulled away and smiled down at me.

"Time to slow down, pretty girl," he whispered.

I could feel his restraint in my own bones. Stopping or slowing down wasn't something that was easy for him, and it made me feel good that he respected me enough to make himself uncomfortable. He brought me up with him and planted a tiny kiss on the corner of my mouth.

As much as I feared getting caught with him in my room, I didn't want him to leave. Spending the night with him the night before had been so nice. Falling asleep in his arms had been one of the best feelings, and I wanted to feel that way again.

He stood and adjusted his shirt. I got a glimpse of his belly button and the hair that disappeared into his jeans. My eyes moved lower on their own, allowing me to see his long legs. He really was such a nice-looking guy. When I looked back up, he was smiling.

"Stop looking down there like that. You're not making this easy for me." He bent down and gave me a small kiss on the lips. "I better go. Have fun at school tomorrow."

Before he could turn away, I reached out and grabbed his hand. I didn't want him to go. I felt amazing when he was around. I could forget about how sad my life was when he was there making everything better.

"Stay."

The minute the word left my mouth, I kind of regretted it. I didn't want him thinking I was making any promises that something would happen. I just wanted to fall asleep in his arms the way I had the night before.

He didn't say anything. Instead, he kicked off his shoes, pulled back the cover on my bed, and climbed under it, pulling it back up around us.

We spent the next few hours quietly talking. He told me about his life, the band, and how he'd come to live with his mom. I held him close as he told me about what growing up in different foster homes had been like. He was such an emotional guy, which probably had a lot to do with why he was so guarded around everyone.

Once I was done telling him the sad little tale of my boring life, I lay there while he played with my hair and sang some songs. I'd never heard the songs before so I assumed they were the band's music. His soft melodic voice relaxed me to the point that I could no longer tell if I was asleep or awake. At some point, I felt his lips against my forehead and I heard him whisper goodnight.

When I woke up the next morning, I was alone in my bed. I rolled onto my side and pressed my face into the pillow where he'd been. I could still smell the light scent of his cologne. When I sat up in bed, a pink rose from my mom's rose bush lay on my bedside table on top of a scribbled note.

If it looks like an angel, talks like an angel, and sleeps like an angel, then it must be an angel.

See you soon, beautiful.

Love,

Finn

If my parents noticed I was acting different, they didn't say anything about it. I probably wouldn't have heard them anyway since my head was so far in the clouds. On the ride to school, I had to push my smile down so my mother didn't see it.

I spent the rest of the day floating and riding my Finn high. Amanda stared at me from across the picnic table at lunch like my head was on fire.

"Tell me again how you slipped in the shower and bruised your face." She said suspiciously.

Rolling my eyes, I laughed as if it was nothing. "Just me being clumsy as usual."

I took a bite from my apple and smiled secretly to myself with thoughts of Finn.

"Okay, what's up with you? You've been acting crazy all day."

When I didn't answer right away, she threw a grape at me. I picked it up and playfully threw it back at her.

"It's nothing. I'm just having a good day."

"Uh-huh. When did you start lying?"

I didn't bother telling her anything about Finn. I still wasn't exactly sure what it was we were doing. I didn't want to look like a fool by telling Amanda that Finn and I were together and then have him show up the following weekend with some new girl.

I didn't know much about guys, but I knew Finn was a ladies' man. He had to be. He was too attractive and too confident not to be.

A sickness sank into my stomach with the thought of Finn saying and doing the things he was saying and doing with me with some other girl. An earlier conversation we'd had before ran through my mind and I could remember him telling me that he had girls in his life.

Maybe I was moving a little too fast with my emotions. Maybe wrapping myself around Finn so quickly wasn't a good idea after all, but it was so hard not to. Especially when he was saying and doing things I'd been yearning for.

That afternoon after dinner I finished up some homework, got ready for sleep, and then relaxed in bed with my favorite book until I could feel myself getting tired. Part of me tried to stay awake in hopes that Finn would swoop in and stay the night with me again, but soon my eyes were heavy and I fell asleep.

By the time Wednesday came around, it had been two days since I'd seen or heard from Finn. I was starting to worry that maybe he really had been messing with my head. I spent the day feeling sick to my stomach and worrying a hole in my heart. I was willing to do anything that would take my mind off of Finn.

When it was time to go to church, I rebelliously slipped into my only long jean skirt instead of the normal khaki and pretended I didn't see my parents' disapproving eyes when I met them at the car. Once we were at church, my cross warmed my palm as I sat through my dad's sermon on sinful ways and remaining holy.

I could feel the congregation's eyes on me since it had already gotten around the church about my night out with Finn. They knew Daddy's sin sermon was for my ears only and seemed to praise Jesus a little louder for my sake. It hurt. My church family was supposed to love me no matter what, but it felt as if they were all turning their backs on me and condemning me.

Stephen wouldn't even look at me anymore, which was fine by me. The last thing I wanted was more attention. His parents had no problem keeping their eyes on me, though, and I spent the entire time wishing I could disappear under the pew and sneak out the back.

The next day at school, I decided I'd had enough wondering about Finn and that talking to Amanda was my best option. I watched her stuff her face with her lunch and text from across the table.

"When's the last time you saw Finn?" I asked abruptly.

There was no need to beat around the bush. Pulling the Band-Aid off fast was less painful.

She looked at me with her mouth open before she recovered and answered. "I saw him last night. Um... why?"

It was time she knew what was going on in my life. It seemed that she was the only person in my life who wouldn't judge or look down on me. It made me appreciate her friendship even more.

I spent the rest of lunch telling all. I could tell by the way she was looking at me that I shocked her. Even though Finn and I hadn't done anything sexually, she looked at me with wide eyes as if she were in awe of me.

"Okay, so you guys are, like, a thing?" she asked.

"I don't know what we are," I said as I covered my face with my hands and growled in aggravation.

The truth was I missed him and I wanted to see him. I wanted to know what was going on between us, if there was anything there to fight for. If not, then I was going to drown myself in schoolwork and church the way I always had and move on.

"I'm going with Kevin to Finn's house tonight for practice. You should come and talk to him." She shrugged.

And just like that, I made plans to sneak out with Amanda once again. It wasn't a smart move, I understood that, but it was necessary as far as I was concerned. I wasn't looking forward to going to the scary side of town, but I could be brave for Finn.

I went straight to my room when I got home and did my homework. At dinner, I was silent as I ate. I felt awful knowing I was being deceitful, but it felt worse not knowing what was going on with Finn and me.

I sat quietly in my room and read until I was sure my parents were asleep. Once I could hear my dad's loud snoring sounding from down the hallway, I pulled out an outfit that I borrowed from Amanda and slipped it on. I thought it was sweet of her to run home during school and pick through her clothes for me. If I was going to go back to Finn's garage, I didn't want to stick out too much.

The dark jeans were tight and hugged my hips like a second skin and the black shirt barely covered my stomach. Every time I lifted my arms, I felt a breeze on the skin just above the waist of my jeans. Even though the clothes were tighter than I was used to, I felt more comfortable in them.

I pulled my hair back in a ponytail and tucked my cross beneath the collar of my shirt. When I finally took a second to look in the mirror, I was amazed at how different I looked. I felt good—comfortable in my skin and ready to take on the wrong side of town. It was amazing the confidence a pair of jeans could bring.

When Amanda tapped on my window, I slid out with little problem. Turns out it's much easier to move around in a pair of jeans than it is a long skirt. I padded across the damp yard to Kevin's car and was once again met with Tiny sitting in the back seat.

I didn't even look back to check to see if my parents had woken up as we pulled away from the curb. The nerves that I felt last time I snuck out were nowhere to be seen. The only thing I felt was happiness as we made our way through town and closer to Finn.

TWELVE

FINN

I sold the last of my stash, fixed my car, and bought a new tire. It felt damn good to have the Mustang back on the road. I was determined to get my life in order and be good for Faith. I didn't want to sneak around with her. I wanted her dad to be okay with me dating her, and if I wanted that, I had to go straight.

I spent the day after getting my car fixed going around and putting in applications everywhere I could. My drug-selling days were over and I wanted to earn honest money. Mom, who never even knew I was dealing, agreed that it was time I stepped up and got a job. She needed my help, but she also understood that I had to make my own way—be a man and all that.

I missed Faith like crazy, but I wasn't going to approach her dad with anything until I could show him that I'd changed and was doing better for myself. My plan was to go to church the following Sunday to speak with him. He needed to know that I was in love with his daughter and I meant her well.

By Wednesday, I didn't think I could take it anymore. All I could think about was sneaking in her window and spending the night with her again. At the very least, I wished I could hear her voice over the phone. Instead of giving in, I wrote songs for the band. Who gave a shit if they were ballads? It felt good to get my feelings out on paper.

Once Reynolds showed up at my house for practice Thursday night, I was hungry for just a glimpse of Faith. I'd never known what it felt like to miss someone so much. He beat on his drums and bullshitted while we waited for Kevin and Tiny. I turned him down when he offered to do a line with me and I was proud of myself.

I watched from my couch as he lined it up on my coffee table and then sucked it up through a dollar bill. He captured the rest of it from the table top with his finger and rubbed it on his gums with a big goofy smile.

"You need to lay off that shit, man," I said as I took a swig from my beer.

"Oh come on, Finn, not you, too. I got this, dude. No worries." He ran the back of his hand across his nose.

Overdosing was a real thing where I came from. I'd only ever seen it happen once, but I knew people over the years that had taken their drug habits too far. I was well on my way out of that shit. The people around me could do what they wanted, but I was done.

I walked toward my mic when I heard a car pull up. I was ready to take my frustrations out in my music. Expecting Kevin and Tiny to walk into the garage, I was taken back when Jenny, my ex girlfriend, walked in.

"What's up?" I asked as I fell back onto my couch. "Haven't seen you around lately."

She shyly smiled at me as she sat next to me on the couch. I'd never noticed before how trashy she looked—her hair was too blond, her makeup too dark. Everything about her was just wrong, and I found myself feeling sick to my stomach that I'd ever touched her.

"I thought I'd stop by and watch you practice. I miss it... I miss you," she said as she laid her hand on my knee suggestively.

I picked up her hand and dropped it in her lap.

"Nah, I'm good, but you're welcome to stay and listen if you want." I trashed my empty bottle and went to the cooler and grabbed another.

She followed me and when I turned around, she threw her arms around my neck.

"Are you seriously going to turn this down?" she asked as she pressed her tits to my chest.

I looked down at her cleavage and almost gagged. She smelled like cigarettes and stale hairspray, and I wanted her as far away from me as possible. I pulled her arms from around my neck, turned her, and pinned her up against a wall.

Excitement filled her eyes and she licked at her lips.

"That's what I'm talking about," she said as she leaned in to kiss me.

I pulled back. "Hell no. We're done. As a matter of fact, I think you should go."

I was about to release her when I heard Kevin's loud voice behind me.

"Damn, man! I thought we were going to practice. Knock that shit off. You can fuck her later."

I turned around and started toward my mic again, but I stopped when I came face to face with Faith. The wounded look in her eyes shot right through me. I knew exactly what she was thinking.

She turned and left the garage quickly, and I cursed and followed behind her. It was going to take some quick talking on my part and a lot of trust on hers.

"Wait up!" I said as I grabbed her by the arm and spun her around.

A single tear rushed down her cheek and broke my heart. I reached up to wipe it away, but she turned her head and looked away from me.

"Faith, nothing was happening. I was telling her to leave, I swear."

She swiped at her face and rolled her eyes. "Yeah, that's exactly what it looked like!"

I'd never heard her yell before. More tears spilled from her eyes and I cussed myself for being so stupid.

"I'm so sorry, baby. Please don't cry." I pulled her tighter to me and wrapped my arms around her.

She tried to pull away and I held tight until she relaxed against me. I felt her body shaking as she cried against my shoulder. I rubbed her back softly.

"I'm so sorry you saw that, but I swear, Faith, I was telling her no. I was asking her to leave. I'll go get her right now and she'll tell you. I promised you that I'd never do anything to hurt you and I meant it. Please just trust me."

She looked up at me and sniffled. Even with a red face covered in tears, she was beautiful.

"This is all so new to me, Finn. I don't know what I'm doing. I don't know what this is that we're doing. If this isn't anything and I'm seeing things that aren't there then just tell me. I'll walk away no questions asked."

I chuckled softly to myself. She was so far off.

I captured her face in my hands and softly kissed her.

"That's the last thing I want you to do. I know I've been quiet lately, but that's only because

I've been out trying to get a job and get my life in order. I want to be good for you, Faith, and right now I'm not."

It was weird putting my emotions out on the table like that, but I trusted her with my life. She would never hurt me and I felt safe giving my all to her.

"You are... you're perfect for me. Since I met you, everything's better. You make everything better and..."

I didn't let her finish. I couldn't take it anymore. I needed to kiss her. So I did. She gripped the front of my shirt and I filled my hands with her hips and pulled her closer to me. There's was no such thing as too close when it came to Faith.

We held hands as we went back into the garage. The guys, who were lounging on the couch, waiting, rolled their eyes and bitched about me running out.

"It's about fucking time, dude. Are we going to do this or not?" Reynolds asked.

I smiled at Faith as I sat her on the couch. It was then that I was able to actually look at her. Her hair was pulled back and I could see every inch of her face and neck. The top she wore was black and low on her shoulders, revealing even more of her creamy skin. Her tight jeans accentuated every curve and dip of her hips and legs.

She looked so fucking sexy and sweet that I almost scooped her up right then and took her to my room. Leaning over, I whispered in her ear.

"You look so sexy tonight."

Her cheeks turned pink, and I softly kissed her lips before turning away from her.

I sang my heart out that night. Not once did I break eye contact as she watched from the couch. Every word I sang was for her, and when she smiled up at me and bobbed her head a little to the music, I felt accomplished. I'd always loved being a part of Original Malice, but something about singing with Faith as my audience made it feel real.

When practice was over, everyone left but Faith. I promised Amanda that I'd get her home safely, and I would, but I wanted to spend some alone time with her. It had been days since we'd seen each other and I since she'd already snuck out anyway, there was no need to waste a perfectly good night.

"You have a beautiful voice," she said as I sat beside her on the couch and pulled her onto my lap.

She wrapped her arms around my neck and kissed my cheek. She felt so good against me, but I remained in control of myself. My body begged to be with her and my mind spun every time she moved in my lap.

"You have a beautiful everything," I said as I captured her lips with mine.

I'd never been so happy in my life. I'd never made plans for the future. There was never a person in my life that was a constant. I wanted Faith to be that person. We were young, but it didn't matter. She was the one I wanted and I wanted her until I was no more.

I made sure to take my time with every move I made. As badly as I wanted to have sex with Faith, I knew I needed to take it slow, and as unmanly as it sounded, I wasn't really ready to take that step with her. It had to be perfect for her since she was so perfect.

An hour later, I took her home and walked her to her window. I kissed her again and helped her climb in. Her ass and hips felt amazing in my hands and I had to stop myself from squeezing and pulling her back out against me. She was going to be the death of me.

Once she was in, she turned around and smiled. “Same time tomorrow night?” she whispered.

I couldn’t help myself, I chuckled. My little angel was turning into a devil. I didn’t like the idea of her sneaking out, but I also didn’t want to deny her anything. If she wanted to see me, then she was going to get what she wanted.

“I’ll park at the stop sign. My car’s louder than Kevin’s. Goodnight, beautiful. I’ll see you tomorrow night.”

“Goodnight.”

She kissed me one last time and then slowly pushed her window closed.

I didn’t even remember the walk back to my car. She made me higher than any drug I’d ever taken and I was becoming addicted to her.

THIRTEEN
FAITH

I was definitely in love. Period. There was no longer any doubt in my mind about that. Finn was it for me. There'd be no other. I understood that the minute I stepped foot into his garage and saw him standing there holding another girl against the wall.

The look on his face when he saw me could only be described as broken. Pain filled his eyes and his mouth fell open as if he'd just been told someone he loved dearly had died. The moment seemed to pause as everyone around us looked in and tried to figure out why the world felt like it was crumbling.

I didn't care. I felt like a fool. Amanda knew everything about me and Finn, and she walked in on the same thing I did. I couldn't get out of that garage fast enough. I didn't want to cry like a big baby in from of a room full of strangers. I'd had enough humiliation.

When he stopped me and told me what had really been going on in the garage, I had no choice but to believe him. He'd never given me any reason not to trust him and the look in his eyes sealed the deal for me. He was just as heartbroken for me as I was for myself.

Thankfully, his ex left as soon as we went back inside. Maybe I was being a jealous freak, but I didn't want her there. She looked like the complete opposite of me and I didn't want Finn having any reminders of what he could have if he wasn't stuck with a church girl who was clueless to anything sex related.

He spent the rest of that night singing sweetly to me in front of everyone, and once the garage cleared out and it was only us, he spent the rest of our time showing me and telling me how perfect he thought I was. It was amazing. He was amazing. I knew in the back of my mind that I was far from perfect, but he truly believed it and as long as he thought I was, then that's all that mattered to me.

I spent the next day at school watching the clock. I couldn't wait to be alone with him again. I'd decided that I was going to throw caution to the wind and do whatever it took to be with Finn. I accepted the fact that I had to lie and sneak out. There was no way my dad was going to allow us to be alone together, and after the whole leaving the movies incident, I was put on restriction until I graduated practically.

I made sure Amanda brought me a set of clothes to school, and once I heard my parents snoring down the hallway, I shut my door, locked it, and changed. I giggled to myself as I looked down at my bare knees. I'd never worn a skirt that landed above the knee, but there was a first time for everything. The truth was I kind of liked it.

A few old welts remained, but nothing that was so noticeable that I couldn't feel comfortable showing my legs. I hadn't thought about it much, but it had been a while since dad pulled off his belt for me. Not since the incidence where he actually broke skin. I wasn't complaining. Maybe seeing me bleed is what it took to make him stop.

The shirt that Amanda sent over for me could never really be called a shirt since it barely covered anything. Instead of wearing it, I threw it in the back of my closet and pulled out one of my sweaters. Doing one last check in the mirror, I decided to leave my hair down and put on a little lip gloss that I'd also borrowed from Amanda. By the time I heard Finn knock softly on my window, I was ready to go and full of excitement.

We held hands in his car as he drove us toward the coast. He didn't think I noticed, but he kept peeking down at my legs, checking me out. I liked it. It made me feel attractive. I gasped when he slid his warm palm over my knee and rested it there.

"Where are we going?" I asked.

The truth was I didn't care where we were going as long as we were together.

"To our spot." He grinned over at me and shifted the gears when we hit the interstate.

He looked so good driving his car. It wasn't in the best shape, but it purred loudly and vibrated beneath us, letting us know it was powerful. It fit him well since he was such a powerful guy. I felt safe with Finn, like nothing or no one could ever hurt me when I was with him.

When he turned onto the familiar wooded street, I smiled to myself. I remembered the first time I'd gone down that road and the beach that it led to. That night had been so perfect and it was romantic of him to bring me back there.

Once we parked and got out, we walked down the beach holding hands and stopping for tiny kisses along the way. I had no idea what time it was. I only knew the water was beautiful beneath the moonlight and Finn couldn't keep his hands and lips off of me.

"So I think I got a job," he said as he kicked at a seashell.

He leaned over and picked it up for inspection.

"That's great. Doing what?" I asked.

He shrugged like it was no big deal when we both knew it was.

"Kevin's dad owns a construction business. I'm supposed to go up there on Monday and talk to him, but Kevin said he's positive his dad will hire me. It's not big money, but it's money." He stuffed his hands in his pockets and continued to walk.

"I think that's great." I slipped my hand through his elbow and pressed my cheek against his arm.

He smiled sweetly down at me before kissing me on the forehead.

"So how's Sister Francis and everyone doing?" he asked.

I was shocked that he cared enough about my church family to ask about them.

When he finally took me back to his car, it was two in the morning. He opened the car door for me, but before I got in, I turned and kissed him.

For someone who once thought kissing was gross, I sure couldn't get enough of it. He didn't seem to mind as he kissed me back. His fingers mingled in my hair and I heard myself moan loudly. He pulled back and stared down at me—his heavy breaths landing against my lips and cheeks.

"What happened to sweet, innocent Faith?" he asked with a grin that showed his dimples.

"She had a taste of Finn."

A tiny growl sounded against my mouth when he pressed his lips to mine. His kisses felt different—harder and desperate. I didn't push him away. I was enjoying it too much.

I gasped in his mouth when I felt his fingers against my stomach. He worked his hand up and rested it on my ribs just below my bra. I was embarrassed that he could feel my hard breathing against his hand, but when he moved it down and gripped my bottom, pulling me closer, I no longer cared.

I moaned when his palm wrapped around my upper thigh. His lips left mine and worked their way down the side of my neck. I leaned my head to the side and gave him working room, and then without realizing I was doing it, I grabbed on to his shirt and pulled him closer.

"Is this okay?" he asked as his hand moved higher into my skirt.

The warmth from his hands mixed with the cool beach breeze that was rushing up my skirt felt exotic against my flesh.

"Yes. Please don't stop."

I couldn't believe I'd even said that. It didn't even sound like me, but I was begging him and I didn't even know what I was begging him for. I just knew that everything he was doing felt right and I wanted more.

My shoe left a line in the sand as I slowly opened my legs for his hand. My skirt bunched up around my thighs to accommodate my stance. I sighed loudly when his hand moved up higher and I felt his knuckles brush my panties.

"You like that?" he asked as he brushed his knuckles against me again.

My knees were starting to feel weak and when I tried to answer him, no words would come out of my mouth. Instead, a tiny humiliating whine slipped past my lips and earned me another dimple-filled grin.

"I love those sweet noises you make," he whispered against my lips.

And then he kissed me again, and again his kisses were harder and more passionate. His tongue moved against mine and tickled the top of my mouth. The noise that I made when he slipped his finger in the side of my panties didn't even sound human.

I'd never known anything like his touch, but while I was mentally clueless, my body seemed to understand and moved on its own. My hips rolled for more of his fingers. The dinging from his car door being held open sounded with the throb of my body as I leaned my head back against the cold rusted steel.

The next thing I knew, my legs were no longer holding me up and somehow, instead of leaning against his car, I was lying in the sand and he was above me. It was as if the things he was doing to me were coming in flashes. The stars above me twinkled with my excitement and the sound of the waves became muffled.

His fingers moved against me in ways I didn't know were possible. My body was strung tight and my breaths came out in pants. He kissed me until I was dizzy and then when I thought I was about to lose my mind, his hands disappeared from my body.

He leaned back and pushed my skirt up more and I lay there needy and greedy for more of what he was offering. In the back of my mind, I knew what we were doing was wrong, but I couldn't make myself stop. It felt too good, but once he started to move down, my body I froze.

I could remember Amanda telling me about what couples did to each other with their mouths and I couldn't fathom Finn doing that to me. I leaned up and grabbed him around his shoulders to keep him from moving lower. He looked up at me beneath his lashes and grinned.

"Just relax. You'll like this, I promise."

Still, I couldn't make myself relax. Things were moving too fast and I wasn't so sure I was as ready as I'd originally thought. He softly kissed my ribs and it tickled. I pulled on his shirt again and tried to make him come back up.

"Finn?" The desperate question in my voice was answered when he kissed me around my belly button.

I had no idea what I was asking for. My mind was telling me to stop him, but my body was begging for him to keep going. I was so confused and scared. My body was so tense with anxiety and the need for a release I didn't know existed.

"Just relax, baby. It's only fair. I sang for you. Now lay back and I'll make you sing for me."

When his mouth touched me, I gave in and fell back. Sand collected under my nails as I dug my fingers into beach around me. His hands and mouth were all over me, pushing and pulling me over the edge of a line that I'd always been afraid to cross.

My toes curled in my shoes and my back lifted from the sand as my insides turned to liquid.

"Let go, Faith. I promise I'll catch you."

His whisper floated in the wind around me and then my body dissolved into the sand. I clutched my cross, the blunt tips of it digging into my palm as I called out my release and sang into the wind. Finn's mouth never left my body, and his fingers dug into my thighs, holding them to the earth as my body trembled and bucked.

When I came down, the sound of the waves was the first thing I heard. My arms and legs tingled and felt heavy. Everything was so sensitive that even the cool breeze felt too thick against my skin. In a daze, I stared at the stars above me and tried to understand what had just happened.

Finn collected me in his arms and kissed the top of my head. His warmth seeped into my skin and spread throughout my body. I continued to clutch my cross. I fully understood that what we had done was wrong—sinful—but what I couldn't understand was how something so beautiful could be bad.

I began to question everything I'd ever been told in my life. For the first time, I wondered if maybe my dad didn't know what he was talking about. I refused to believe that Finn was bad. I wouldn't accept the fact that my soul was in danger with him. Not when I'd just been so close to heaven in his arms.

This time when I closed my eyes, I didn't think about protecting my soul in my cross. There was no need for it anymore. Finn had my soul, and I knew that no matter what, he'd protect it.

FOURTEEN

FINN

I'd promised myself I'd wait until she was ready, and I'd failed. That wasn't surprising since I'd spent most of my life fucking up. I hadn't planned on going down on Faith in the sand. I really had been trying to be romantic and take her on an actual date. Walking the beach was supposed to be sweet, but once she started kissing me and pressing against me, I was done for.

I kept thinking that at least I hadn't taken her virginity. I wanted to. Damn, I'd never wanted to so badly. The noises she made when she came almost did me in. I was sure I was going unload right there in my jeans. The amount of willpower it took to hold her afterward and not finish the job was amazing. I had no idea I was capable of shit like that.

I wanted to show her how good I could make her feel. I wanted to hear her say my name over and over again like she had. It wanted it so badly for her, but at the same time, I couldn't help but feel like I'd pressured her into it.

The last thing I wanted was for her to clam up and never talk to me again out of fear. I never wanted to scare her. She seemed okay when I dropped her off. I promised her I'd come by the following night and that made her smile happily, but I knew girls pretty well and I knew they reacted after the fact. I just had to hope that the following day when I saw her, she didn't hate me.

When I got home, Reynolds was waiting in my garage for me. His long legs were resting on the coffee table in front of Mom's old leather couch. He pulled at a ripped piece, exposing more of the yellow sponge inside.

When I stepped in, he looked up at me with hard eyes.

"Where the fuck you been, man? I've been waiting here all goddamn night."

His eyes were dilated and he couldn't sit still. He crossed his leg over the other and shook his foot so fast it started to blur. No doubt about it he was fucked on the white wizard again.

The tiny bit of white power stuck on the tip of his nose caught my attention and gave him away more than his behavior. He'd been on the decline for a while, but I hadn't noticed how badly until I sobered up and stepped away. Usually I was along for the party, but since I'd met Faith, I was clean—minus a few beers every now again. That was yet another reason I knew she was good for me. Even my mom had commented on my changes.

"I was out with my girl. What's up?" I asked as I fell onto the couch beside him.

It was late and I was exhausted. I could still smell Faith on my skin, and I was determined to catch some relief in my palm before hitting the sheets.

He reached into his pocket and pulled out a blunt. The smell of lighter fluid swarmed around me when he lit his Zippo. The tip of the blunt crackled as he hit it hard and held it in.

"Man, fuck that shit. Relationships are for the birds and bitches. Don't get yourself all caught up. It's bad for business."

I had to force myself to remember that he was fucked up. Otherwise, I would've punched him in the mouth. Since I'd known Reynolds, I was always fighting his fights. He had a mouth on him and never knew when to shut it. It also didn't help that he wasn't afraid of anyone or anything. Whenever he got in over his head, which was most of the time, I was always there to pull him out.

He usually never pushed my buttons, but something was up with him tonight. I was starting to worry that he was on something much heavier than usual. He kept making shitty remarks, but I ignored him and turned down the blunt when he held it out to me. His arm hung suspended and he eyed me hard like he was challenging me to smoke. Still, I shook my head no.

"Nah, man, I'm good—high on life and shit." I tried to lighten the mood. "You need a ride home or something? Looks like you've partied extra hard tonight."

I'd seen his car parked out front, but if he needed a ride home, I'd take him. Whatever got him out of my garage so I could get some sleep.

I was caught off guard when he flicked the blunt at my face. I barely swatted it away quick enough. "What the fuck, Reynolds?" I stood tall.

He stood, too, but I towered over him. I tried to keep myself in check. He was pushing some serious buttons and I was starting to get pissed off. I didn't want to fly off the handle and kick his ass and feel bad about it the next day when he didn't remember.

"You don't know shit about a party anymore. Man, you're supposed to be our front man. A real front man doesn't let himself get pussy whipped."

I'd had enough. I pushed him. "Get the fuck out of here. I'm done with your shit tonight."

I walked away. At least I tried to, but he had other plans. I didn't see his fist coming, but it was hard against the back of my head. The oil-covered concrete garage floor dug into my cheek. My ears rang and the world around me shifted for a few seconds. I blinked rapidly and gathered my wits.

Once I realized what happened, I was up and on top of him. I'd had enough of Reynolds's shit.

He blocked and fought back hard. Punches were thrown and words were said. The drums sounded and the cymbals clanged as we tumbled into them, knocking them everywhere.

Once I had him on his back, I continued to hit him. I told myself to stop, but I was so pissed and disoriented from his initial hit that I no longer cared.

Hard fingers dug into my arms and pulled me back. Instead of continuing to fight, I stopped once I saw that Reynolds wasn't coming back for me.

"Woah! Chill the fuck out, Finn! What happened, man?" I heard Tiny say from behind me.

He was young, but he had a grip on him.

I wiped the blood from my lip and cheek as I tried to catch my breath.

"He started the shit. I'm getting about sick of him getting all fucked up on coke and acting crazy." I shook Tiny's hands from my arms and turned to see Kevin and Amanda staring at me from across the garage. "Get him the fuck out of here until he sobers up," I said to Kevin.

I sat on the couch pressing a cold beer to my lip and watched as Tiny and Kevin helped Reynolds up and dragged him to Kevin's car. No way would he even remember the fight the next day, but I was done. I fully planned on sitting his ass down and having a long talk with him about his drug problem. If we were serious about Original Malice, then we needed our heads in the right place. Being fucked up all the time wasn't going to cut it.

Kevin came back in once everyone was settled into the car.

"He's getting worse," he said as he pulled out a cigarette and lit it.

"I know. We'll go over tomorrow and try to talk some sense into him."

"Yeah, that sounds good. You're different, too, you know?" he said as he exhaled smoke through his nose.

I hadn't expected Kevin to say that. I looked up at him and nodded my head. I knew I was different and that wasn't a bad thing. "I know."

"I've known you for a long time, Finn. You're like my brother, man, and since you got Faith, you seem a lot happier. I'm glad to see that. You deserve it." He stepped over toward me and grabbed my shoulder. "She's a nice girl. Be good to her."

Kevin and I weren't big on heart to heart talks, so I nodded my head, acknowledging what he was saying. "I will. Thanks, man. Be safe getting his crazy ass home. I'll see y'all tomorrow."

We brought it in for a hug and smacked each other on the back. He really was like my brother and no matter what, he always had my back. I couldn't have asked for a better sidekick.

After they left, I went inside, got a shower, and crashed. My face hurt like a bitch, and a tiny bit of guilt for kicking Reynolds's ass was starting to seep in. Needless to say, I slept for shit. It wasn't long before I heard my mom screaming my name and pounding on my door.

I woke up disoriented and reaching for anything in the darkness. In a panic, I jumped out of my bed and tripped over my shoes. After stubbing my knee on a few things and almost falling and breaking my neck, I managed to make it across my room in the dark.

I swung the door open and flipped on the light at the same time. When I did, my mom fell into my arms crying. I held her close to my bare chest. Her tears dripped from her chin and streamed down my torso. She was saying something over and over again, but it was muffled. I leaned back and looked down at her.

"What is it?" Fear gripped my heart. I'd only ever seen my mom like this once before and it was when Mr. Charles, her husband, had died.

My thoughts went straight to Faith. Panic set in until I remembered Mom didn't know Faith.

"Oh, thank God you're here. I thought you were gone. I thought you were with them and I'd lost you." Her words weren't making any sense and with her crying so hard, I could barely understand what she was saying.

"I'm here, Mom. What's going on? Did you have a nightmare or something?"

I held her up and she continued to bawl. "Jimmy, I'm so sorry. God, Jimmy, I'm so sorry, baby," she said over and over again.

Still I had no idea what she was talking about. Her entire body was shaking and her breath was beginning to hiccup.

"For what, Mom? You didn't do anything."

She slowed her crying and looked up at me. She looked older with tears on her cheeks and red eyes. Her hair was coming out of its bun and stuck out in random places. She'd been awakened from her sleep too.

"There's been an accident—a bad one. They're gone. Reynolds and Kevin, they didn't make it."

Her words swam around me. I was still half asleep and confused, but finally they made it to my brain and I realized what she was saying. She had practically adopted Reynolds and Kevin as her own since they were always at my house. She was freaking out and I could feel myself starting to freak out, too.

My head spun and I felt like I was going to be sick. My boys—more like my brothers, the only brothers I'd ever had—they were dead. Gone—never coming back again.

I gripped the edge of my dresser to hold myself up, but then I began to dig my fingers into the wood as anger set in. I wanted to pick the dresser up and put it through the wall. My breath was coming too fast and hard as I began to hyperventilate, yet I couldn't breathe. I needed to breathe.

Mom wrapped her arms around me and I felt like I was suffocated even more. I moved away from her and pressed my head against the wall. The place where Reynolds had punched me earlier that night started to throb when I ran my fingers through my hair, reminding me of our last moments together.

I couldn't help it from then on out—I cried. It was hard and loud as I pressed myself up against the wall as if I could go through it and disappear. This wasn't happening. No way was this really happening.

So many people had walked away from me all my life, and Kevin and Reynolds had been two out of the few that stuck with me no matter what. Yeah, Reynolds had a drug problem, and yeah, Kevin knew exactly what to say to piss me off, but they were like my family. Other than my mom, they were the only real family I'd ever had.

I reared back and put my fist through the wall. Pieces of paneling splintered into the air around me. My hand throbbed with my heartbeat and it hurt. I needed something to hurt—anything but my heart, which ached so badly I thought it would stop completely. I collapsed on my bedroom floor and I felt my mom holding me and wiping the tears from my cheeks.

Once the sun came up, all the details started to come out. Kevin had been intoxicated and Reynolds took over the wheel. Why hadn't I seen how drunk Kevin was? I was so caught up with Reynolds and his bullshit, so caught up in my new way of life, that I hadn't paid enough attention to him.

I'd already been at the hospital with Tiny for an hour before he woke up. He'd survived, but barely. Both his legs were broken and a large piece of metal had gone so far into his side that the doctors were saying it was a miracle he was alive. He looked like shit—barely recognizable—and I couldn't help but feel like it was my fault.

I found out soon after that Amanda, Faith's friend, also died in the crash. My heart broke for Faith and all I wanted to do was go to her and make sure she was okay. She didn't have a lot of friends in her life and she'd known Amanda since they were little girls. She wasn't going to take it well.

I gripped my steering wheel hard as I drove to the church. It was Sunday and I knew that's where Faith would be. Fuck the rules her dad had laid down. If she already knew about Amanda, then she would need me, and if she didn't already know, I wanted to be there for her when she found out. Plus, I needed her. I needed her so bad. I felt like everything was falling away from me and I wanted to see her face—know she was okay and still breathing.

I didn't bother going in the front door of the church. Instead, I went into the side door that went straight to the kids' room. If she wasn't in there, she would be at some point. I looked like shit and I didn't want the church people looking down on me. Not then—not when I was breaking apart piece by piece.

I heard her soft crying from around the corner. Once I made it into the room, I found Faith sitting at a table with her head down. Her dark hair spilled over her arms and shined in the sunlight coming through the closest window.

I wasted no time going to her. I sat in the chair next to her and picked her up from her seat, placing her in my lap. She collapsed against me and wrapped her arms around my neck. I held her close as she wet my shoulder with her tears. Rubbing her back, I tried my best to console her.

She leaned back and swiped at her red face with the back of her sleeve. "I'm so sorry about Reynolds and Kevin. I can't believe they're gone, Finn." Again, she started to cry. I felt a tear of my own roll off my chin.

I held her that way until people started to come into the room. When it was time for me to leave, I kissed her cheek with a promise in my eyes that I'd see her again very soon. If she needed me, she knew how to reach me and she knew she could no matter what.

Reynolds was buried first. Mom and I stood next to his grave as he was lowed into the ground. I felt like I was suffocating, both because of the fact that my boys were gone and the stupid fucking tie I had to wear. I could practically hear Reynolds laughing at me. No doubt about it, if he were still there, he would have gotten a kick out of me wearing a suit.

I helped his mom make it to her car. She wasn't even walking on her own. Reynolds's cousin, Mike, and me were practically carrying her. She was on so many drugs to cope that she was talking out of her head and calling Mike Reynolds. It was so fucking sad to watch.

That night, Faith called to check on me. It pissed me off that she had to hide being on the phone and I only got to talk to her for three minutes. I missed her and I needed her—she needed me.

Kevin and Amanda were buried on the same day. By the time they lowered Kevin in the ground, I felt numb. His little sister, Erica, cried on my shoulder as I held her. She was only five; she shouldn't know what it felt like to lose someone. Kids shouldn't hurt, but I'd seen enough in my life being tossed from one home to next, and the one thing I knew was that kids were always getting hurt—and somehow they survived.

Before leaving the graveyard, his mom made me promise to stay in touch. As if I wouldn't have. Mom and I drove in silence back to the house. By the time we got home, it started to rain. She ran inside and I went into the garage for the first time since the night of the accident.

I stood there with my hands on my hips—my tie loosened around my neck—and took in the space. Reynolds's drums were still strewn around the room from our fight. I sat on his stool and started to put them back together again. Our last moment together beat into my head over and over again. What a fucked-up way to spend your last moments with one of your best friends.

I picked up his sticks and set them on top of the snare. Reaching up, I wiped away a tear that had slipped down my cheek.

"Are you okay?" Faith asked from the garage door.

I hadn't known she was standing there. She looked so beautiful. Her hair was pinned back and tiny strands had escaped and were dangling around her face. The long black dress she wore touched the ground and black lacey flowers were stitched around the neck.

Her eyes were red and puffy. Her nose looked raw like she'd just gotten over a bad cold. Seeing her instantly made me feel better. I held my arms out to her and she came to me and sat on my lap. I held her as she cried on my shoulder.

When she stopped, she looked up at me and softly kissed me on the lips.

"I missed you," she said.

I twirled a piece of her hair around my finger.

"God, I missed you, too." I buried my face in her hair and breathed her in. It had only been a few days, but it felt like forever since the last time we'd seen each other.

"Are you okay?" I asked as I used my thumb to brush away a tear from her cheek.

"I'll be okay. You?"

"I'll make it. As long as I have you, I'll make it."

I kissed her again. Her kisses were so sweet and undemanding. I could almost forget what it had been like to kiss anyone else.

"How did you get here? Where's your dad?"

She peeked up at me. She looked so guilty that I was almost afraid of her answer.

"I took my dad's car. He's at the church with Amanda's family. I had to get out of there."

I cupped her cheek and smiled. "You shouldn't have done that. I don't want you to get in trouble, baby."

"I needed to see you."

There was no way she could comprehend what her words did for me. I needed her just as badly, and I was thrilled that she was with me, but still worried at the same time. Thinking of consequences was new for me, but when it came to Faith, it's all I could think about.

Before she left, I introduced her to my mom. Watching the two women that I loved as they hugged each other and talked like they'd known each other forever did my heart good.

And just like that, it hit me. I loved Faith. I was crazy in love with her. I couldn't tell her that yet since I didn't want to freak her out, but I felt it. I'm sure she knew. She had to know.

"Faith, I'm so glad I got to meet you," Mom said as she patted her hand. "Finn hasn't been the same since he met you—in a good way, of course."

She winked over at me and I blushed for the first time in my entire life. Faith laughed and grabbed my hand with a tiny squeeze.

"I'm so glad I got to meet you, too."

I walked Faith to her dad's car and kissed her once more before she got in.

"I'll see you tonight?" she asked.

I smiled down at her and nodded my head. She really was so adorable. "I'll pick you up at the stop sign—same time."

Her smile lit up my heart that had been so heavy for the last few days. I watched her drive away and smiled to myself. She was so amazing and I was one lucky son of a bitch to have her.

FIFTEEN

FAITH

Burying your best and only friend kills a part of you—the part that held the memories the two of you made over the years. I couldn't believe Amanda was gone. She'd always been there. Her laughter had sometimes been the only thing that could make me smile after a night with my dad and his belt.

Her coffin was pink and her mom welcomed all of her friends to sign it with multi-colored permanent markers. The marker shook in my hand as I wrote a message and told her I loved her.

Flowers took over the space as the entire church community bought bouquets for the family with condolences and donations for her burial. The room smelled of a fresh garden and ladies' heavy perfume. I couldn't tell if it was the smells that made me feel sick to my stomach or the fact that her mom had decided on an open coffin.

I found myself upset at the fact that Amanda was being buried in such a boring dress without a stitch of makeup on her face. No way would she be okay with that. I stood beside her coffin and cried silently until Sister Francis pulled me away.

Life—it was taken away so quickly and I'd spent all of mine afraid to live. Almost eighteen years of wasting my life following the rules, walking a straight line, afraid that if I stepped off track, the world would explode around me or the devil himself would appear in front of me and pull me into the underworld for eternity.

Some of the best things I'd experienced in my life so far had been when I was breaking the rules. This was my thinking process as I sat on a chair in the back of the church. Everyone came back there to mourn and eat. Amanda's mom asked that everyone gather there instead of her house.

My dad took center stage as he proceeded to talk about how bad the teenagers these days were becoming and how Amanda had gotten caught up with the wrong crowd. I listened with my eyes glued to the plate of food in front of me. Finn was a part of the group he was talking about and I couldn't help but feel a twinge in my stomach. I missed Finn so much and I needed him.

Without a second thought, I stood and slipped out the back of the church, grabbing my dad's keys from his desk on the way out. I already knew because of the accident the reins on me were going to become even tighter. I figured I might as well go out with a bang and at least get to see Finn as much as I could before then. Seeing him somehow made things tolerable.

I was shocked when he introduced me to his mother. Amanda used to tell me when a guy introduced you to his parents, they were serious about you. Finn was serious about me and I was more than serious about him.

When I got back from my visit with Finn and his mom, I was happy to see no one even noticed I was gone. Dad's keys were back on his desk in the nick of time and soon we were going home for the night. I stopped out by Amanda's grave once more before getting in the car with my parents. I plucked one of the pink roses from the bouquet on top of the fresh dirt.

"I hope you don't mind if I take this. I was thinking I'd dry it and close it in my journal." I paused to take a much needed breath. "I'll miss you, girl. Be good up there. Try not to give God too much hell," I whispered into the wind.

I smiled to myself as I wiped a tear from my cheek.

As soon as we got home, my mom excused herself and went to her room. She was complaining of one of her stress headaches, but I knew the only thing that gave her a headache was my dad. I headed toward my room as well, but before I got to the hallway, my dad called me back into the living room.

"Faith, we need to talk."

I hated the sound of that. I tucked my dress under me and took a seat on the couch across from him.

"What is it, Daddy?"

He pulled off his dress shoes and relaxed in his recliner.

"Me and your mother have been talking and we've come to a decision about something." He cleared his throat and mine tightened. "We're moving."

I started to panic for a second, but then I realized that he might be talking about another house in the same area. I knew my dad, and he would never leave the church.

"A house closer to the church?" I asked.

He shook his head and my chest got heavy. "No, we're moving to California."

His words echoed throughout the room, ricocheted off the walls, and pierced my heart. I was on my feet in that instant, and I was irate. He wasn't going to do this to me. I couldn't let him do this.

"No, we aren't!" As soon as the words left my mouth, I knew I was going to regret them.

I'd never spoken to my father that way—ever. I patiently waited for him to jump out of his chair, pull off his belt, and beat me until I couldn't see straight. He stood from his chair and towered over me with angry eyes.

"Excuse me?"

I swallowed my nerves and looked him in the eye.

"I'm not going anywhere." I flinched when he lifted his hand and ran it across his bald head.

"You're going. There's too much for you to get into around here, and with Amanda's death, I realize I'm not willing to lose you because you can't stay away from that boy. I heard about him coming to the church the day we found out about the accident, and I won't have you following in her footsteps."

That boy? He didn't even have the decency to say his name. Well, I didn't care what he said. I wasn't going anywhere without Finn. Without thinking, I blurted out the first thing that came to my mind.

"I love Finn, Daddy. I'm not leaving him. I'm sorry, but I'm seventeen and—"

The back of his hand connected with my cheek, knocking me back onto the couch. I sat up quickly. My face felt like it was about to explode. The taste of blood rolled across my tongue, making my stomach turn. I placed my palm against my face and looked up at him like he was crazy. I was positive he was. I was older and I knew more. I understood.

He clawed at his belt before he pulled it off and used it on me. This time I fought back. I grabbed at his belt and pulled at it. Still, he managed to catch me on my arms and even once across my face. The entire time I screamed for him to leave me alone and even once clawed at his arm.

When he was done, he swiped at the sweat on his forehead and pointed a finger at me.

"You're going. As a matter of fact, you're not leaving this house again until it's time to go. I've already put in a call with some friends on the West Coast. There's a good church there that could use my services. I think this is the best thing."

Backing away from him, I turned toward the front door. I grabbed the knob and prepped my feet to run. I had to get to Finn. He had to know what was going on so we could figure out what to do. I wasn't going to leave him. I wouldn't. He was everything to me and the only person left in the world that I cared about.

My head lurched back when my dad grabbed the back of my hair and pulled me back into the house. Tiny pins pulled from my hair and strands were released into my face.

"Don't even think about it. God don't like ugly, Faith, and you're disgracing yourself and this family. I hated to do it this way, but you leave me no other choice. I'm a respected man around here. One call to the police and I could have that boy put in prison for a long time. Did you know he sells drugs from his home? I knew that and so does his probation officer." He jerked me closer to him; my hair was being ripped from its roots. "All I have to do is make a call. Quit being a selfish girl. Think about that mother of his. She can barely make it around without him. Do you really want to take him away from her like that?"

"You're lying!"

He spun me around and again his hand connected with my cheek.

Then he pulled out a video tape—one that went to those old style VCRs that no one used anymore. He shoved it in my face, the black plastic dug into my cheek.

"Do you know what this is, Faith?" An angry vein poked out of his forehead. "Of course you don't. Well, let me tell you what this is. It's Finn on tape, selling drugs. I bet you know all about drugs and such now that you're a sinner." I smacked the tape out of my face and pulled away. “Leave this house, even think about leaving this house, and he’s going to prison for a very long time. You’re no longer allowed to see that boy. It’s over and we’re leaving.”

I tried not to believe anything he was saying, but it was hard since for my entire life, I’d looked up to my father like he was good and saintly. It also didn’t help that I could remember all the drugs that bounced around Finn’s garage. He didn’t have a job yet, but somehow he’d been able to fix his car and buy things. I didn’t know much about the way drug deals worked, but I assumed Finn was in a good place in the world to be able to do such things. His neighbors alone would make great customers for him.

I pulled away from my dad again and this time he freed me. I took advantage of the moment and of his age and I ripped open the front door. I knew I was taking a chance on getting Finn into some major trouble, but the thought of just disappearing on him didn’t sit well with me. I knew Finn and I knew he’d want to know what was happening with me, even if it meant false accusations on him.

I collided with the screened door and went right through it. Tiny pieces of wood splintered into the air. I heard my dad calling out behind me, followed by my mother's high-pitched voice. Tripping on the broken door, I fell to the ground. My dad latched onto my ankle with strong fingers and I kicked with all my might until he let go. Jumping up, I ran.

I ran until my lungs ached, my flats beating into the asphalt and echoing into the wind that rushed past me. Tears that I didn't know I was shedding spread across my cheeks and cooled, leaving my face feeling stiff and swollen. Hair flapped against my face and tangled into the chain around my neck. My cross dug into my palm until I felt like it was bleeding.

Night was settling in and the air was getting cooler. When I saw a pair of headlights coming my way, I freaked out, knowing it was my father coming after me, so I turned and fled into the patch of woods on the side of the road. I ducked down into the brush as my dad's car zoomed by.

I'd done the unthinkable, and I already knew it wasn't going to end well for me. I was seventeen. I could leave. I could tell my dad to shove it and run away with Finn, but I needed to make sure Finn was on board first. I needed to make sure that he wanted the same from me.

It took a while, but I finally made it to the closest gas station. My feet burned and lungs ached from breathing in the night air. The cashier looked at me like I was death walking in the store, which made sense since that's exactly what I felt like.

"Do you have a phone I can use?" I asked.

I pulled the chord as far as it would go and punched in Finn's home number. I prayed as it rang that he would answer and when he did, I nearly burst out into tears again.

"Finn, I need you. Please come and get me." The minute the words left my mouth, I began to cry.

SIXTEEN

FINN

I couldn't get to her fast enough. From the second I heard her crying on the phone and telling me she needed me, I was out the front door. I broke the speed limit the entire way to her side of town and left most of the rubber from my tires on the road. When I pulled up to the gas station and saw her sitting on the sidewalk in her pretty black dress and her hair all tangled up, I was angry. I wanted to put my fist through her dad's face—pastor or no pastor.

She stood, my headlights blinding her, and adjusted her dress. She looked like a weeping willow in a spot of sunlight. I jumped out of my car and went to her. Pulling her into my arms, I held her close and breathed her in.

"Are you okay?" I asked.

"I am now."

She looked up at me with a broken smile. I caught a wayward tear on her cheek with my thumb.

"Come on. You're coming home with me."

I held her hand on the ride back to my house. By the time we got there, she was asleep. Instead of waking her, I went around to her side of the car, opened the door, and carried her in my house. She wrapped her arms around my neck and breathed softly into my ear.

Mom had gone to bingo with some friends in hopes of hitting the big-ass jackpot and paying some bills, so the house was empty and quiet.

I carried Faith straight to my room and laid her on my bed. She turned and sighed into my pillow. Her hair spread across my pillow and a tiny smile formed on her mouth. She looked so peaceful. She fit perfectly there, and I silently wished that she would sleep there every night.

I left her there, turned everything off in the house, and then went to shower. The bathroom steamed up as I let the hot water wash away the bad memories of the week that passed. So many life-changing things happened to me in the last week—the loss of my brothers and hopefully, the permanence of Faith.

I turned off the shower, wrapped a towel around my junk, and then crept into my room to get some clothes. My room was dark—the only sound was the osculating fan that I couldn't sleep without. I pulled open my top drawer and grabbed a pair of boxers.

Turning around, I was about to drop my towel and slip on the boxers, but I stopped when I realized Faith was standing across the room, staring at me. Her eyes burned me as they moved down from my face, past my neck and chest, and landed on the part of my towel that was slowly lifting.

I expected her to turn away or leave the room, but instead, she walked up to me and slid her arms around my neck. Her fingers moved across the droplets of water that lingered on my back before she worked them through my wet hair. I sucked in a breath when she pressed her sweet mouth to my chest.

I tangled my fingers in the back of her hair and lifted her face to mine. I kissed her slowly, memorizing her mouth with my tongue. She pressed into me and dug her nails into my back as if she couldn't get enough.

I turned, pressing her up against the wall. Lifting her dress, I wrapped her legs around my hips. She didn't stop me; instead, she began to move her hips like she knew what she was doing. Our panting breaths filled the room as we kissed. Dropping my mouth to her neck, I kissed softly, nipping at her earlobe before sucking it into my mouth.

"Please Finn," she said over and over again.

I knew what she was asking me for, but it was too soon. Things were too emotionally fucked up right now, and I didn't want her searching for consolation in the wrong places. Her friend had just died and her father had just attacked her.

Thinking about what she told me in the car before she fell asleep was making me crazy. He hit her and from what she'd said, it was for no reason at all. That son of bitch hit her!

I growled a little before taking her mouth again. I felt like an animal—wild and ready to rip someone apart. She tugged at her dress, making it move up past her hips, before she began to grind against my towel, against my hard cock. It was then that I knew I had to stop. I was ready to go all the way, but it was wrong. It was the worst time for her to lose her virginity. Once she was done grieving for Amanda, she'd hate me for taking advantage.

I pulled away from her and used my hand to block my hardness. "Faith, we have to stop."

I was breathing like I'd just run a marathon. Every muscle in my body was tight as if I'd been working them all at the same time.

She shocked me as she followed me, slid her arms around my neck again, and then started kissing me again. She tasted so sweet and her body felt so amazing against mine. I wanted to keep going. I wanted it more than anything, but again, I pulled away. I had to be the levelheaded one.

She looked up at me with pain in her eyes. "Please, Finn, just give me this night. Please."

That made no sense to me. We had all the nights of our lives if we wanted them.

"There'll be other nights. We have the rest of our lives, Faith. A lot has happened this week. Let me hold you and when you're really ready and only when you're really ready—"

She captured my face in her hands and kissed me again, harder. I kissed her back and then pulled away. "I'm ready, Finn. I've never been more ready. What if this is the only night we have together?"

I was confused.

"But it's not. Don't even say that."

"I know, but what if it was? What if someone tried to take me away from you?"

I couldn't even fathom the idea.

"That won't happen," I said.

I clenched my jaws so hard my teeth ached.

"But how do you know?" she asked.

"Because I'd kill anyone who tried to take you away... either that or I'd die fighting for you. No one will ever take you away from me—ever."

The truth of my words burned in my chest.

Her eyes filled with tears until they broke free and rolled down her cheeks. "I love you, Finn."

My heart shifted. She meant it. I could see it in her eyes that she meant it, and I'd never been so happy to hear those words. I needed them. I wanted to wrap them up and stick them in a box for safe keeping. They meant everything to me since I felt exactly the same.

I looked her in the eyes and took a deep breath. It wasn't every day I confessed my love to someone. "I love you, too."

She smiled up at me before leaning in close. "Then show me."

She stepped back and reached for the hem of her dress. I could hardly believe my eyes when she pulled it up and over her head. She wore simple white cotton panties with a matching bra. My eyes dropped from her breasts, down her stomach, and landed on her thighs. Her body was beautiful. Her hair was pushed across one shoulder as she shyly peeked up at me from her dark lashes. She'd never looked more like an angel.

And just like that, I gave in to her. Taking her by the hand, I led her to my bed and laid her down. She held her arms out to me and welcomed me into them when I climbed on top of her. I took my time kissing her and touching her in all her secret places. She moaned my name over and over again, and when I felt her fingers make their way into my towel, I moaned, too.

She squirmed beneath me, her breath coming in rampant pants. I removed her bra and panties and blew softly on different parts of her body, making her arch her body and shiver. Once my towel was gone from between us, I pressed and teased her with my body. She shifted her hips and whined.

"Please, Finn. I want you." Her eyes were wide as she looked into mine.

"Are you sure?"

I had to make sure before I took something from her that I could never give back.

Her fingers dug into my back, pulling me so close to her that I could feel her heartbeat against my chest.

"Yes. Please." The desperation in her voice matched my own.

Reaching into my night table, I pulled out a condom. The foil crackled as I ripped it open. She looked down and watched as I slid the slippery rubber over my hardness. Swallowing, she looked back up at me and I saw the nervousness in her expression.

I braced myself above her and adjusted my hips. I knew it was going to hurt her, so I leaned down and began to kiss her hard and deep to take her mind off of it. Once she was into the kissing and wrapping her arms around my neck, I pulled back and pressed into her in one swift movement.

She broke the kiss and gasped in pain. I stopped moving and sat there seeded deep inside of her.

"Are you okay?" I asked.

She felt amazing wrapped around me. It took everything in me not to let loose and go hard and fast.

She nodded with big, shocked eyes. "Yes."

I wasn't so sure, and the last thing I wanted was to hurt her more. "Do you want to stop?"

"No. Don't stop."

So I didn't. I waited and kissed her more, letting her get adjusted to the feel of me. After a while, natural instinct kicked in and she began rolling her hips beneath me. It felt amazing. I began moving my hips as well—withdrawing slowly before moving back in.

It felt different with Faith. Even with the condom on, I felt as if I could really feel her. She was warmer and felt better than anything I'd ever felt in my life. I told her so over and over again as I rocked into her and angled my body in ways that made her make more noise.

The world around us ceased to exist as we panted each other's names—our bodies slid together in a way I'd never experienced. It was as if I were the virgin. Sex with Faith was beyond words. I wasn't only physically connected to her; I was emotionally connected as well, which made it feel a hundred times better.

Fingernails dug into my back as she threw her head back and cried out her release. It was my undoing. I buried my face into her neck, held her closer, and released my all for her. I died a little in that moment, and Faith was my heaven.

Seventeen

Faith

I lay next to Finn and watched him sleep. The alarm clock beside his bed blinked twelve midnight and lit the corner of his room red with every blink. His chest moved up and down with his deep breathing. Every now and again, he'd make a sweet noise of contentment and I'd smile to myself.

I could hardly believe I was no longer the innocent girl I once was. I'd sinned in the worst way, but I'd welcome hell if it meant being with Finn. We were in love and being with him that way, I could almost forget the drama with my dad. I had until the sun came up to decide what to do. Either I'd risk Finn going to jail and stay with him, or I'd give in to my dad's commands and walk away from love and everything that I wanted for myself.

I knew if I told Finn the truth and gave him my options which one he'd pick, but the thought of Finn in jail made me feel nauseated. He was too good for that. He was too good for the life he was living. Technically, I hadn't seen Finn dealing drugs, but would my dad lie to me?

His abs felt hot against my fingertips as I ran them down his body. He turned toward me in his sleep and gathered me in his arms. I felt so safe there, like no one or nothing could reach me. My eyes grew heavy, but I fought sleep for as long as I could. I needed to stay awake and at least try to contemplate what to do. I was practically asleep when I heard Finn whisper, "I love you, Faith," in my ear.

It felt like five minutes later when a loud crashing noise woke me. I sat straight up in an empty bed. The alarm clock blinked two a.m. in my face, letting me know I needed more sleep.

Throwing back the sheet, I slid from Finn's bed and pulled my dress back over my head.

Bright light spilled into the room as I silently pulled his bedroom door open. There was no one outside his room, but every now and again, I'd hear someone talking from down the hallway. I followed the voices and ended up in front of the master bedroom.

I didn't want to be rude and go in, but all I could think was what if someone in there needed help? What if Finn needed me? When I heard his muffled voice through the door, I knew I had to go in. I should've knocked, but if Finn was in the room doing something drug related, I wanted to see it with my own two eyes.

I reached out for the rusted doorknob and gave it a turn. The door was silent as I pushed it open enough for me to peek in. A mauve-covered room stood before me. My eyes skimmed the room carefully, taking in the matching bedspread and curtains. Then my eyes landed on Finn and his mom. They were in the master bathroom across the room from me. Finn held back her hair as she puked in the toilet and cried.

"It's hurts so bad, Jimmy." She moaned.

My heart broke for her. Finn told me before that she had multiple sclerosis, but I had no idea what that really meant.

"I know, Mom. I'm here. I promise I won't leave you," Finn said softly.

I saw another side of him in that moment. I'd always known he was a guy who would take care of anyone he loved, but seeing it with my own two eyes made it more real. He was a caretaker—a good man—and I was a lucky girl to have him.

I felt awful for prying into their business, but it was such an honest moment that I couldn't look away.

"Don't leave me. Please just stay until I'm not dizzy anymore," she asked as Finn wiped at her cheeks with a rag.

I stood there until he helped her back to her bed. Something happened to me as I watched a very personal story unfold in front of me. Whatever it was changed my entire thought process, and I knew in that moment that I couldn't stay with Finn and risk my dad having him arrested for drugs. His mom needed him too much. She was sick, and as badly as I wanted to be with Finn, I couldn't be selfish.

I quickly made my way back to his room, peeled off my dress so he wouldn't know I'd been awake, and fell back into his bed with my eyes shut tightly. His door squeaked a little and I could see the light through my eyelids when he came back into his room. Darkness consumed me, and the door clicked into place as he shut the world out again.

I pretended to sleep as he slid back into bed with me. His side of the mattress dipped and pulled me closer to him. Warm arms came around me and he snuggled his body up to mine and spooned me. I wanted to cry for what I would be losing if I walked away. I was almost positive it was what I had to do.

He kissed the side of my neck and sighed happily. Once I heard his breathing even out again, I stared at the wall and watched it blink red again. I sat in the same spot for an hour as I went over my options over and over again. In the end, I came to the conclusion that I had to do the right thing. I had to move to California with my parents, and I had to do it without telling Finn.

I knew Finn and I knew he would fight for me… He'd said so himself earlier that night. If the situation had been different, I would've fought harder for him, but someone else needed him more than me, and if I stayed, it could mean prison for Finn. That wasn't something I could live with.

Hot tears streamed down my face as I quietly slipped from his bed. I put my bra and panties back on and then I pulled my dress over my head. My cross warmed my palm as I stared down at Finn and his sweet face. I imagined that everything I was poured into my cross. More than just my soul, more than my emotions that were crumbling at that exact moment, but my essence—all that was Faith.

I didn't need any part of myself anymore. I was going to be lifeless without Finn anyway. I loved him and since he couldn't have me, I wanted him to have the biggest and most important part of me—my soul.

Unhooking my necklace, I let the cross slide from the chain and into my palm. It felt hotter than usual, and the back of my neck felt weird without the weight pulling against it. Closing my eyes, I said a silent prayer that my cross would always keep Finn safe, and then I made a promise to the air in the room that when I could, I'd come back to Finn.

Kissing the cross, I laid it on the pillow next to his head. My heart was breaking into pieces and everything ached. I felt like I couldn't breathe. I leaned down and pressed my lips to his cheek. He smiled in his sleep, his dimples popping out for me one last time.

Wiping my face with the back of my sleeve, I stepped away from him. I crept through his house like a criminal until I stepped into his yard and into the cold morning air. The world was silent as I walked toward the closest store and called my parents. I didn't pass a single person on the way, not that anyone could hurt me any worse than I'd hurt myself at that point.

An hour later, I was in the back of my dad's car on my way back to hell. There was a belt and a plane ticket waiting for me when I got there. By ten a.m., my father had me on the way to the airport. My plane left at noon. I cried the entire time.

A week later, I was dying. I couldn't take it anymore. Dad had yet to prove to me that he had any evidence against Finn, and when I pushed it too much, he'd pull off his belt. Except, instead of taking it the way I had before we left South Carolina, I fought back. It made the beatings worse, and I was forced to live at the church to pray for my sins, but I refused to lie there and take it anymore.

I wrote letter after letter to Finn. I told him everything in those letters and left him phone numbers where he could reach me, but I never heard anything back from him. I drove myself crazy trying to figure out why he wasn't responding to me or at least calling me. Every time I tried to call his house number, I would get the disconnected signal, and the cell he shared with his mom always went straight to voicemail. I must've left at least fifty messages, until finally I called and that number, too, was not in service.

When I'd had about all I could take, I told my parents I wanted to go back home—back to Finn. My mother was stressed out of her mind and my father refused to hear anything I had to say. Every time I'd try to run away, they'd find me, and I never got very far. The whole needing a plane ticket thing made it difficult, too.

Finally, one day I got a letter in the mail from Finn. Except when I opened it, it wasn't the response I was hoping for.

Faith,

I don't care why you left. You leaving was the best thing that could've ever happened to me. I can't believe I got mixed up with a girl like you. Please quit sending me letters. I no longer care what you have to say. There wasn't any other point to this letter. I just wanted you to know I'm over you and I hope you have a nice life in California.

Finn

The air was sucked out of my lungs, and I had to sit down. The room spun around me.

"But you said you loved me," I whispered to myself as I clutched the letter to my chest.

The words were there and he had signed it, but it couldn't be right. Finn loved me; he wanted me. He never would've treated me that way. The only thing that I could think was that it was a lie. My father had to be a liar.

"This is a lie!" I cried as I held up the letter.

My father didn't even respond. Instead, he knocked me into my seat with a backhand.

I sat on that letter for three days as I contemplated my next move. Love made you do crazy things, and so I became a liar and a thief. I waited until my parents were asleep and then snuck into their room. I brazenly stole my dad's debit card and ordered a plane ticket on my older-than-dirt computer that I'd always hated. Turns out it was handy to have around after all.

When I tucked his debit card back into his wallet, I took all his cash and his keys. When I got back to my room, I quickly packed everything I could into a duffle bag and left before they had a chance to wake up and stop me.

I spent the next two hours getting lost all over California, trying to find the airport. I'd never been so happy to see an airport in all my life when the sign finally came into view. I'd almost missed my flight so things moved quickly once I got there. Thankfully, I was on a plane back to the East Coast before the sun even broke through the clouds.

I looked at my watch and smiled to myself at the exact moment that I knew my parents were figuring out that I was gone and that I'd taken their car. They couldn't come after me as quickly as they'd like since their car was parked in the airport garage.

When I landed, I got a cab and gave the driver Finn's address. I needed to see him. I needed him to hold me and tell me that everything would be okay. I missed him so much it hurt.

The driver kept looking at me through the rearview mirror, which was kind of creepy. I was relieved when I saw Finn's house come into view.

"Thanks," I said to the driver as I paid him.

He pulled away as I stood on the sidewalk, clutching my duffle bag. It was nearly two in the afternoon already in South Carolina, and already there were cars everywhere in Finn's yard. It bothered me a little that he was inside partying while I'd been in California, dying without him.

Music played loudly from the garage as usual as I made my way to the door. I nervously smoothed out my skirt and shirt before I stepped inside. I was so excited and scared at the same time. What if the letter had really been from Finn? What if he never wanted to see my face again? I'd be stuck with no one to turn to and nowhere to go. I didn't want to have to run back to my dad, and I didn't even know if he'd let me come back again after the stuff I'd pulled.

I held my breath and stepped through the doors into the smoke-filled space. The smells that stung my nose were awful—a mixture of sweat and alcohol made my stomach turn. My eyes took in the crowded room as the smoke burned them. And then I saw him across the room and everything around me disappeared. I smiled to myself as I walked closer to where he sat. The smile slowly disappeared from my face once he was in full view.

He was leaning back against the couch with his eyes closed. He wasn't smiling. Actually, he looked like he was in pain, but the memories of our night together reminded me that sometimes when Finn looked like he was in pain, he was in ecstasy. Jenny, his ex-girlfriend, straddled his lap and worked her body back and forth. Her long hair bobbed with her movements.

I felt sick to my stomach. My knees went weak beneath me, and I used the wall of the garage to hold myself up. I couldn't take my eyes away from them. Finn just sat there with his eyelids closed tight. He didn't even bother to touch her. Instead, his arms were thrown out at his sides.

My heart shattered into a million soulless pieces. It was true. Finn had really moved on just that quickly. I was nothing to him. I never was. I'd read his letter, but I'd refused to believe it. I should've believed my dad. Maybe he really did mean well. Maybe he really did have my best interests at heart.

My legs felt numb as I turned and left the garage. When I escaped the terrible smells, I took deep breaths of fresh air. The breeze that moved around me cooled the tears pouring down my cheeks and dripping from my chin. I turned and started toward the gas station that was the closest. I died a little more with every step I took away from Finn, but I had to do what I had to. So I left and I never looked back again.

Thankfully, my father let me come back to our new home in California and even paid for my return. I ran back with my tail tucked firmly between my legs and salty tears on my cheeks. The beating I got when I got home was one that would stay with me for the rest of my life, but still, it didn't hurt as much as seeing Finn with Jenny.

I settled into the life my dad wanted me to have and tried with all my might to block out Finn and everything I felt for him. It worked as long as I shut off my brain and stayed so busy I literally fell into bed each night. But then things took a turn for the worse and before I knew it, I was kicked out in a strange state with no one to turn to and nowhere to go.

Part Two: Old Wounds

Four Years Later

EIGHTEEN

FINN

I placed my hand on the back of her head as she continued to suck my cock. She wasn't the best I'd had, but she was damn good at it. It felt even better when I closed my eyes and imagined she was a certain brunette that I loved to hate. In the end, imagining things like that only made me even more of an asshole.

I looked down at my hands and the blond hair clasped in my fingers. It was bleached. There was nothing natural about the girl on her knees in front of me. She looked up at me with big blue eyes and I had to look away. She wasn't the woman I wanted, so I kept my eyes closed and wished it would be over already. I'd give her one thing, though; she won a ton of extra points when I told her I was going to come and she kept going until I was dry.

I tucked my junk back into my boxers and zipped up my jeans. The blonde adjusted her shorts as she sat on the couch next to me and attempted to snuggle. There was once a time in my life when I enjoyed snuggling, being close to the woman I cared about and breathing her in—not so much anymore. In fact, I fucking hated it. Not to mention, I didn't give a shit about the girl I was with. I hadn't even asked her name. I think at one point she'd told me, but I'd heard a lot of names. She had given me no reason to remember hers.

"Listen, babe, I appreciate the good time, but I think it's time I get some sleep," I said as I yawned.

I hated bringing girls on the bus, but a man had needs, and when there was a girl all ready to fulfill those needs, then what else could you do? It wasn't like I forced them to do anything. They should've thought twice before they dropped their panties for just anyone.

"Should I give you my number?" she asked sweetly.

She ran her knee suggestively across mine, and I slid over and grabbed my beer.

I hated the part when they thought there'd be more. I always made it clear beforehand, but they all thought they'd be the one that did the trick—like they had a magic mouth that would snap me into some romantic Romeo. Not so much. I'd been burned before. No way in hell was the shit happening again.

"Nah, I'm good," I said carelessly. "Thanks again, though."

Her eyes widened and she looked at me like she couldn't believe I had the audacity to say something so rude to her. I had all the audacity in the fucking world since she'd been dumb enough to drop to her knees in a strange bus with a guy she was never going to see again. Her purse swung close to my face when she grabbed it and ran from the bus. I chuckled to myself and shook my head. It was just another day in the life.

"Dude, tell me you got some of that," Chet said as he stepped onboard the bus.

He turned back around and watched her walk across the parking lot. Licking his lips, he said, "Damn, look at that ass."

I ignored his words. "Grab me another beer, man."

Reaching into the refrigerator, he grabbed two bottles and threw one at me. The table beside me became a bottle opener as I popped it open on the edge. Six beers and three blunts later, we were laughing with Zeke and Tiny and getting ready to play our asses off in front of the thousands of people who'd come from all over to watch Blow Hole play.

I could hardly believe the life we were living these days. We'd definitely moved up in the world. We'd gone from shit to shoe shines in less than a month. Everything had happened so fast. One minute we were getting a contract, and then next we were moving to California and rubbing elbows with the big dogs. I loved being the front man for Blow Hole. When I stood before thousands and sang the lyrics I'd burned inside to write, it did something to me—took away my anger for just a few hours. It was the therapy that I definitely needed.

When I was on the stage with my boys, nothing else mattered. Girls in the front row screamed my name, and I knelt down to run my fingers across theirs. To my right, Zeke, the lead guitarist, shook his head at me with a knowing grin as he jumped up on the large speaker at the front of the stage and played his guitar solo.

That fucker could play guitar like no other, and he reminded me so much of Kevin. It was fitting that he'd be my right-hand man. I felt okay with him taking Kevin's spot, and I knew if Kevin had the chance to meet Zeke, he would've agreed. Maybe that was why I'd accepted him into my world so easily. It wasn't every day that someone walked straight into my life the way Zeke had. He had a fucked-up home life, and Mom and I had taken him under our wings until he was able to fly on his own.

Although he flew crooked, getting all mixed up in drugs and sex, he was making his way. Truth be told, Zeke was a fucking wreck until he'd gotten with his girl, Patience. I knew all too well what that was like. She straightened him right out and smoothed away his permanent frown. I liked the new Zeke, even if I did bust his balls about being all domesticated and shit. I was happy for him.

Patience was a sweet girl, and I could see her appeal to Zeke, but settling down wasn't for me.

I stepped back toward Chet's drums to grab my drink. Red mystery liquid mixed with something strong slid down my throat as I tipped back my red Solo cup. I didn't care what it was as long as it took away my inhibitions, not that I had many.

"Blonde, front and center," Chet called out to me as he nodded his head in the direction of the girl he was talking about.

He was always pointing out the girls he wanted to bring back to the bus. I did what I could to help him out since he was stuck at the back of the stage behind the drums most nights. As the drummer, he got lots of ass, but he liked to pick his own.

I beat on Chet's drums with my palms, making a loud rumble, and he pointed his drumstick at me during a break as he mouthed the words "fuck face" at me. The crowd went wild at our display. I loved giving Chet hell, and even though he acted like he hated the shit, I knew deep down he liked it.

Chet was the one to worry about. He had no fear, and fearless men were scary as fuck. Of course, he also had no filter, which meant he was the funniest piece of shit I'd ever met. Him and Zeke were younger. They were like my badass little brothers, and even though I'd bite off my tongue before I said it, I guess I loved the assholes.

We'd just started touring and getting adjusted to the larger crowds. Back home in South Carolina, we mostly played small clubs. One of our favorites was The Pit, an underground concrete club. On a good night there, we'd play for maybe five hundred people. Looking out at the crowd in front of me, I couldn't believe how far we'd come.

Once the show was over and I'd crowd surfed and had my cock grabbed too many times to count, we ran off the stage and were ushered to our bus by security.

"We love you, Finn!" girls screamed as I passed by.

A particularly bold one flashed her tits at me. They were fake and I preferred the real thing, but that didn't stop me from telling her they were nice and letting her hug me with her top still up. I grinned down at her, and the girls around us screamed louder. Fuck it. I gave them what they wanted… always.

I looked back just in time to see Chet peel off his sweaty "Fuck me. I'm pretty!" shirt and throw it to a chick standing on the side. Since he was the jokester, the girls responded to him and he took full advantage. A different girl every night wasn't enough for Chet most times, and he was into some pretty hardcore shit sexually. To each his own, though.

Zeke walked a straight line to the bus and ignored the girls. He was the hard-ass the girls loved to hate. I never understood how he could be such an asshole to them and still they'd flock to him. Of course, since he'd been seeing Patience, the sleeping around had stopped. I could respect that.

I was totally against finding *the one*. The rest of the group would probably agree with me, but Zeke was good and whipped. He was the last one I expected it from, but you could tell by looking at him that he was crazy in love. I just hoped he didn't get his heart ripped out the way I had so many years ago.

"That was a hell of a show, Finn. We rocked that shit," Tiny said as he hugged a girl in passing.

Camera flashes lit up the path, and I had to blink away the balls of light that stuck to my vision. I looked over at Tiny and threw my arm around his neck.

"Hell yeah, we did."

Tiny stuck with me no matter what. Believe it or not, he'd actually grown more since he was in high school. He towered over the rest of us and worked out constantly. The working out had started after the accident that almost took his life. I was thankful to still have him around. He didn't have much family so he stuck around my place a lot. I never asked questions, but he was a loner and needed Mom and me. At least that's how it seemed. Mom hadn't only adopted me; she took in my boys, too. I loved that woman.

Tiny hadn't only gotten taller; he'd gotten better at a lot of things. Even his bass playing had improved. Not that he was bad before, but after the accident, he had a hard time with his nerves. Playing hurt him, and even though he didn't complain, I think it still did. I didn't push. I only knew I wouldn't pursue anything musically without him, and I'd always keep his secret. No one but me knew about the awful scaring under his clothes, and no one else needed to know. He was strong and loyal to the fucking core, and I'd be the same to him. We'd been through it all together.

The funny thing about Tiny was the fact that even though he didn't realize I noticed, he never slept with girls. He made out with them plenty, but I couldn't remember a time when he'd actually broke the back out of one of them. And he could do it easily since he was every bit of three hundred pounds and hard muscle.

At one point, I'd almost asked if he batted for the other team, but there were times when I'd catch him checking out girls. Either way, he'd been there for me through a lot of shit and I'd always been there for him.

All in all, I was pretty happy with the way things were going for the four of us. We were Blow Hole since there was no way in hell I could continue using the name Original Malice with half of the band gone. The name Blow Hole fit. After Faith left, I went back to selling cocaine. Uncle Lester, my old supplier, used to call it blow, and since my garage was the place to go when you wanted some blow, my garage became known as the blow hole. The name stuck.

It was good, though. You couldn't turn on the radio without hearing a Blow Hole song, and after signing what could only be described as a kickass contract, we'd been living a much different lifestyle than what we were all used to. None of us were complaining.

"Zeke, pack us a bowl, man. I'm going to change. Some bitch poured her entire beer over me when I went surfing," I said as I went to the back of the bus.

We spent the rest of the night bullshitting on the bus and getting high out of our minds. Zeke kind of chilled on the side. I got it, being all domesticated and shit, but it wasn't for the rest of us. We playfully teased him about it, but even though we didn't believe in only one girl, we understood and respected him.

A ton of shit had happened since we'd been on the road. We practically lived on our bus or on a plane, but home was a big-ass condo in California.

The next morning, I called my mom to check on her. I called her at least twice a week no matter what.

"I'm good. Rick planted a garden in the back yard and I was helping him. You should see how nice the tomatoes came out."

Mom was now settled down with her new husband, Rick. He was a nice guy. He treated her good and took good care of her. I couldn't ask for more.

"That sounds great, Mom. Listen, we'll be heading that way here soon. I miss you and was hoping we could get together for a nice dinner or something."

Even though she hated it and swore she wouldn't use it, I sent her a couple thousand dollars a month. Needless to say, she didn't live back in the old neighborhood or drive that piece of shit Jeep anymore.

"Of course, Jimmy! I can't wait to have you home for a little while. Y'all be careful out there with all those crazy people. Be good and try not to get into any trouble."

I got the same speech every time I called and I loved it. It was nice after being on the road with a bunch of bitches that only cared about your wallet or your name to have someone who actually gave a real shit about you. My mom would always be the only woman in my life for those exact reasons.

"We will. I love you, Mom. See you soon."

We got a break in our tour a week later and went back to California for some downtime before going on the run again. Our lush condo was nice and decorated with some of the most expensive shit our label could find. I remember the moment we all stepped into the massive place and how we all flipped out over how nice it was. None of us were used to living in such splendor. We'd each came from the other side of town, living in either a shitty little house, a fucked-up trailer, or the ghetto apartments where all the single moms and meth heads lived.

I threw my shit on my bed and went into my bathroom for a shower. I didn't even notice how nice our place was anymore. After staying in some of the nicest hotels in the world, I was accustomed to the best.

I stepped up to my shower and turned the water on full blast before stripping down naked and tossing my dirty clothes onto the floor. I'd called a temp agency for a maid. We were a bunch of messy asses and none of us wanted to clean when we were home from being on the road for so long. I could tell by looking at the bathroom that she'd already started her job and was damn good at it.

I turned around to grab a towel, and when I did, I ran straight into the maid, who was holding a large pile of fresh laundry in her arms. She screamed loudly before dropping all the laundry to the floor. The smell of fabric softer and washing detergent filled my senses as a thick white towel fell over my face.

I pulled down the towel, ready to see the shocked face on the maid when she realized that she'd just walked in on her employer naked as the day he was born. My eyes started at the top of her head and took in the long chocolate locks. Big brown eyes stared back at me. I'd thought I'd shock her with my nakedness, but instead, the shock was mine. I took in the woman in front of me and my chest got tight. Faith stared back at me with flushed, embarrassed cheeks. Her plump lips opened in a gasp before she collapsed at my feet.

NINETEEN

FAITH

"What do you mean I'm fired?" I asked Jesse, my manager.

I couldn't afford to lose my second job. It was the only one that worked with my busy schedule and it was the main reason I was able to keep us above water. I was drowning and I hadn't slept properly in four years, but my family was taken care of and that was all that mattered to me.

"I'm sorry, Faith, we can't afford to keep you, and the owner's pretty pissed at you still for giving away free gas," Jesse said as he slid my final paycheck over the counter to me.

"But I paid for that out of my pocket!"

"I'm sorry." He turned and walked away from the counter, letting me know our conversation was over.

The truth was I hated working in the gas station after dark. Especially in that neighborhood, but luckily some of the Spanish guys who lived in the trailer park nearby kept watch over me after I gave them a free tank of gas one day. But regardless of not being safe working there at night, it paid well enough.

I hated searching for a new job. With my day job at the grocery store by my apartment, it made it hard to get away to find another job, and honestly, I couldn't afford to take a day off to search for another one.

After grabbing my final check, I ran outside to catch my mom before she pulled away. Thankfully, she'd needed gas before she went home. Otherwise, she would've been long gone.

"You aren't working tonight?" she asked, confused.

"Nope. I got fired," I said as I climbed into the front seat and slammed the door behind me.

She got into the driver's seat and cranked up the car. It was hard to believe Mom's old Taurus was still kicking. "I'm sorry, honey. I'll start looking for something. It's not fair for you to be working two jobs when I could find something."

Mom had a stroke right after she and my dad divorced, and I was determined that she wasn't going to have to work. I think it was the stress of the entire ordeal that did her in. I'd been so shocked when Mom had come into the room while Daddy was beating me and stood up to him. She'd done it once before, but that last time had been different. It might have had something to do with the fact that I was six months pregnant by that point.

"No, Mom, I got this." I smiled over at her.

"Mommy, is work over?" Jimmy said from the back seat as he rubbed his sleepy eyes.

He must've fallen asleep right after I got out of the car. I turned around and ruffled his soft brown curls. The last thing I wanted was for Jimmy to get upset over me being upset.

"Yes, baby, work's over. I'm going to take you home and we can watch your dinosaur movie until we fall asleep. Does that sound fun?"

Mom and I laughed at his excitement as we drove home, but still, I couldn't help but feel stressed about our situation.

Both Mom and I had always lived under Daddy's thumb. He worked and took care of us. When we first started out on our own without him, we were both lost as to what to do. Daddy no longer had anything to do with me since I'd shamed our family, so it wasn't like I could ask him for help even if I wanted to, but we were making it. Barely, but we were making it.

The next day, even though I hated to do it, I took the day off. I spent the entire day job searching. At the advice of my mom, I went to a local temp agency and applied, even though I knew nothing would come of it. I'd only ever had four jobs in my entire life and none of them required any real skill since I didn't get a chance to graduate from high school.

Daddy forced me quit the minute he'd found out I was pregnant, so I only made it to the end of my junior year. I had dreams of going back and getting my diploma and going to college. I wanted to make a life for Jimmy and me, but that was hard to do when you had to work every minute of every day just to make ends meet.

There were days when I thought about contacting Finn. I'd followed his career even though it killed me to do so. He was a big-time rock star now; he could afford to pay some child support. But then I'd realize the error in my thoughts. I hated Finn and Finn hated me. He had the money and the ability to take Jimmy away from me, and I knew he would. I'd die before I let anyone try to take my baby.

So instead, I pulled through and did the single mom thing the only way I knew how—I worked my fingers to the bone and slept when I could. I did, however, try my hardest to always make time for Jimmy. Having a three-year-old boy who loved me unconditionally was the best thing that had ever happened to me, and I'd always make sure he knew he was the most important thing in my life.

I was in a bad place emotionally when I'd found out I was pregnant, and I thought for sure my world was ending. I went through my pregnancy practically alone, with the exception of my mom, who was dealing with health issues and a divorce, but I'd done it and every day that I looked at that precious boy with his daddy's eyes and dimples, I knew that I couldn't give in to my depression. Not ever. Little Jimmy saved my life in so many ways.

I got a call from the temp agency exactly a week later. Even though I hated to do it and I needed the money, I called in at the grocery store again so I could meet with them to find out about other jobs. I dressed in my best pants and a nice top. I hadn't worn a long skirt in four years, and I swore I never would again.

The blonde behind the front desk of the temp agency reminded me of Amanda. There were a lot of blondes in California and many of them reminded me of her. I was constantly doing a double take even though I knew it was impossible for her to be anywhere.

I missed Amanda so much. It was hard to believe it had already been over four years since she died. Not a day went by that I didn't think about her. I remember crying the day I delivered little Jimmy because I'd done it alone. Mom was in the hospital at the same time as me. Amanda would've been there for the entire thing. I know she would've. I would've had a baby shower and she would've been there helping me push when it was time.

Instead, I screamed my head off since I'd gotten there too late for drugs, and the only people who'd been in the room were the doctor who I was positive hated me and a nurse that said I was acting like a baby. It was a good memory and a bad one all wrapped in one.

I filled out some paperwork that the blonde behind the desk gave me and then I was called back into a tiny office with an older lady sitting behind a massive desk covered in papers. She stood and smiled when I entered.

"Hi, Faith, I'm Mrs. Cooper." She shook my hand. "Please, have a seat and let's see what we can do for you."

I sat there silently as she went through all of my papers and my application and tried her hardest to find a job for me. It was hard considering I had limited experience and no educational background. It stung when I told her that I hadn't graduated or gone to college.

"It looks like I may have found something," she said in relief.

I appreciated her trying so hard for me.

"How do you feel about cleaning? As in being a maid?"

"What are the hours?" I asked.

I had to make sure it either had hours that worked with my grocery store job or paid enough that I could work only the maid position.

"Monday through Friday, and the hours are as long as the job takes. If you go in early enough and you get the job done right, I don't see any reason why you'd have to stay in the house. It's not a live-in position."

"What does it pay?" I asked.

She smiled over a piece of paper. "Well, it seems the job pays six hundred and fifty dollars a week, after taxes, of course. How does that sound?"

How did it sound? It sounded amazing! I barely brought home four hundred after taxes from my two jobs a week. That barely covered rent in our small two-bedroom apartment, the bills, groceries, and everything else that went along with living.

"It sounds perfect," I said with a smile. "When can I start?"

I left Mrs. Cooper's office feeling better than I had in a very long time. Things were looking up. God was starting to answer my prayers. With a job like that, I'd get to spend time with Little Jimmy and possibly go back to school.

I brought home pizza as a surprise for Mom and Jimmy. When I walked in the front door, he jumped out with his dinosaur mask on, and I pretended to be afraid. He giggled as he hugged my leg.

"It's okay, Mommy. It's me, it's me!"

We all sat in the living room, ate pizza, and watched dinosaur movies. Once Jimmy fell asleep on my lap, I lifted him and took him to our bed. We shared a room and the room was big enough for two beds, but all I had was my small full-sized bed from when I lived at home. At least Dad had let me take that.

Some nights, I'd relax in bed and sift through my memories. My bed always reminded of the time when Finn had spent the night with me. It was a bittersweet memory that started out making me feel better, but then I'd get angry all over again and I'd end up in an even worse mood.

The truth was I was lonely. Other than Mom and Jimmy, I had no friends, and even though there were some men who flirted with me, I couldn't bring myself to date. Even thinking about being sexual with another man made me feel sick to my stomach. Finn was my only, and as far as I was concerned, I got the best part of him. Every time I looked at my baby boy, I knew I could never regret being with Finn, even if he'd broken me beyond repair.

I started my new maid job three days later. Mrs. Cooper had informed me that the owners of the condo I was cleaning were almost never home, which made me even happier. The last thing I wanted was to clean someone's toilet as they watched me.

The condo was massive with contemporary furniture like you'd see in a dental office and abstract paintings of different instruments all over. The kitchen was covered in stainless steel and granite, and the five bathrooms were all bigger than my entire apartment.

Why someone would need so many bathrooms and bedrooms was beyond me, but once I started cleaning, I realized there were quite a few people living there. Each room was well lived in and dirty as all get out. Actually, considering how rich the apartment looked, it was pretty filthy—like maybe a bunch of men lived there.

I didn't get the entire place cleaned the first day, so I was extra happy that the owners didn't seem to be returning anytime soon. I'd return each day to an empty condo and continue to clean, making it further and further every day. After four days, the place was spotless.

By the fifth day, all I had to do was the laundry that was left over. It was all men's clothes, but by then, I'd already figured out that I was cleaning for a household full of guys. Maybe a sports team or something like that? There weren't any personal pictures lying around. Nothing letting me know what the people looked like or whether or not they had families. It was kind of spooky, but I didn't care. As long as the check came every Friday and I could pay my bills, I was happy.

I folded all the towels in the laundry area and began to put them in the linen closets located in every bathroom. When I made it to the gray-and-black room, which is what I'd named it, I had an armful of towels and a happy smile since I knew it was payday and I'd have enough money to stop and get Jimmy the stuffed dinosaur he'd been wanting.

I could hardly wait to see his face when I came through that door with that thing. It was expensive, but my baby deserved it.

The sound of water sounded somewhere and I stopped. The agency had warned me that the owners would be returning, but I hadn't seen anyone yet. I felt relief knowing that I was almost done and that I wouldn't be stuck cleaning while they were there.

I raced across the room and straight into the bathroom with my arms full of towels. I wanted to hurry and get out of the condo and on my way home. I expected the room to be empty since the running water sounded as if it were coming from the kitchen.

I screamed loudly and dropped all the laundry when I ran straight into a naked man. My cheeks lit up with a red rush of fire. The embarrassment made me dizzy, so dizzy that I was afraid I might faint as my eyes took in his naked chest and lower half, but it was when my vision clashed with Finn's shocked blue eyes and dark features, that I went crashing to the floor.

Twenty
Finn

I could hardly believe my eyes. For a brief moment, I wondered to myself if I was still high from the last shit I'd smoked. I was shocked that I almost didn't catch her when she fainted right there on the bathroom floor. My hand kept her head from smashing into the expensive flooring.

Not that I cared much about what happened to her. Or did I?

I scooped up her small frame. She felt smaller than she had four years ago. I tried not to think about what she felt like in my arms as I crossed my bedroom and laid her on my massive king-sized bed. Her head was back and her mouth was gapped open. I appreciated the fact that she still had her long hair, even though I couldn't see it since it was piled on top of her head in a messy bun.

It was only natural for my eyes to take in her body. They followed her graceful neckline, down past her chest and flat stomach, and landed on a set of long legs that I could remember being wrapped so tightly around me. My cock started to grow hard and I had to step away.

"Snap the fuck out of it, Finn. This bitch is the devil. Remember that," I said to myself.

I went into my closet and pulled out a change of clothes and dressed as quickly as I could. In the bathroom, I turned off the water. By the time I was back in the bedroom, she was coming around. I sat in the chair beside my bed and watched as she opened her eyes and blinked rapidly at the ceiling above us.

The words that I longed to say to her for the past four years felt sour against my tongue. She'd burned me so badly—sucked out any bit of good that was in me and spit it in my face. When she disappeared on me, I went so far into a depression that my mom feared for my life. I drank until I couldn't keep my eyes open and did so much drugs that any bit of money I made selling anything went straight into my habit.

I didn't touch another girl until after I'd been with Blow Hole for a while. I remembered Jenny coming over not long after Faith had left. She'd tried so hard to get me to fuck her, and I ended up passing out on her. My boy Leroy informed me the next day that he'd found Jenny straddling me while I was passed out. Being the kickass friend that he was, he pulled her off of me and kicked her out of my garage.

I couldn't even remember the first girl I'd slept with after Faith. I just remember being drunk and crying the next day. I'd felt as if I'd cheated on her. It took me a long time to build up so much anger toward Faith that I could be with another woman, but I always made sure to never get involved with a woman more than once, and feelings were something I never planned on having again. It worked and that was all that mattered.

I could easily say without blinking that I hated Faith, and I'd spent a good chunk of the four years contemplating the havoc I'd wreak on her if I ever saw her again. So while seeing her lying on my bed reminded me of a bad moment in my life, it also made me happy that I'd finally be able to get revenge for the heartbreak she'd delivered without a care for me.

When she finally realized what had happened, she sat up quickly and grabbed the back of her head like it hurt. Her eyes scanned my room until they landed on me. They widened as took me in.

"Finn?"

"Faith?" I responded.

"What are you doing here?" she asked.

"I live here. I'm assuming you're the new maid the temp agency sent over?"

She shook her head yes slowly, her eyes still relaying her shock.

"I didn't... I didn't know you lived here," she stuttered.

"And here I was thinking you'd come for a second dose," I said sarcastically.

I praised myself when she frowned.

"I assure you that is *not* the case," she said as she swatted at a piece of hair in her face.

She quickly slid from my bed and went into the bathroom to gather the towels she'd dropped. She folded them and placed them into the linen cabinet without saying another word. I didn't take my eyes off of her as she worked. I enjoyed the fact that I made her so nervous. The bitch deserved it.

When she came out of the bathroom, she started across the room as if she were going to leave. Something told me she wouldn't be returning to the condo to clean, and I had to take my chance to get my digs in before she left.

"My, my, how the mighty have fallen." I shook my head. She stopped with her back to me, and I continued. "When exactly did you start cleaning toilets for a living?"

She swung around like she was going to say something rude. Her eyes blazed and her cheeks turned fire red. I longed for her to say something fucked up so I could fire back and burn her, but instead, she closed her eyes, took a deep breath, and walked away.

I couldn't help myself. I followed behind her. Thankfully, no one was in living room or kitchen when we got in there. She went to the kitchen counter and grabbed her purse. She turned toward the door and I decided to give one more slap in the face before she left.

"Bye, Faith. Beware of Daddy's belt when you get home." I chuckled to myself.

It was fucked up, but so was her walking out on me like I was nothing. If she could treat me that way, then I could treat her the same way.

Again, she paused with her back to me. I waited anxiously for her to turn on me and give me a reason to verbally cut her, but again, she walked away. The front door shut quietly behind her. She didn't even have the backbone to slam the fucking door in anger. What I'd ever seen in such a weak woman I didn't know.

That weekend we threw a big-ass party and instead of getting pissed at the fuckers who trashed our place, I smiled to myself, knowing that if Faith had enough balls to come back to clean, she'd have her hands full.

I drank so much that Tiny had to help me to my room. I knew in the back of my mind that I was trying to drown the old hurtful memories that kept popping up. I'd never admit that to anyone else, but the only thing that seemed to make those thoughts and feelings that I loathed so much go away was liquor and drugs.

"Leave it. Let the maid get it," I said to Zeke's girlfriend, Patience, the following Monday when I walked into the kitchen.

She was stacking the dishwasher and collecting the trash. I didn't mind her being at our place. I actually enjoyed her company. It was nice having a girl around that I could be friends with.

"It's not a problem." She smiled over at me. "There's some Tylenol in the cabinet there for that hangover I'm sure you have."

I reached out and stopped her from cleaning. "Patience, get your cute little butt back in that bedroom with Zeke and spend some time with him. I got this."

After I'd gotten rid of Patience, I downed another beer to bite the dog and swallowed enough Tylenol to knock out my headache.

I stood in the shower for an extra long time, letting the hot water clear my brain. Once I got out and got dressed, everyone was ready to head out and do some fun stuff for the day. Zeke and Patience were obviously going to do their own thing, so Tiny and Chet tried to talk me into getting into some trouble with them.

"Nah, I think I'm going to hang out around here today. I feel like shit."

It was a lie. Really, I wanted to stay just in case Faith came back. I didn't want to miss the chance to talk shit while she cleaned up after me and my boys.

Once the place was empty, I chilled on the couch and watched TV. I couldn't believe my luck when I heard the front door open and then close. When I turned around, Faith was standing there looking back at me. She said nothing as she set her purse on the kitchen counter and went to work. I was already thinking of everything I wanted to say to her. When I was done with her, she'd never come back in my home again.

TWENTY-ONE
FAITH

His words cut me deep. So deep, in fact, that I cried the entire drive back to my apartment. I cursed myself for letting him lure more tears from me. I'd sworn I'd never cry over Finn again, yet I had, but the things he said to me were so cold, so hurtful.

As soon as I got home, I called the grocery store and tried to get my old job back, but the position had already been filled. I took Jimmy with me to the temp agency to pick up my check.

"Mrs. Cooper, is there any chance you might have another position for me?" I asked.

Her brows pulled down in confusion.

"But I thought you were enjoying it. Is it because the owners came home? Did something happen?" she asked.

Something had definitely happened, but I couldn't tell her, especially in front of Jimmy.

"No, nothing like that. I was just asking."

"Unfortunately, Faith, with your lack of education, it'd be hard to find you something else, but I'll keep an eye out."

I wanted to cry when I left her office. I was stuck. If Finn didn't fire me, I'd have to work for him. I'd have to see him over and over again, and that made me feel sick. Not to mention, I didn't want to be anywhere near him. What if he found out about Jimmy? I could not under any circumstances let that happen. He'd take him, and then I'd really die inside.

I took Jimmy to the toy store and bought him his dinosaur. On the way back to the apartment, I kept looking at him in the rearview mirror. He loved his new toy and it was nice to give him something and make him smile. It made me sad that I couldn't do that whenever I wanted. He was a great kid and deserved so much more, but I could give him all the love in the world. Hopefully, that would be enough.

The fact of the matter was I'd continue to look for something else and hopefully Mrs. Cooper would continue to search, but until then, and as long as Finn didn't fire me, I was stuck cleaning up after him. I didn't like it, but I'd swallow my pride if it meant taking care of my son.

The worst thing about it was that I was working for something that Finn should've been giving me anyway. Jimmy was his son. There was no denying that one. Not only had Finn been the only guy I'd ever had sex with, but Jimmy looked just like Finn—same eyes and dimples, the works.

On Monday, I went back to the condo to clean. I felt relief when I unlocked the door and found no one inside. That relief was instantly replaced with nerves when I looked around the corner and saw Finn staring back at me from the couch. Quickly, I turned away, set down my purse, and went to work. The place was trashed—all my hard work from the week before undone in just a weekend.

"Look who it is, the preacher's devil daughter." He chuckled from the couch.

I ignored him as I loaded the dishwasher.

"I have to admit, you look nothing like the girl I used to know. I guess age is catching up with you, huh?"

He sounded closer, but still I continued to ignore him. His words stung. I'd already started to feel unattractive. I had dark circles around my eyes from lack of sleep, and I worked so much that I was finding it hard to gain or keep on weight.

I turned on the dishwasher and started on the trash. There were bottles and drugs everywhere. I shook my head since obviously nothing had changed in Finn's life. It was probably a good thing that things turned out the way they had all those years ago. I deserved better and so did Jimmy.

Once I was done cleaning and mopping the kitchen, I turned to start on the next room. When I did, Finn was standing behind me with a bottle of soda in his hand. He grinned down at me with sinister eyes as he set the soda on the counter. I started to step away from him, but then he purposely pushed over the soda. It spilled all over the clean countertop and began dripping onto the floor.

I moved quickly to pick up the bottle. When I stood again, he was walking away, laughing. Once he was completely gone from the room, I let go of the tears that had formed in my eyes. I swiped them from my face before I grabbed the cloth and began to clean up the mess.

Three hours later, I was finally done cleaning the rest of the condo. The only room that was left was Finn's, and I knew that's where he was. I stepped up to the door and tapped softly.

"Come in!" he called from inside the room.

I pushed the door open and stepped into the room. The smell of beer assaulted me and made me gag a little.

"Come to try me out again?" He took a hard swig from a beer, his bloodshot eyes never leaving mine.

He was propped up in his bed without his shirt on. His body looked just as amazing as it had years ago. With the exception of a few new tattoos that I refused to look at, he looked exactly the same—more stylish maybe, but still just as beautiful as he always was. I secretly hated him for being so stress free. He didn't have a kid to worry about. He didn't have bills to worry about or whether or not he had to put food on the table for a kid who wouldn't eat anything but pizza and chicken nuggets most of the time.

There were so many things I wanted to say to him, but he wasn't worth it.

His glassy blue eyes devoured me from across the room. Beside him was a half-empty bottle of liquor, and there were clothes everywhere. His jeans were unbuttoned, leaving a space between his abdominal muscles and his jeans. I knew what was under those jeans. I'd been in those jeans, and although I knew it was wrong, I had a brief moment of weakness. I wanted to climb in that bed with him.

Something about the way he looked at me was alarming. It was like I didn't affect him at all. Like he couldn't care less that I was there. He didn't blink. He just stared right through me. Saw all the shattered faithless parts of Faith and disregarded them completely. I couldn't help myself. I responded.

"Try you out?"

"So you do speak? I was starting to think you'd gone dumb, too." He took a big swig from his liquor bottle and chased it with his beer. "I'll admit, the last time you had some of this," he said as he grabbed himself, "I wasn't as good as I am now. I've learned my way around a woman's body. I could do things to you that you wouldn't believe, and I could do it with my eyes closed. Maybe then you wouldn't run off the next day like a bat out of hell." He was drunk, slurring.

I felt his seductive words in my thighs. How was he able to do that? How was he able to send his words across the room and make them dance inside my panties that way?

"I didn't..." I started to defend myself and my actions.

"Don't. I don't care what you did or didn't do. Either you're here to screw or we have nothing to talk about." He finished his beer and set it next to the liquor bottle.

I said nothing. Instead, I turned around and left the room. I grabbed my purse and left without cleaning his bedroom. I was almost to my car when the tears came. At least I could be happy that I'd gotten out of there before he saw my tears. He was nothing like the guy he used to be. Although, the letter I'd gotten four years ago should've told me I was wrong about him.

As soon as I walked into the front door of my apartment, Jimmy attacked me with hugs and kisses. He erased every bad thing Finn said to me in that moment. I scooped him up into my arms and blew raspberries on his tummy. He squirmed out of my embrace and ran back to his toy box.

"You're back early," Mom said from the stove.

Whatever she was cooking smelled amazing but made my stomach turn. The thought of food made me sick. All I wanted to do was go take a hot shower and sleep.

"Grandma's making meatballs!" Jimmy said as he ran around the living room with his dinosaur.

I silently wished I had a tenth of his energy. I laughed and gave him a kiss on the cheek before I went to get a shower.

Once I was undressed, I took the time to look in the mirror. I really did look awful. I was twenty-one, almost twenty-two, yet I looked like a thirty-one-year-old who'd lived a rough life. I pulled the hair away from my face and looked hard at the circles around my eyes. I'd never worn makeup, but I was starting to think maybe I really needed it.

Finn's words moved through my mind once more, and I hated myself for letting them hurt me like they did. I didn't care about him anymore. At least that's what I kept telling myself over and over again. I'd spent the last four years of my life hating him just to make it through the day.

Why did he have to come back into my life now? Why couldn't I be cleaning for some old author or a really hip starlet?

I spent the rest of my night lounging in bed with Jimmy and watching cartoons. It had been so long since I'd watched an adult movie or TV show that I could almost forget they existed. I fell asleep to the soft rhythm of a singing dinosaur buzzing in my ears.

The rest of that week, every day was the same. I'd go to work and clean. Every now and again, Finn would say something hurtful or rude and I'd choke on tears until I could make it to Mom's car and drive myself home.

On Friday, I met the rest of the band. They were all really nice and it was good to see Tiny again, even though he looked at me as if he'd never met me before, which only made me feel uglier and older. It had only been four years, yet even Tiny, who'd always been nothing but nice to me, didn't even recognize me.

I'd never been so happy to see Friday. As soon as I was done with work, I picked up my check and paid bills. I spent the rest of the weekend spending time with my mom and Jimmy. I even got a chance to take him to the jump castle place that he loved so much. It was nice to have a little bit of money to have fun with him.

The following Monday, I was happy to find out that the guys were on the road again. I spent the first two days cleaning the condo, and on Wednesday, I even got to leave early since the place was already spotless.

I stopped by on Thursday and Friday to make sure nothing needed to be done, and then I spent another great weekend with Jimmy and my mom. I even took the time to go by the library and look into going back to get my diploma.

"I'm so proud of you, Faith," Mom said when I told her my plan. "You've been through a lot, yet you still push hard for what you want."

She kissed me on the forehead as she passed me. I was sitting at the kitchen table, filling out paperwork to go back to school.

The following Monday after I went and checked the condo and dusted, I stopped by the adult education place and got an appointment with the advisor. I'd never been more serious about getting back in school and making a better life for me and my son.

Tuesday, when I went to work, the boys were back. They were lounging on the couch and laughing about random stuff. The pretty blonde girl, Patience, was with them again, and I thought it was cute every time I saw her and her boyfriend, Zeke, the lead guitarist, being all sweet alone in the corner.

I longed for some form of male attention. Not sex so much, but at that point, someone telling me I was pretty would be enough. I felt awful all the time and it reflected on the outside. Now that I wasn't stuck under my father's thumb, I could take the time to clean myself up. Maybe dress a little better or put on makeup, but who had time and money for that kind of stuff?

"Man, I would've tapped that ass two times, and then when I was done that second time, I would've tapped it again since all good things come in threes," the one named Chet said loudly.

The guys around him laughed, including Finn.

"I still can't believe you didn't fuck her, Finn. You should've sent her my way if you weren't feeling it."

"Chill with the language, man. My girl's in the room," Zeke said as he pulled Patience closer to his side.

Finn looked over at me and I turned my head quickly. Apparently, Finn was still living his wild playboy life. I remembered the way he looked sitting on that couch with his eyes closed as Jenny, worked her body on top of him. The thought of them together still made me sick four years later. Actually, hearing them talk about Finn getting laid while on tour made me sick, too.

I ignored them and went straight to the back bedrooms to get to work. I made the bed and cleaned up trash in Finn's room first so I didn't get stuck in his room with him again. I was working on his bathroom when I felt someone behind me.

I wasn't in the mood for him. I didn't think I could take any more rude remarks. I'd woken up that morning with my period and I had a severe case of PMS. I was angry and emotional and I honestly didn't think I could sit there and take his crap without responding this time.

When I turned around, he was standing behind me, watching me work. I turned my head and continued. If I could get it done as soon as possible, then I could leave. Water from cleaning the countertop had spilled onto the floor, so I grabbed one of towels from the little bucket I took to work with me and started to clean it up. I was positive I had it all, but when I started to clean the shower, I slipped on a slick spot and fell face first into the hot shower water.

Embarrassment set in as the hot water ran over my hair and into my eyes. I put my hands out to lift myself, but the chemicals I'd sprayed on the slick tile kept making me slip. I couldn't get up.

A set of large hands grabbed me around the waist and lifted me like I weighed nothing. Once I was on my feet, I pushed my sopping wet hair from my face and reached for a towel to dry myself.

"Thank you," I said to Finn.

The words felt like bees stinging the back of my throat. I would've much rather endured the bees than to have to say thank you to him. Still, it was the right thing to do, and even though I didn't go to church every day the way I used to, I still knew the difference between what was right and what was wrong.

"Don't worry about it," he said.

I looked up at him, but he wasn't looking at my face. Instead, his eyes were glued to my chest. I hadn't noticed it, but my light-blue shirt was plastered to my body. My simple black bra was showing clearly through the thin fabric. It was the only colored bra I'd ever owned, and I only bought it because I could once my parents divorced.

I pulled at my shirt and then wrapped my arms around myself. I started to walk away, but Finn grabbed my arm and pulled me close to him. I hated my body for reacting as my nipples hardened and my breathing accelerated.

He stared down at me, blue eyes taking me in. I felt naked even though I was still fully covered, and I was starting to shiver. I couldn't decide if that was because of Finn or because of my swim in the shower.

“No more boring white cotton?” he asked with a sexy smirk.

He was playing with me again. I reached up and pried his fingers from around my arm. I jerked my body away from him and turned and left the room. I think I hated him more in that embarrassing moment than I had over the last four years.

He laughed behind me and then I heard him saying something that made me so angry I had to go to another bathroom and cool down.

“I tainted the preacher’s daughter and now she thinks it’s okay for her to wear black. Only sexy women make black look good.”

He was right. I had no business wearing black anything. I was still a boring, white cotton girl.

TWENTY-TWO

FINN

Black had never looked so fucking sexy—never. An angel in the devil's clothing, holy shit, it was a turn on. The way she felt in my arms when I pulled her from the hot shower had been a thing that my memories were made of. I guess some things never changed and Faith's body was one of them.

I hated that my cock got hard just by looking at her bra through her shirt, but I couldn't take it anymore. I hadn't had sex since Faith came back into my life. Not for lack of trying, but I couldn't seem to go through with it. It was like I'd turned into the biggest puss the world had ever seen.

I stuck my hand in my pocket and wrapped it around the cross that I carried around with me everywhere. It was the only thing I had to show for having ever known Faith, other than the hurtful letter she'd sent me right after she left. That I kept in my wallet. For a while, I'd worn the cross charm on a chain around my neck, but after having a particularly rough night, I'd ripped it off. Ever since that night, it was in my pocket, always.

At first, it had been a reminder of what I was holding on to, but these days, it was a reminder of what I was running from—love. I'd run from that shit for the rest of my life. I couldn't go through what I'd gone through before. I could hardly believe I'd made it through it the first time. I'd lost my friends in a terrible accident, and then within days, I lost the only girl I'd ever loved.

It seemed as though the more time I spent with her, the more the memories of the past came to me. Some of those memories were so sweet my stomach hurt just thinking about it, but some had taught me all I knew about being a hard ass and not letting anyone in. I was starting to think that keeping her around and taunting her wasn't worth the old memories and that maybe I should fire her.

I opened my wallet and pulled at the crinkled letter. I unfolded it and read it to myself. Every time I felt myself slipping, I'd read the letter and regroup.

Finn,

I can't be with someone I'm ashamed of. As a God-fearing Christian, I think it's best if I stayed away from you. Please do not contact me ever again. What we had was nothing more than me trying to get back at my father. It was not love, and I think the best thing is to never speak to each other again.

Have a nice life.

Faith

Even her handwriting hadn't been sweet. Most girls had bubbly, easy-to-read handwriting. Faith's had been jagged like the letter itself, and I used to have a hard time reading it. It was memorized after four years, but still, it hurt so good to read it to myself every now and again.

After the whole black bra situation, I made it a point to stay away from Faith. I hadn't decided yet if I wanted her gone from the job completely, but until I figured it out, staying away was the best I could come up with.

I went out with the guys every chance I got and flirted with beautiful women in hopes that something would spark interest for me and I could take one of them home, but every time, I ended up going home alone.

When we were on the road, girls swarmed our bus and offers were laid on the table for me left and right, but I couldn't do it. The boys were starting to take notice and ask what the hell was wrong with me.

"Dude, when's the last time you had a piece? You're starting to look pale and shit. It's not natural—especially when there are hot-ass females begging to slob your knob," Chet said as he took a hit from his blunt.

He passed it my way and instead of turning it down like I'd originally thought I would, I took it from him and hit it three times before I passed it back.

"You worry entirely too much about my cock, Chet. Is there anything you want to tell me?" I laughed.

His face got serious. “Yes. Please give it to me, big Daddy.” He joked before he jumped on top of me and pretended to hump my leg.

“Get the fuck off me!” I laughed.

Zeke stepped onto the bus and looked at us like we were crazy. Tiny was right behind him.

“What the fuck?” they said at the same time.

We played three shows in Texas after that, and it was going to be another month before we went back home. I was glad I wouldn’t have to see Faith again for a while, and I hoped by the time I did, I’d have my shit straight.

Over that month, I stayed high the entire time. I’d sing to the crowd with my eyes closed some nights, unable to keep them open. The crowd didn’t seem to give a fuck. As long as we were there and I opened my mouth, they were happy.

One night in particular, I’d gotten so drunk before the show that I accidently fell off the stage. Thankfully, the crowd below caught me and surfed me out and back. I played it off to the rest of the band as if I’d done it on purpose.

A few times, I took a couple of girls back to my room or the bus, but I’d always leave them hanging or call Chet in to entertain. He didn’t seem to mind having all the ladies to himself. I couldn't force myself to be interested. Zeke was in love, and Tiny was whatever he was. Who fucking knew when it came to him?

By the time I walked in the door to our place, I was exhausted. All I wanted was a hot shower in my own bathroom and my bed. The condo was spotless, as usual, as I walked through. When I got to my room, I tossed my bags on the bed and pulled off my shirt.

Grabbing some towels out of my linen closet, I turned on the shower and started toward my closet to grab some clothes. I pulled open the door and almost stepped on Faith, who was sitting Indian style on the floor, surrounded by books.

She looked up at me in shock before she started to hurry and clean the space around her.

"I was wondering when you were going to come out of the closet." I joked.

I reached down and picked up one of the books sitting by her feet.

"What the hell are you doing in here anyway? And why are you reading about..." I read the title of the book. "Economics in America, when you should be scrubbing my toilet or something?"

She practically hissed at me, her eyes tiny slits in her face. She was pissed and she'd never looked so fucking hot.

Snatching the book from my hand, she stuffed it in an old purple backpack with her name written in whiteout on the strap.

"I was just catching up on some reading, but don't worry, your *toilets* are nice and clean." She gave me a sarcastic smile before trying to walk around me.

I moved so she was stuck in the closet and placed my arms against the doorframe around me. Her eyes dropped to my chest and roamed across my tattoos. I had a lot more than I had the last time she'd been this close to my body. I liked the way her eyes felt on me.

When she looked back up, her eyes were softer.

"Let me through," she said calmly.

I shook my head. "Nope."

She took a deep breath and looked away from me. "Finn, let me out of here. Seriously, I don't have time to play games with you."

Her words struck a chord, and I felt myself going from playful to pissed off just that quickly.

"Why not, Faith? You had plenty of time to play games with me when you were younger. Why not now?"

Her eyes clashed with mine as we angrily stared each other down.

"I never played games with you," she said sternly.

"The hell you didn't. I bet you felt good—the innocent girl who *played* the player. Well, think again, little girl. You can't play someone who doesn't give a shit about you!" I shouted.

The minute I said it, her face went pale and dropped. I felt sick to my stomach after saying those words—mostly because they were a fucking lie. I'd been so in love with Faith and she'd taken me apart piece by piece when she left. I was still trying to put myself back together four years later.

It was unexpected, but out of nowhere, she exploded. Dropping her bag to the floor, she used her fists as she starting pounding against my chest. She was screaming things I couldn't understand uncontrollably as she had a breakdown right in front of me.

I let her hit me until my chest became tender from her tiny fists, and then I grabbed her by the wrists and pushed her up against the wall. Still, she tried to kick me in the shins and knee me in the balls. Using one of my legs, I trapped hers. She struggled a little more before finally giving in.

She turned her face away from me, her hair sticking to her flushed cheeks.

"Look at me!" I shouted.

No one was allowed to put their hands on me like that—ever. Grown-ass men had gotten their asses kicked for less.

When she refused to look at me, I used one hand to capture both her wrists and used my other to turn her face to me. When I did, her hair slipped from her cheeks and I could see she was crying. I felt like the biggest dick in the world, but I had to hold strong. I couldn't be fooled by her again.

Her big brown eyes met mine and her slow flow of tears turned into much more when she burst out crying even harder.

"Please just let me go, Finn," she cried. "I swore I'd never let you see me like this."

I was so shocked that I let go of her arms. She grabbed her right one and rubbed it, making me feel bad that I might have held her too roughly.

I wasn't one to hurt a girl, but she had made me so fucking angry.

She wiped at her eyes with the back of her hand and then reached over to grab her bag.

"Just go ahead and fire me already. I'll find another job," she said as she walked out of my closet.

I wasn't sure what had just happened, but I was pretty sure the girl was having a mental breakdown. If she was still living with her dad, which I was sure she still was, why was she working as a maid? I hadn't even thought about that. It made me wonder what Faith had been up to all these years.

When I went back into my bedroom, she was nowhere to be found. I wasn't going to give her what she obviously wanted—I wasn't going to fire her. If it was torturing her to be around me as badly as it was torturing me to be around her, then I could take it as long as possible.

The following day, I stayed in again just in case she showed. I sat around and watched TV while the guys went out shopping and hit up Disneyland. I waited until later in the afternoon, and when she still didn't show, I put in a phone call to the temp agency.

"Hi, Mrs. Cooper, this is James Finn. The maid didn't show up this morning and I was wondering if everything was okay?"

I didn't want to admit it, but I was nervous that I might've hurt her arms or something. I was angry, but I didn't think I was angry enough to actually hurt her.

"Hmm... that's weird. Let me call Miss Warren and find out if she's okay. Thanks for the call, Mr. Finn."

I hated that it made me happy that Faith's last name was still Warren. Why the fuck did I care if she'd been married? I shouldn't care about anything that had to do with her, but when I thought of her being with another man, which I'm sure she already had been, I felt a strange pressure in my chest that I didn't like.

An hour later, she showed up at my door. She said nothing to me as she moved around the condo straightening up and bagging the trash. I couldn't keep my eyes off of her. I hated that my body responded to her so easily, yet all the girls who threw themselves at me did nothing for me.

"So since when do you read books about economics?" I asked.

I was sitting on a barstool at the counter she was cleaning.

She didn't answer, which only made me mad. Who the hell did she think she was? I stood up from my stool and snatched up her backpack from the floor. Unzipping it, I had all the books pulled out before she even noticed what I was doing.

"Put them back," she said as she came toward me.

I looked down at the books in my arms. English, Chemistry, Economics, High School Biology—books that any college student would've been done with years before.

She snatched the books from my hands and stuffed them back in her bag.

"Did anyone ever teach you it was rude to go through other people's things?" she yelled.

I'd never heard her yell so much when she was younger. Actually, the idea of Faith yelling was almost comical. Her voice was too soft and sweet for it to sound forceful. It came out sounding completely wrong.

"Nope. Didn't your holy rolling daddy ever tell you it was a sin to have premarital sex?" I responded.

Her tiny hand across my cheek caught me off guard. I could tell by her expression that she had shocked herself as well. She gasped and covered her mouth with the hand she'd hit me with. Fire shot through me, but the wrong kind. Instead of being mad, I was so turned on that I could barely hold myself together.

I reached in and pulled her to me, locking my arms behind her back and trapping her in my embrace. My cheek stung and by the way she was staring at the stinging spot, I was sure there was a fierce little handprint there.

"You hit me." I stated the obvious.

She pressed her palms to my chest and tried to wiggle her way out of my arms. All that did was press her tiny body against my already rock-hard cock.

"You're not strong enough," I said. "Isn't there something you should say to me?"

I couldn't have given a shit less if she apologized. I just wanted a reason to hold her against me a little longer. The way she was moving was rubbing against the front of my jeans, and it felt like a damn good dry hump. Her hair pulled away from her face again and every timc she moved, the sweet scent of roses and fresh power, her familiar scent, would invade my senses.

She stopped struggling against me and looked up at me with big wounded eyes. For a brief moment, I felt my heart melt a little before I realized my mistake and put my guard back up. It was so easy to forget the past when I held her so close. It was easy to forget what she'd done to me. For a moment, I wished to myself that I could forget.

"I guess you want me to apologize?" she said as she rolled her eyes. "Fine. I'm sorry, but you have to admit you deserved it."

"I deserved to be hurt?" I asked.

My voice cracked and it made me sound weak.

I wanted to know what I'd done for her to just up and leave four years ago. I really felt like I deserved some kind of explanation. As soon as the question left my mouth, I regretted it. I never wanted her to know how badly she'd hurt me—

never. Thankfully, she thought I was talking about her slapping me.

"I seriously doubt my hand hurt you that bad. I'm sure you've been hit worse than that before," she said.

I had been. One of the worst hits I'd ever taken had been by one of my best friends, and he'd died in an accident that same night. Her making me think about Reynolds upset me worse than her hitting me. I felt my arms tighten around her and all the playfulness left me.

"Don't hit people. You never know if they might hit you back," I said as I released her suddenly.

She grabbed the counter behind her and had the nerve to look like I'd hurt her feelings.

"I know I never really knew you, Finn, but I find it hard to believe that you'd ever hit a woman."

And just like that, I was more pissed off than I'd ever been in my life. How could she say she never knew me? She knew me better than anyone else in my life ever did or ever would. I wanted to turn and put my fist through anything that wouldn't feel it. I wanted to release my anger on anything but the girl in front of me.

I settled for a big expensive vase on the top of the breakfast table behind me. It crashed to the floor. Bits and pieces of blue glass shattered everywhere and sounded like raindrops on the expensive tile flooring.

Faith looked at me like I was a monster, and that was just fine by me. Let her think what she wanted to think. I turned and walked away before I did anything I truly regretted. I wanted to hurt her the way she'd hurt me, but emotionally only. She was right about one thing; I'd never lay a hand on a woman. No matter how badly she'd ripped my heart out and or how badly she'd changed me for the worse.

TWENTY-THREE

FAITH

I couldn't go back there. It was obvious that Finn wasn't stable and I couldn't handle him. I was too sensitive to anything that involved him. I couldn't deny that anymore. I still had feelings for Finn. I was pretty sure they'd never gone away, but the minute I found myself sitting his closet to study, I knew I was going down the wrong road.

The closet smelled familiar to me. It smelled of a time long ago when I'd spent stress-free nights with Finn. Only after sitting in there with the lights on and a book in my face did I realize it was his cologne that was so familiar to me.

He wasn't the boy I'd once thought he was, though. I'd been fooled, and I swore that I'd never be fooled again. Having him treat me so badly wasn't something I was willing to put up with—ever.

He didn't have any right. I understood that I left him first, but he moved on without me entirely too fast. That made it more than clear that he never really cared about me and that letter—the letter that ripped out my heart and destroyed it, I could never get over it. As a matter of fact, it was still tucked away in my old journal. I'd filled that particular journal with all the things I'd longed to say to Finn. I'd recently pulled out that journal in particular to remind me of anything I might've forgotten.

I'd almost quit altogether, but when Mrs. Cooper called to check on me, I had to go in. Not to mention the lack of groceries in the apartment was a big kick in the butt, too. But I had to find something else and I had to find it fast. Continuing to work for Finn wasn't a good idea anymore.

I made up my mind the next morning that Finn wasn't going to scare me away. I had no choice but to continue to clean until I found something else. I was taking adult education classes at night so that was going to make things a bit more difficult, but I could do it. If I'd learned one thing about myself over the last four years, it was that I could do anything as long as I worked hard enough.

When I got to the condo, no one was there. I let out the breath I'd been holding, then made my way to the bedrooms. I wanted to be done with those before anyone came back. The first room I came to was Zeke's. I stepped up to his door, ready to push it open, when through the crack, I heard soft panting noises.

I should've backed away. I should've gone back into another part of the house and cleaned until the back of the condo was empty, but I didn't. Instead, I peeked in through the crack. It was Zeke and his girlfriend Patience. They were completely covered, thank God, but he was on top of her, looking into her eyes as if she were the only thing holding him on Earth.

It was mesmerizing. He whispered sweet words of love to her as he slowly moved his body against hers. Their kisses were sweet, and again, it made me long for the affection I was missing in my life. I was tired of being alone and shouldering all the responsibilities. I wanted a partner in life—someone who could hold me on the nights when I felt like everything was falling apart and tell me that

I was going to be okay—that Jimmy was going to be okay.

I backed away from their door slowly, ready to turn and go back into the kitchen to clean. Instead, I walked straight into Finn. He looked past me into the crack in the door and then looked back down at me with a knowing smirk.

My face lit up with a deep blush. I could hardly believe that I'd been caught watching a couple make love.

I tried to move around him quietly so I didn't interrupt Zeke and Patience, but Finn caught me around the waist and turned me back around to face the door. His arms locked around me the way they had the day before and then I felt his hot breath against my ear.

"So you're into voyeurism now?" he whispered.

Chills broke out across my body.

I tried again to get away, but he was holding me so tightly that I couldn't move. The fear of Zeke and Patience seeing us standing in their doorway watching was too much. I didn't want to say anything to him. I didn't want to make any noise at all. I just wanted him to let me go so I could be out of the embarrassing situation.

"Let me ask you something, Faith. What do you see in there?" His lips brushed my ear. "Are you into Zeke now? Because if so, let me go ahead and squash your fantasies now. He wouldn't touch you." He was still whispering, but it sounded so loud to me that I was positive Zeke and Patience would hear it, too.

The noises from their room were starting to get louder, and instinctively, I pressed back away from the doorway, but all that did was press me harder up against Finn. He hissed softly in my ear and cursed under his breath.

Everything was so quiet that I could still hear the things that Zeke and Patience were saying to each other.

"I love you so much, baby. God, you feel so good," Patience was saying to Zeke. "Please. Please don't stop." She moaned louder.

Again, I pressed myself back. I wanted to run. I wanted to be anywhere in that moment but where I was.

My eyes locked onto Zeke's tattooed back as the covers slid down around his waist. Patience dug her nails into his back so hard that I was sure he would bleed. Instead of yelling, he kept telling her how beautiful she was and how he couldn't live without her. It was the most disturbing yet most beautiful thing I'd ever seen.

"Tell me, Faith. What do you see?" Finn whispered in my ear again.

I felt his words all over. My knees were getting weaker by the second. My stomach dug into his arm as my body slowly melted.

Finally, he released me enough that I could move. I turned in his arms and looked up at him. I was so mad that he was making me watch them. I didn't want to be there. I didn't want to see people engage in something that I'd never know. I'd probably never feel a man's touch again, and I'd probably never hear someone call me beautiful or tell me they loved me. I wanted to scream at him. I wanted to hit him again.

Instead, I pushed him back away from me. He moved out of my way and grinned down at me like he'd been playing a joke.

"I see love," I said. "Something you know nothing about."

His face dropped and he attempted to say something, but instead of waiting to listen, I walked away. He didn't follow and I was glad. I wanted to be rid of him. I couldn't get into the kitchen fast enough, and once I was in there, I cleaned the fastest I ever had. Once I was done with the place, I left as quickly as I could.

I stopped by the grocery store on the way home and grabbed some essentials. A few of the people I worked with were happy to see me and kept telling me how great I looked. They were just being nice since I knew my stress level had only gotten worse since I'd taken on my new job.

When I got home, Jimmy was jumping on the couch and singing loudly.

"Baby boy, get off the couch and quiet down some. The people next door are going to start complaining." He jumped down from the couch and into my arms. "Where's Grandma?" I asked.

"I dunno!" he sang playfully.

Worry set in. I set Jimmy down and started searching through the apartment.

"Mom?" I called loudly. "Mom, where are you?"

I went to her room and pushed the door open. She was nowhere to be seen. I started to panic. She would never leave Jimmy alone. Something was wrong. Something was definitely wrong.

When I got to the bathroom, I tried to push on the door, but it wouldn't budge. Something was keeping the door from opening all the way. I pushed harder and when I did, I saw my mom's leg.

"Mom! Oh my God! Mom!"

I ran into the living room and picked up the cheap flip phone that Mom and I shared. I called 9-1-1 and screamed my address into the phone. Jimmy sat on the couch in front of me and started to cry.

"It's okay, baby. Everything's okay. Just sit there and be a good boy for Mommy."

Ten minutes later, the fire department and an ambulance showed up at our apartment. They were able to get into the bathroom and get Mom up on a stretcher.

Jimmy and I followed behind the ambulance to the local hospital. We sat in the waiting room until we were allowed to go back and see her. Apparently, she'd had another stroke.

When we got into her room, I was shocked to see my father sitting next to her bed.

"What are you doing here?" I asked, disgusted.

I hadn't seen him in forever, and I couldn't think of a single time when he'd seen Jimmy.

"I'm still the first person on her contact list. They called me and I came straight here." He reached down and cupped her hand.

He looked older. The little bit of hair he did have was gone completely and there were new wrinkles around his eyes and mouth. He looked down at Jimmy and gave him his fake preacher smile.

"I was just leaving," he said as he stood.

He walked right by us and left without saying good-bye. It hurt that he barely acknowledged my son, or me for that matter. It was amazing how easily he'd given up his family. As a mother, I couldn't understand it. There was nothing in the world that would make me disown Jimmy—nothing.

I sat by Mom's side. Jimmy ate some vending machine food and fell asleep in the chair on the other side of Mom's bed. When she finally woke up, I called a nurse in and she examined her. Her blood pressure was way too high and the doctors were concerned that she might have another stroke.

The following morning, I called in to Mrs. Cooper to let her know that I wouldn't be making it to work. I explained what had happened to my mom and she said she'd take care of it.

After running some tests, the doctor determined that Mom would have to stay in the hospital for a few weeks.

"I'm so sorry, Faith." Mom apologized when we found out she wasn't going to be released soon. "Who else are you going to get to watch Jimmy so you can work?"

"Mom, do *not* apologize to me. Don't you worry about Jimmy. I'll take care of everything. You just get better," I said as I held her hand.

I was happy that Mom and I had a decent mother-daughter relationship. I hadn't had that since I was younger and I missed it.

When I left the hospital, I sat in my car and gathered my thoughts. I had to figure out what to do with Jimmy while I went to work. Missing an entire week, or however long it took for Mom to get released, wasn't something I could do. I wasn't even sure Mom would be able to watch him anymore. I couldn't take the chance of something else happening to her and Jimmy being left alone again.

I called around to daycares, but the prices were insane. I'd have to pay them half of what I made a week for him to stay there. The only way I was going to make this work was to get a second job. So the following day, while I was at one of the daycares applying for Jimmy to get a spot, I also applied for a job.

The daycare director hired me as soon as I turned in the application, and thankfully, my hours were eight to two Monday through Friday. That gave me enough time to go to the condo after the daycare and clean. Mrs. Karen, the daycare director, said it would be perfectly fine for Jimmy to stay at the daycare all day. I'd still have to pay, of course, but all worked out well.

The only thing I couldn't get around was school. So once again, I had to drop out. I hated to do it, but Jimmy and work always came first. If I didn't feed him and put a roof over his head, then no one else would.

From that day forward, my schedule was nuts. I worked the daycare every day from eight in the morning until two in the afternoon. From that point on, I'd go to the condo and spend the next three to four hours cleaning. Once I was done cleaning, I'd go back to the daycare, pick up Jimmy, and go home, where I'd make us dinner. After dinner was bath time followed soon after by bedtime.

I continued to study my books just in case I was able to go back to school. So once Jimmy went to sleep, I'd pull out the books and study until I couldn't keep my eyes open. Every morning it was the same routine and every day was the same. I hardly ate, I barely slept, but I worked constantly.

Luckily, I hardly saw Finn. Coming later in the day was apparently the trick. Not to mention, Blow Hole had been doing a lot of shows lately and were out of town constantly. It worked. I was too busy to be happy or unhappy about my situation.

Even after Mom came home from the hospital, I continued this way. Watching Jimmy was just too much for her. He was a rambunctious three-year-old and Mom was getting up there in age. Her health was most important, and I wanted to be sure to keep her stress levels down like the doctor had suggested.

After a few weeks of the same schedule, I could feel myself wearing down. I hardly got to see Jimmy at all since I took care of the babies and he was in a separate class at the daycare. I missed him so much it hurt. Mom was having issues with her memory and her right hand, and that was making it hard for her do to things on her own.

I spent my days working and silently cursing all the men who were major factors in my life—Finn and my father. They were doing whatever they wanted while Mom and I continued to struggle to hold it all together. Then I'd spend my nights trying to sleep and having nightmares in the moments when I did catch a brief nap.

I'd never before been so happy to see Friday roll around. Even if I did spend my weekends lying around with Jimmy or running around the park, it was time with him and that's all that mattered.

I scrubbed the guest bathroom vigorously. It was one of the last rooms I had to get done before I left for the day and spend the weekend with my baby boy. I was leaning over the tub and rinsing the cleaner from the bottom, when I felt someone standing behind me.

I didn't bother turning around. The soft scent of Finn's cologne wafted in on the bathroom steam that was floating around. I'd gone a while without seeing him, but I'd always known that I'd run into him again. I was cleaning his condo after all. The heat from the hot water in the tub was no match to Finn's heat when he moved up behind me.

"No backpack full of high school books today?" he asked.

"No," I said as I continued to scrub.

"Gave up on tutoring high schoolers already? That's so unlike you to give up on someone, Faith. Oh wait, maybe it's not so unlike you after all."

His sarcasm made my stomach turn. I knew exactly what he was getting at, but I was too exhausted to play battle of the wits with him.

"I wasn't tutoring anyone but myself."

I gave the tub a final rinse and stood full, stretching the ache out of my back. I was too young to feel so old.

"Tutoring yourself? You're a little too old for high school, don't you think? You graduated a few years ago. I'm sure you're getting close to graduating from whatever fancy Christian college your daddy forced you to go to." He continued to verbally poke my nerves.

"You don't know what you're talking about," I said as I collected my things and moved on to the last room.

"Oh, come on. Enlighten me on this one, Faith. How's your dad feel about the fact that you're in my home every day?" He chuckled to himself.

I'd had enough. I was exhausted and tired of Finn's smart mouth.

"Just stop already! I've seen my father once in the last three years, okay? I was going back to school to try and get my diploma. I was forced to quit school before I graduated. I'm sure it makes you happy to know that my life isn't all peaches and cream, but that's what it is."

I turned and attempted to move away from him.

"What do you mean 'was' going back to school? Are you not going anymore?" he asked.

His eyes moved across my face, leaving me feeling entirely too exposed.

"I had to quit. It's no big deal," I said as I sidestepped him and made my way into the laundry room to drop off the dirty towels.

Again, he followed behind me.

"Please, Finn, just drop it. I'm tired and I don't feel like this today."

I was starting to feel weak. I didn't know if it was his poking into my personal life, the lack of sleep I'd been getting, or the fact that I hadn't really eaten anything in the last two days. Either way, it didn't matter. The room was moving under my feet and the gray laundry room walls were starting to blur.

"Are you okay?" he asked with pinched brows.

I wasn't sure what he was seeing, but I definitely wasn't feeling okay. I just wanted to finish the job and go home and relax for the weekend. I turned toward him again.

"I'm fine. Just let me finish my—"

I never got to finish my sentence. The room danced around me a few times before going completely black.

Twenty-Four

Finn

She dropped like a sack of potatoes in a mix of dirty towels. I flew across the room and scooped her into my arms. She felt lighter than the last time I'd carried her. Something was up with her and as much as I tried not to care, I couldn't help it.

All this time I'd wanted nothing more than to watch her suffer, but now that the pieces of Faith's life were coming together, I wasn't so sure I was happy to see her so unhappy. She never smiled—ever. It was as if she didn't know how to anymore. I wasn't sure if she just hated being around me, which was understandable since I'd gone out of my way to get under her skin, but she always looked so damn miserable.

I laid her on my bed and got a cold rag to press against her flushed cheeks. I was the only one in the condo since everyone had gone out for the night. I contemplated calling an ambulance, but by the time I got my cell, she was already starting to come to.

I sat on the edge of the bed and watched as she blinked and slowly figured out where she was. The room was so silent that I could hear her stomach growling loudly. Had she not been eating? And by the look at the dark rings around her eyes, she was either strung out big time or not sleeping. I had to go with no sleep since I knew Faith would never touch drugs. At least the girl I thought she once was never would have.

She tried to lean up on her elbows, but she wasn't successful.

"When's the last time you ate?" I asked.

She looked over at me as if she was just realizing I was there and closed her eyes again.

"I ate earlier. I can't believe I fainted. Just let me finish up around here and I'll be out of your hair." Again, she tried to get up.

It was obvious she was weak, and I was starting to feel bad for her.

"Don't worry about the damn condo. It's fine the way it is. Earlier like when? An hour ago? Lunch at noon?" I asked.

Something told me she was lying. No way would her stomach be growling so loudly after only a few hours. I knew hunger and I also knew that stomachs that growled like hers did had gone a few days without food.

"I ate lunch."

She couldn't even look me in the eye with that lame-ass lie.

"You're lying," I said.

She glared over at me.

"I don't lie," she growled.

I chuckled. "That's a lie."

She jumped off of my bed, grabbing the edge when she lost her balance.

"What are you doing?" I asked.

"I'm leaving. I don't have to take this crap," she said as she tried to walk to the door. I stopped her and forced her to sit back down.

"You're not going anywhere until you can walk straight." I crossed my arms over my chest as I stood above her.

She looked up at me and rolled her eyes. "You can't keep me prisoner here, Finn. I have somewhere I have to be."

Did she have a date? Why the fuck did I hate the idea of her dating? She was beautiful. Of course, she was dating. Why wasn't the guy she was dating making sure she was eating properly? What if it was someone who treated her badly? What he beat her or some crazy shit like that?

My brain wouldn't stop as I thought every bad scenario she could've possibly gotten herself into.

"You can stay put right here while I go make you a sandwich or something. You need to eat."

"You don't know anything about what I need. What I need is to be away from you!" she yelled. Her voice sounded rough and it cracked.

Her words stung a little, but I guess I deserved them, considering I'd been a dick since we ran into each other again.

"You yell a lot. I don't remember you yelling you so much before. You've become a bit of a bitch over the years, huh?" I shook my head and sighed.

"Don't call me that!" She stood up and pushed me.

"And you're awfully abusive, but I guess I know where you got that bad habit."

I hadn't meant to sound so rude and I hadn't meant to be mean when I said that. It was the truth. We both knew it was. Her father used to beat her. It only made sense that she'd pick up the habit.

She didn't like what I said. She pushed even harder and literally growled at me. I almost laughed, but I figured laughing in her face would only piss her off more.

"Come on. Sit down and I'll get you something to eat."

"I don't want anything from you! I just want to go home!" Again, she pushed me.

I was disgusted by the fact that her pushing me around was kind of turning me on. It wasn't every day that anyone stood up to me and the fact that this tiny girl did just that was kind of hot.

"Why are you so angry all the damn time? You need to relax. Let's call a truce until you eat something."

I was trying to be reasonable, but she wasn't having it.

"Why am I so mad? Maybe because of you! You push my buttons and you make me so... you make me so damn mad!" She covered her mouth when the word came out. Her face was bright red in anger and embarrassment. It was probably the cutest fucking thing I'd ever seen. Faith had probably never said a cuss word in her life.

I couldn't help myself. I burst out laughing. It was uncontrollable laughter that hurt my stomach. Apparently, laughing at her was all it took. She charged me with tiny hands and pushed me up against the wall. I could have stood strong, but it was too funny to watch her rough me up. It was super hot and I was getting hard.

"Don't you dare laugh at me. I'm so mad!"

I didn't know she was capable of such anger. She'd always been so meek and mild—always letting people run over her like she was nothing. It was one of the main reasons I'd been so shocked when she up and left me hanging. Part of me knew it had to be someone else's fault, but at the same time, I was upset that she didn't care enough to stay.

"I'm sorry. I can't help it." I continued to laugh. "You're like a rabid Chihuahua puppy."

Anger flared in her eyes again. "Are you calling me a dog?" Again, she pushed me up against the wall.

I stopped laughing and took a good look at her. She was so different—so jaded. What had happened to her to change her so much? For me, it was her leaving me high and dry—literally—but her leaving me couldn't have done this to her. Someone else had to.

The thought of anyone else hurting her made me irate.

"What happened to you?" I asked. "Who made you this way?"

The better question was why did I care?

She stepped away from me with sad eyes. Her face dropped and for a second I thought maybe she'd pass out again.

"You happened," she said as she looked me straight in the eyes.

A tear wobbled on her lashes, but she swiped it away before it had a chance to fall.

"No. *You* happened to me. *You* left me," I said as I dug my finger into my chest. "You don't get to be altered. You don't get to be hurt by it. I do."

Her face paled before her cheeks filled with red heat again.

"You're joking, right? I hurt you? Yeah, you were so hurt that a week later you were screwing your ex-girlfriend? Wow, Finn, you must've really been heartbroken." A tear leaked down her cheek before she turned and hauled ass out of the room.

I was on her heels. I had no fucking idea what she was talking about, but I hadn't had sex with anyone for a freaking year after Faith left. She didn't know what the hell she was saying, but I wasn't having it. She wasn't allowed to play the victim in this. I was the victim. I was the one who was hurt—not her. She was the one that left me.

Before she could open the front door, I caught it and slammed it shut.

"Are you fucking kidding me right now? You don't know what you're talking about. I suggest you get your story straight before you start pretending like the poor preacher's daughter with me," I yelled back.

"Oh, I don't know what I'm talking about? I saw you, Finn. I saw you with my own two eyes. I came back. I ran away from California and I came back to you, but you were there with her on your couch. I turned and walked away and I never looked back."

Again, she tried to pull the door open to leave. She was talking out of her head. Maybe she was medicated or something. She had to be on something. Her story was nuts and there was no way in hell I was falling for it.

"You're crazy. You're really crazy," I said as I released the door for her.

I'd dealt with crazy bitches before, but Faith took the cake. She was talking out of her head and making up stories on the spot. I hadn't touched Jenny and I knew for fact that Faith never came back. I knew that because I'd received a letter from her saying how much she hated me a week after she left. She was nuts. It was impossible for her to be in two places at once.

"Yeah, you're right. I am crazy. I should've never gone back to South Carolina. Especially after that awful letter you sent me," she said before pulling the door open and running out.

She left me there staring after her like she was a fucking nutcase. She left me there with doubts about the past and the way things really happened, and she left me there wondering what fucking letter she was talking about. I'd never sent her any letter.

An hour later, after sitting and thinking over the argument we had, the memory of Leroy telling me he had to pull Jenny off me came back quick and clear. Had Faith really come back for me? And if so, was it at the exact moment that Leroy told me about? Things were getting complicated, and as much I knew I should've just let the past go and move on, I couldn't. I wanted answers and I wanted to not feel things for Faith.

TWENTY-FIVE

FAITH

I couldn't get food into my body fast enough. I was so embarrassed that I'd fainted in front of Finn again. I was turning into a weakling who was passing out at the drop of a hat. I needed meat and veggies, and I needed them as soon as possible.

Instead of cooking, I took the three of us out to dinner. Jimmy always got excited when we ate dinner out, and I enjoyed seeing him get excited about all the food on the buffet.

I ate my food and mulled through the argument Finn and I had earlier. I silently wished I could take back everything I'd said. I hated that I'd shown him my weakness like that. But mainly what bothered me was the fact that he had looked seriously offended when I said I knew about him sleeping with Jenny right after I left. Maybe I'd seen it the wrong way. When I closed my eyes, I could still play the scene over in my head and every time I did, I could clearly see Finn's eyes closed with his arms at his side. Was he passed out?

It wasn't like I could ask him. I needed to drop it and leave the past in the past, but the problem with that was every time I looked at my son, the past was there to haunt me. Those blue eyes, those sweet dimples, and a smile that was a perfect match to his father's—it was all too much.

Saturday and Sunday I spent cleaning my own apartment. I started calling Jimmy Hurricane Jimmy, since the boy could destroy a room in less than two minutes flat. It wasn't that he had a ton of toys; it was that he turned everything into something to play with. Boxes became cars and ships, and paper became people and airplanes. I was happy that my baby had an active imagination. It worked well since I couldn't afford to buy him much.

I hated to do it, but the following Monday after work at the daycare, I went to the condo to clean. I hadn't heard anything back from any of the places I'd applied to, so I called Mrs. Cooper to check in and see if she'd heard anything. Sadly, she was still in search mode, but she did have some good news for me. I was happy to hear that the boys were out of town again.

When I got to the condo, no one was there. I went through and checked all the rooms so there were no surprises and then I cleaned the entire place. By the time I was done, I was drenched in sweat and I had something gross all over the front of my clothes. I knew I was there alone so I thought I'd throw my clothes in the wash and grab a bath. Finn's massive tub had been calling my name since the first time I'd cleaned it.

I took a towel with me to the laundry room and put all my clothes in the machine. Wrapping the towel around myself, I went back to Finn's bathroom to a filling tub. Dropping my towel, I lowered myself into the hot water and sighed in contentment. The tub at my apartment was always full of kid's toys and was so small. I'd never taken a bath there and my body longed for a nice long soak in steaming water.

I adjusted my hair into a tighter bun, closed my eyes, and lay back in the tub. Every ache and pain in my body felt better as all my muscles relaxed and melted into the heat. The steam opened up my sinuses and somehow I felt like I could breathe better. I used my hands to scoop up the hot water around me and lapped it over my breasts and shoulders.

"Oh my God, this is amazing," I said to myself.

"Yes, it is," a deep voice said from beside me.

I sat up and covered myself. Turning to reach for my towel, I found Finn leaning against the counter with the towel thrown across his shoulder.

His smoldering eyes touched every part of my body as I tried to sink farther into the water.

"Give me my towel, Finn," I said with a growl.

"That's no way to ask for something you want, Faith. I know you have better manners than that."

He had no shame in looking at me. I, on the other hand, couldn't stand the thought of him seeing me. I'd had a baby and things were different. Not to mention, he'd already said how awful I looked. It was beyond embarrassing and I knew the minute I got home Mrs. Cooper was going to call about my little swim in my employee's bathtub. Of course I'd get fired over something so stupid.

"Please, Finn, give it to me," I said in the nicest way possible, considering I was dying of humiliation.

"Oh, I'll give it to you, baby. You only have to ask once," he said as he dropped the towel and stalked over to the tub with a grin.

I held my hands out to stop him. "I meant the towel!" I said quickly.

His eyes dipped down and took in my bare breasts. I hadn't even realized I'd stopped covering them to hold out my hands to stop him. His smile grew as I covered myself again.

"Your mouth says no, but your nipples say yes. What does the rest of you say?"

His voice was so low and smooth. It worked itself over my wet skin and rippled inside my thighs and lower stomach.

"Don't talk to me like that," I said.

Not that I didn't like it, but the way he was making my body feel was wrong. Everything about the situation I had myself in was wrong.

"What's wrong? Don't like it when a man talks dirty? Are you too innocent for that still?"

I ignored his questions. He was making me uncomfortable. He was waking up parts of my body that had been asleep for a long time, and it was making me anxious.

"Can I please have my towel?" I asked again.

His dimples popped and for the first time since I'd run into him again, he looked like the old Finn. The way he was looking at me was playful and sweet—not playful and sinister.

"Let's play a game. Say something dirty to me, and I'll give you this towel," he said as he reached down and plucked the towel from the tile.

My cheeks ached from the heat of my embarrassment. I wasn't going to talk dirty to him. I wasn't going to give him what he wanted. I hated that he had the upper hand over me. Not to mention, I had no idea how to talk dirty.

I silently wished I wasn't so embarrassed by my body. Any other girl would have the confidence to step out of the bathtub and walk away. Not me. The thought of getting out in front of him made my nerves jump into my throat.

"I'm not." The water was cooling and I could feel myself starting to shiver.

"Then you're not getting this towel. You're welcome to get out. Where are your clothes anyway?"

He had me there.

"They're in the wash. I spilled something gross on my shirt."

He put his head down and chuckled to himself. When he looked back up at me, the amusement in his eyes angered me. "No clothes either. Whatever will you do, Faith?"

"Okay, enough screwing around, Finn. Please give me my towel so I can get out of here."

"But we haven't screwed around yet. How can that be enough?" He countered. "I'm still waiting to hear something dirty. Come on, you can do it. It will only hurt a little the first time."

Everything he said sounded like sexual innuendo and every time he spoke, my memory flashed back to that night on the beach when he pleasured me with his mouth or my first time when he'd held me so close and took to me heaven.

He was winning and I hated it. He had the upper hand and that frustrated me beyond words.

"Fine! What do you want me to say?" I gave in.

The water was beginning to feel colder and I wanted out of it.

He had the nerve to laugh at me. "I don't know. Surprise me," he said with a grin.

I racked my brain for something dirty to say, but I'd only ever had two sexual experiences and they were both with Finn. Our past together was the last thing I wanted to bring up. Nothing was coming to me, and the longer I sat there, the colder the water was getting. Every time I moved and the water swished against my skin, I trembled.

"I don't know what to say," I said honestly.

This time he didn't laugh. Instead, his serious eyes settled on me and consumed my body.

"Tell me something that's true," he said.

Of course he'd make it even harder. Telling the truth was difficult when I was around Finn. The truth could cause heartache when it came to him.

The truth was he was my only and I didn't want him to know that. I didn't want him to know how special our night together had been for me. My mind moved across my memories and settled on the night on the beach—the night when he'd shown me the stars and heaven all at the same time.

"Sometimes when I touch myself, I think about our night at the beach and what you did with your mouth."

As soon as the words left my mouth, I wished I could take them back. Fire filled his eyes and his mouth pinched into a frown. At first I was afraid I'd offended him, but then he swallowed hard and stepped toward me with my towel in his hand.

Leaning over the tub, he pushed a strand of my hair from my face and ran his knuckle softly down my cheek.

"That was probably the sexiest thing I've ever heard a woman say. Was it the truth?" he said as he handed me my towel.

I stood and covered myself at the same time. Cold water dripped from my body and I shivered. I stepped out of the tub, but he stood his ground. He was so close, so big and tall compared to me. I looked up into his eyes once I had my towel wrapped around myself.

"Yes," I said.

I could hardly believe I was talking to him like that. It wasn't something I ever did. My cheeks burned as usual and I wanted nothing more than to leave immediately—even if I had to do it in wet clothes.

He shocked me when he cupped my cheeks with his hands and ran his thumb across my bottom lip. His touch did something to me. Pushed away the past and brought me into the future—one where Finn hadn't broken my heart. The chill in my body slipped away and was replaced with a heat I hadn't felt since I was seventeen.

I swallowed hard and licked my dry lips. His eyes darted to my mouth and he slowly started to move in. Nerves loosened my knees and made me wobble a little. I leaned my head back a bit and closed my eyes. It was wrong letting him kiss me, but when his lips pressed again mine, it felt so right.

A soft moan slipped from my mouth. I'd waited so long to feel that way again. I'd waited so long so be touched or kissed. I hadn't planned on it being Finn, but there was something almost comical about the fact that it was.

His arm slid around my waist and warmed me more. I didn't resist when he pulled my body to his. I should've. I should've pulled away and slapped him, but my body was begging for just a taste of what Finn could give me. I'd had it before. I knew what he was capable of, and I was seconds away from begging him for it.

My body throbbed with the beat of my heart, and I feared he could feel it when he wrapped his other arm around me and held me tighter.

I opened my mouth and let him in as he slid his slick tongue across mine. His kisses were so strong and intense. He took so much from me but gave a lot. The minute I gave in completely, my body melted against his. I wrapped my arms around his neck, forgetting about the towel that was covering me.

He started to back me up against the bathroom counter and I let him. The cold granite stung my backside and I gasped into his mouth. As if I weighed nothing, he lifted me onto the cold counter and continued to kiss me. My mind was screaming for me to stop him, but my body longed for everything he was doing.

The pulse between my thighs was beating hard and begged for his touch. When his finger pressed against that moist pulsing point, I called out against my will. It felt so amazing and I needed it. I'd deserved to feel this good. After the four years I'd had, I deserved it. When he slid his fingers into me, I almost cried happy tears.

"God, you're so wet, baby," he said against my mouth.

His words slid down my throat, past my stomach, and straight to the sensitive part of me he was stimulating.

My body tensed up, on the verge of release, when suddenly he pulled his hands away from me. I opened my eyes and looked up at him. He stared down at me with aqua irises and ran his nose across mine.

"I've wanted this for so long," he said as he unzipped his jeans.

My conscience was kicking in, but the sinner inside me pushed it away. The crackle of his condom wrapper echoed into the bathroom. The sounds of our heated breaths muffled it a bit.

My mind was going a hundred miles per hour. He'd worn a condom before, too, but that obviously didn't work. I should've stopped him. I should've said no and walked away, but once I felt the tip of him pushing inside me, every thought I had crashed and burned.

I threw my head back as his hips began to thrust over and over again. My palms held me up enough so my back didn't touch the cold mirror behind me.

"I want you to think of this moment the next time you touch yourself," he said as he moved hard and fast against me.

The room around me faded away and my body began to tingle. A rush of heat moved through my core and dropped down into my thighs. My release was just out of reach, but it was definitely there.

The sound of our bodies coming together echoed throughout the room. It was an exotic sound that intensified everything I was feeling.

He pushed his fingers into my hair and forced me to look at him. His mouth slammed against mine and his tongue worked with the rhythm of his hips—fast and hard—nothing like that the last time we'd had sex. I didn't hate it.

I tried to close my eyes again, but he wasn't having it.

"Look at me. I want you to look at me when you come."

His words sent me over the edge. Every nerve in my body climbed high before crashing and colliding where our two bodies met. I kept my eyes on him like he'd asked as I moaned and cried out my release. It felt like nothing I'd ever known.

Within seconds, he threw his head back and growled before slamming his body into mine one final hard time.

His breathing was hard against my neck as he trembled between my legs. I leaned up and wrapped my arms around his neck, holding him close to me. Residual shivers went through my body and caused me a jerk a little every now and again.

I expected him to look up at me and smile. I somehow thought things might be different since we'd come together so beautifully again, but when he pulled back and looked down at me, it wasn't happiness I saw on his face. It was anger.

"What did you do to me?" he said as he pulled away. I slid down from the countertop and collected my towel. I wrapped it around myself and followed behind him as he left the bathroom and righted his clothes.

"Finn? Is everything okay?" I asked.

I couldn't believe what we'd done. We hated each other, but apparently the attraction was still there for both of us. A lot of things were still there for me when it came to Finn, although I'd never admit it.

"No! Things are definitely not okay. We shouldn't have done that. It was a mistake," he said.

His words slammed into my chest and broke my heart all over again. He thought I was a mistake. He was looking at me like I was disgusting. Maybe he wasn't so attracted to me after all.

A mistake. The word burned through my brain and spiked my anger. I went to his dresser and pulled out one of his T-shirts and a pair of his boxers. I folded them; I knew where they were.

"What the hell do you think you're doing?" he said loudly.

I looked over at the clock and knew I was running late to get Jimmy from the daycare. I'd been playing around with someone who obviously never gave two shits about me. I couldn't believe how stupid I'd been. How could I have fallen for his games again?

"My clothes are wet and I need to get out of here."

I almost let it slip that my son was waiting for me. I had to be more careful around Finn.

I tugged on his T-shirt and pulled the boxers up over my hips. He stood beside his bed and watched me like a hawk—a really angry hawk.

"I can't believe I fell for that again," I said clearly as I walked around him and left the room.

I heard him behind me and then I felt his hand wrap around the top of my arm before he swung me around to face him.

"You? I can't believe I fell for *your* shit again. You're not the victim here, Faith. I am! And you know what I say to that? I say fuck it! And fuck you for even thinking for a second that you could slide your pretty little ass back into my life and all would be right with the world. The world ain't got shit on a man with a past like mine."

I flinched at his words and I felt the tears coming. I tried to pull away again. I was sick of crying for him, and I was determined he'd never see them fall again.

All I could think about was Jimmy and how I'd almost died giving birth to him—the pain that I went through all alone because Finn was such a jerk. The beatings I took just to be with him even for an hour to two. I'd bled for him and this was how he was going to treat me again? I was done.

Everything I'd felt over the last four years of my life came together in that moment and filled me with so much hurt that I thought I'd fall to the floor and curl up in the fetal position. Tears slipped from my eyes against my will, and I swiped at them.

"You asshole! I bled for you!" I yelled as I pushed against his chest and tried to get away.

His cheeks flushed red in anger; his nostrils flared as he breathed out hard. Then he was in my face, staring down at me with red-hot eyes. All signs of the heated moment we'd just had in the bathroom were gone.

I gasped when his fingers dug hard into my arms and he tugged me closer to him. His nails burrowed into my skin as he held me close. He was all heat and fury, wrapped around me, scorching my skin in the all the places that we touched. I couldn't decide if I should run like I did before or stay and face the consequences for my past actions. Somehow that didn't seem fair since he still hadn't paid for his.

I decided to stay and face him. Looking up at him, blue orbs swirled back at me, his eyes leaving no part of my face untouched. I couldn't breathe. His hard chest was like a brick wall squeezing the oxygen from my lungs.

"You *bled* for me? Well, I didn't bleed for you, Faith. I *died* for you. There's a big fucking difference. You didn't wound me; you killed me. You murdered the boy I used to be in his sleep and he's never coming back. All that's left of that boy is me, and all you'll ever get from *me* is a quickie and a door in your face."

He released me and the spot where his fingers were digging ached. Wrapping my arms around myself, I rubbed at the sore areas. He looked down at my arms and closed his eyes hard as if he were feeling my pain.

When he opened them, his expression had softened. "I'm sorry if I hurt you." He reached out and ran a finger down my arm. "Even now the thought of hurting you hurts me. It's a bad habit I can't seem to break."

I couldn't take it anymore. I had to get away from him and I had to stay away. I turned and walked away. I snatched up my keys and walked out his front door and out of his life again.

It wasn't until I was about to climb into bed later that I realized I'd forgotten my purse.

TWENTY-SIX
FINN

"Fuck!" I yelled out loud as I punched a hole through my bedroom wall.

I'd fucked up a lot in my life, but having sex with Faith was by far the worse and best thing I'd done in a long time. It was amazing—beyond amazing. It was everything I'd fantasized about for the last four years of my life. And while I'd experienced a release like I hadn't since the last time I was with her, I couldn't help but feel like I'd just royally fucked myself.

After years of dealing with the loss of Faith in my own way, I'd taken one big step back. The only way it didn't hurt to be without her was to hate her, and I'd definitely done the opposite of that in my bathroom. The worst part was all the emotions

I'd spent the last four years burying had resurfaced just that quickly and I didn't know what to do with them. After going so long not feeling, it was scary to feel again. The way I saw it was emotion was a bad thing and Faith brought out entirely too many damn emotions.

It wasn't like when I fucked a random girl, which is what I'd been doing for the last four years. It was so much more. There'd been eye contact and touching. I actually cared about how she felt and whether or not she got off. It felt so wrong and so right all at the same time.

I could hardly believe my eyes when I walked into my bathroom and found her naked in my bathtub. I watched her as she bathed. The way the light reflected off of her moist skin and the way she'd rubbed the water and soap onto her body. I thought for a second I was going to come in my pants right then.

It had been so long since I'd been with a woman, and when she told me she touched herself with thoughts of me, I was done. There was no way I would've been able to control what happened next.

How was she able to pull me back in that way? And why wasn't I able to just blow it off as a fuck like I usually did? It was as if she'd weaved some crazy web of innocent seduction all around me and I was stuck and couldn't get out. I was thoroughly tangled in her snare and I fucking hated it.

When I turned around, Zeke was standing there staring back at me.

"You okay, man?" he asked calmly.

Nothing shocked Zeke and he was always so chill about everything.

"Yeah, I'm good. Just need to blow off some steam," I said as I rubbed my busted knuckles.

"Want to talk? There's some beers in the fridge." He started toward the kitchen.

I followed behind him. He tossed me a beer over the counter and I popped it open and sucked down half of it.

Zeke and I weren't big on heart-to-heart talks, but I guessed if anyone understood relationships, it would be him. And while the rest of the guys would have ragged me about it, Zeke would understand since he was in a relationship.

I spent the next hour telling Zeke all about Faith. He listened carefully and shook his head from time to time. He almost spewed beer on himself when I told him that our new maid was the Faith I was talking about.

"Damn, man. That's fucked up," he said. "So what are you going to do about her?"

"I don' t know. She makes me fucking crazy," I said as I took another swig from my third beer.

He chuckled softly to himself. "That's all women. They're nuts, but love makes you that way. Don't let the past get in the way of your future, dude. If you love her, you have to try. Pride's a bitch, but it's not worth losing the girl you love."

He gave my shoulder a squeeze as he stood up from his stool and walked by me. "If you need to talk again, you know where I am."

I watched him walk away. His words moved around in my head while I finished my beer.

I spent the rest of the night mentally kicking my own ass. I felt bad for the things I'd said to Faith, and even when I pulled out her letter and read it, it still didn't anger me enough to not worry about whether or not I'd hurt her. I clutched her cross in my palm until I was sure it would puncture my skin and I'd bleed all over—bleed for her the way she swore she bled for me.

I drowned myself in vodka with Chet and Tiny when they got home and smoked so much cush that I went into my room and passed out. I had dreams of her face in pleasure. I could practically hear her moaning in my sleep. I had dreams of her body as she took me in and held me like no other woman ever had.

I woke the next morning feeling even worse. I couldn't help but hope she came back to work so we could talk things out. Obviously, there were lies floating around. I figured that out when she mentioned the letter I'd written to her. I never wrote her letter. Honestly, I hadn't even known where she was even if I wanted to send her a letter. If there really was a letter out there from me to her, it wasn't a real one. And if hers wasn't real, who's to say the letter I got from her wasn't real either?

My brain was practically smoking I was thinking so many things. Finally, I had to climb out of bed and move or I was going to make myself crazy. I needed to stop thinking for just a second and take a few deep breaths. Things were getting chaotic in my mind, and I didn't want to have a meltdown.

I went into the kitchen and pulled open the fridge. Orange juice spilled down my chest as I downed it straight out of the carton. After finding a Pop-Tart in the cabinet, I sat on a barstool and devoured it. Anything that made me feel better at that point was my friend—food was my friend.

It was then that I noticed her purse sitting on the counter. I looked around to see if maybe she'd come in when I wasn't paying attention, but she was nowhere to be seen. Everyone else was still in bed so the condo was completely quiet. If she was anywhere cleaning, I would've heard her.

I pulled the purse over to me and unzipped it. It was wrong, I knew it was wrong, but I couldn't help myself. There were so many things I wanted to know about Faith—things about the last four years of her life that I couldn't help but wonder about. Had she been in any other relationships? Was she in one now?

It wasn't a big purse, so I was surprised when I pulled out a full-sized journal. Smiley faces and crosses covered the outside cover. The binding was unraveling it had been opened and closed so much. It sounded like it was cracking when I opened it, and the pages all looked as if they'd been wet by some dark liquid.

I flipped through the pages quickly and landed on a page with a dried flower stuck in the center. The flower was old and cracking. I wondered briefly if maybe a boyfriend had given it to her. I felt bad for that thought when I read the passage and realized the flower was from Amanda's funeral. The words on the page told how Faith had felt when Amanda died and how she wouldn't have made it through without me. I felt tears sting my eyes. I could remember how she came to me and how badly I'd needed her, too.

I slipped the flower back inside the book and moved on. Flipping through the pages, I found my name a few times and every time, it had been something sweet written in there about me. I smiled to myself when I got to the page where she talked about being with me at the beach. When I found the page about the night she'd given herself to me, I had to wipe tears from my cheeks.

It was wrong to read her journal, but it was so insightful. It made me angry that I'd missed so much of Faith's life when she was such a big part of mine. If I went by these words, I was a big part of hers, too.

I flipped through a few more pages until I didn't think I could read another word. There was so much truth. She had so much love for me, yet she had walked away to keep me from going to jail. It had killed her to walk away from me. I could see that in the painful words that were written for me, blurred by stale tear drops on the old paper.

When I flipped through the pages again, a folded-up piece of paper fell out. Unfolding the paper, I looked down at the words scribbled across the page and felt shocked at what I was reading. It was a letter from me, except it wasn't. I'd never written a letter. It wasn't even my handwriting. Not to mention, the words that were written across the page were words I would've never said to Faith. I loved her—I still did. I would've never hurt her that way, and I was already feeling shitty about the way I'd been treating her.

The jagged handwriting that swept across the page looked familiar, and I was positive I knew where I'd seen it before. Rushing back into my bedroom, I grabbed my wallet and pulled out Faith's letter. I ran back into the kitchen and laid the two side by side. As I suspected, the handwriting was almost exactly the same.

Just like that, everything became so clear to me. Someone was hell-bent on keeping Faith and me apart, and I was positive I knew who that someone was. The preacher man, as holy as he pretended to be, had spun so many lies around Faith and me that we no longer knew what to believe.

I hated that bastard for taking away the only woman I'd ever loved. I hated him for taking away a future that I'd longed for my entire childhood. Not that I wasn't happy with Blow Hole, but had I been with Faith, things would've turned out much differently. I could've had a family—kids.

I'd thought a lot about finally having kids and being there for them the way my father never had been. I'd give my kids the life I never got. I'd be in their life no matter what. At least one good thing had come from being a foster kid when I was younger. Because of my time in the many foster homes, I knew exactly what not to be when I had children of my own. I knew that no matter what, I'd be a damn good father.

All of that seemed like an impossible dream. There was no way to make it better. Too many bad things had happened over the years—too many bad memories. I'd said too many things that I couldn't take back, and I wouldn't blame her if she never wanted to see my face again. My chest burned when I thought about never seeing her again. I'd lost her again, and this time I had only myself to blame.

The fact was I loved her. I'd never really stopped loving her, and when I wasn't too busy hating her, I could see that. Faith was all I ever wanted, and I was going to try with all my might to get her back.

I took a shower and got dressed. When everyone woke up and left for the day, I stayed and waited for Faith. Even if she didn't come back to work, she'd have to come back for her purse. That was another thing... Her working for me had to stop. She was the girl I loved, and I wasn't going to have her scrubbing toilets anymore.

Hours went by and still no Faith. I was starting to worry and bite my nails, which I never did anymore. I thought I was about to come out of my skin when I heard the front door open. I was sure it was probably the guys coming back, but when I turned around, I saw Faith standing there with my folded T-shirt and boxers in her hand.

She stood there like the weeping willow I'd always pictured her as. Her hair flowed around her shoulders and her big brown eyes looked wounded. I hurt her. She was hurting and it was my fault.

"I forgot my purse," she said as she turned and went toward the kitchen.

"Faith, wait. We need to talk."

"I think you said enough yesterday," she said with her back to me.

Again, I felt awful for everything I'd said to her from the moment we ran into each other again until the day before when I'd all but cussed her in the hallway.

"I'm sorry," I said easily.

Sorry had never been an easy word for me, but I truly was this time. I was so sorry for everything I'd ever said and done to her, and I wished I could take it all back.

She turned and looked at me, her eyes pulled down in confusion. "What?"

"I said I'm sorry for everything. I was an asshole to you. You didn't deserve that and I'm sorry."

Tears filled her eyes and she wiped them before they could escape.

"I just want you to know some things. One: I didn't sleep with Jenny. I was drunk and passed out. Thinking about it now and knowing that you came back and I didn't know you did makes me sick to my stomach. The last four years have been hell for me."

More tears came and she didn't stop them from falling.

"For me, too," she whispered.

I pulled out the two letters and handed them to her.

"And this is number two," I said.

She unfolded each one and read them. When she looked back up at me, she started crying. Pulling her into my arms, I held her close to me.

"Don't cry, baby. Everything's okay now."

She felt so good in my arms. It was as if the last four years never happened—like we'd just picked right up from the night she left. I'd take care of her. I'd make sure no one ever hurt her again. I had the ability to make everything perfect in her life, and I was determined to do it.

She pulled away and continued to cry.

"Everything's not okay, Finn. There are things..." She stopped. "You know what? I can't do this right now. I need time to think. I need to go and think."

She took off with her purse in hand toward the front door. Following behind her, I grabbed her hand before she could leave.

"Don't do this to me again, Faith. I need you," I said honestly.

She placed her forehead against the door and took a deep breath. When she turned my way again, I held my arms out to her and she melted into my chest.

I breathed her in and rubbed her back. She was everything I ever wanted. She looked up at me and I leaned down and softly kissed her. She kissed me back and moaned sweetly in my mouth.

Things were going great until suddenly she pulled away again. Tears streamed down her cheeks and she sniffled. I used my thumb to wipe away her tears.

"Whatever it is, we can fix it," I whispered in her hair.

That was the trigger. She pulled away completely and turned toward the door again. As she reached out for the knob, I watched her shoulders droop in defeat.

"It can't be fixed," she said sadly.

Then a thought hit me. Maybe she was already with someone else. Maybe he was good to her and she loved him. If that were the case, then my chance to find happiness would never come. If she was already taken, then I'd never be with another woman the way I was with Faith.

"Is there someone else?" I asked. The words choked me as they came out.

My chest ached with my words. I couldn't stand the thought of another man having what I wanted.

Her face went pale as she stared back at me with big brown eyes. "Something like that," she said.

And then she turned away and left. This time she slammed the door behind her. A picture of a guitar fell from the wall next to the door and broke all over the expensive flooring. It shattered into pieces exactly the way my heart did... again.

Twenty-Seven
Faith

I cried the entire drive home. Things were so screwed up and I didn't know what to do. Finn was basically trying to mend things with me and I wanted it—I wanted to be with him so bad. The only problem was I knew the minute I told him about Jimmy, he would hate me again. Either that or he'd try to take Jimmy away.

As badly as I wanted everything Finn was offering me, I couldn't take that chance—not when my child was involved.

I felt bad because Finn deserved to know about Jimmy. He deserved to be a parent just as much as I did. All the reasons that we weren't together were lies spun by my father to keep me away from Finn. Neither of us was theoretically in the wrong, and if we started pointed fingers, technically, I was the one who walked away from him.

Another thing I had to worry about was work. No way could I continue to work for the boys. I couldn't clean up for Finn, knowing everything that happened since we reunited. Plus, the more I went around him, the more likely I was to tell him about Jimmy. I just didn't know what to do. I was stuck between a rock and hard place.

When I walked in the front door, Mom was sitting on the couch. Jimmy was napping on his dinosaur sleeping bag on the floor in front of the TV.

"What's wrong? Did something happen?" she asked when she saw me crying.

I spent the next hour telling her everything. From the moment I left Finn in South Carolina to the moment I'd left him not twenty minutes before. I pulled out the two letters that I was positive my father had written and handed them to her.

She looked down at the letters and then back up at me with tear-filled eyes. Mom and I hadn't been close since I was a little girl, but since she divorced my father, she was her old self again. It was nice having a relationship with her.

"Faith. Your father didn't write these. I did," she said as a tear slipped down her cheek.

I moved away from her and my heart sank. She suddenly looked different to me. She was so quiet and godly. No way could my mother have done such a thing.

"No, Mom," I whispered.

She reached out for my hand and gripped my fingers.

"I'm so sorry. I just wanted our lives to go back to normal. I was tired of seeing you and your father argue, and I thought it was for the best. Now that I see the trouble I caused, I'm so sorry. Please forgive me."

I couldn't believe what I was hearing. It was so unlike anything my mother would do, but as a mother myself, I supposed I could see her way of thinking. Everything was a mess, and Mom and Jimmy were all I had. It was hard, but I had to forgive her. I couldn't deny a person who'd asked for forgiveness, which was why I also had to forgive Finn.

I didn't sleep that night as I snuggled in bed with my son. I held him close to me as I thought about our future and the last four years of my life. Things were hard, but I learned a lot about myself in those hard times. I learned how strong I could be when it was needed. I had to have faith that things would get better, and I had to have faith that Finn wouldn't take my baby away from me if I revealed his existence.

It felt wrong not telling him, and a part of me knew that Finn would make a wonderful father. Jimmy was a great kid and he was really missing out by not knowing him. I had to do the right thing and pray that things would work out okay. By the time I fell asleep, I decided that I was going to tell Finn about Jimmy.

The next day, after I was done at the daycare, I went to the temp agency and told Mrs. Cooper that I couldn't return back to work cleaning the condo. Thankfully, until I found something else, I still had the daycare, and Mrs. Karen, the daycare director, even promised to give me more hours.

I went to work the rest of that week still trying to figure out how to tell Finn about Jimmy. I knew it was wrong to run out on him without explanation, but I freaked out and went about it completely the wrong way.

That night, I watched some adult TV and saw parts of a Blow Hole concert. Finn looked amazing on stage. His voice had only gotten better since I'd last heard him sing. I watched and wished he was there singing sweetly to me the way he had when we were younger. I fell asleep with a dreamy smile on my face and thoughts of the past.

The following week, I finally got up the nerve to tell him, but when I got to his door, there was no one at the condo. I no longer had a key to get in, and if I did, I wouldn't have gone in anyway. I left thinking that maybe fate had intervened. Maybe I wasn't supposed to tell Finn. Maybe I should wait and spend some time with him first.

By the following week, I was already missing Finn, as if the last four years apart had never existed. I'd stop by every now and again, but no one was ever home. I just assumed they were out doing shows like they used to when I worked there.

Money from the daycare wasn't great, but it was enough to keep my head above the bills. I was even able to pick up a few fun things at the grocery store for Jimmy when he asked for it, which wasn't often since he never asked for anything. I was pretty sure I'd raised the best kid in the world.

One day after leaving the daycare with Jimmy, I rode by Finn's place to see if maybe anyone was home. If so, then I could take Jimmy home to Mom and come back. Still, there was no one. I set off for home, feeling deflated and rundown. I'd finally gotten the nerve to tell Finn the truth, but he was never home.

When I got home, we ate dinner with Mom, and then I gave Jimmy a bath and dressed him in his thermal cartoon pajamas. Putting on his dinosaur movie, I left him in the bedroom with his new dinosaur mask. It was the newest thing I'd purchased for him with my most recent paycheck. There was nothing funnier than seeing a tiny three-year-old running around with cartoon pajamas and a big dinosaur mask. He loved it, though, and that was all that mattered to me.

While he was occupied, I took a long, hot shower and took the time to shave my legs. After getting dressed for bed, I ran the brush through my long hair and went into the kitchen to get a glass of water. Mom had already gone to bed so the only light left on in the apartment was the living room lamp.

I turned everything off in the kitchen and made my way into the living room to check the locks and turn off the lamp. I was about to turn it off when a knock on the door startled me.

It was late and we weren't in a great neighborhood. Opening doors all willy-nilly around where we lived could get you killed. I peeked out the curtain, thinking I'd get a look at who it was, but I couldn't get a good view. Finally, they moved and I saw Finn's arm.

My heart started beating super fast. This wasn't the way I wanted him to find out, and if Jimmy came out of his room, there was no way I could deny him. Not to mention, Jimmy looked just like Finn. He'd see him and know instantly that Jimmy was his son.

He knocked again, and instead of risking Jimmy hearing and coming out of the room, I quickly opened the door. Finn's eyes moved from my head to my toes, and then he shyly smiled.

"I know it's late, but I needed to see you," he said.

I could tell it had taken a lot for him to admit that. He looked so incredibly handsome in his dark-wash jeans and black long-sleeved shirt. He leaned against the doorjamb and shattered me with his dimpled smile.

"We just got back in town. I missed you. Did you miss me at all?" he asked sweetly.

Did I ever...

"I did," I whispered.

"Well, aren't you going to invite me in?"

I wanted to. I wanted to so bad, but I couldn't take that risk. Jimmy was just a few rooms away and still awake. I could hear him softly singing the music that was playing on his movie.

"Right now's not really a good time," I said.

His face dropped and he shook his head like he understood. He moved closer and ran a single finger down my cheek as if he were memorizing me.

"I'm too late," he said sadly.

He looked as if he was on the verge of tears, and my heart broke for him.

"What do you mean?" I asked.

"You're with someone else. I'm too late."

It took a minute for his words to sink in, and when they did, I almost laughed out loud. He thought I was with someone else and that was so far from happening it wasn't even funny. I'd never been with anyone but Finn. I hadn't even been on a date with anyone else, much less lived with someone else.

"Does he treat you good?" He looked me straight in the eye with a crushed expression.

"There's no one else, Finn."

I smiled at the relief that moved across his expression.

"Then it's me? Have you still not forgiven me?"

It bothered me that he even said it that way. I was the one that should've been asking for forgiveness. I was the one who was harboring a massive secret that could change his life forever.

"There's nothing to forgive. Finn, can we talk tomorrow? There are things I want to talk to you about, but right now's not a good time."

My nerves were jumping around inside me. Any minute, Jimmy could come around the corner and any minute, things between Finn and me would go downhill just that quickly. He could take my son on the spot. He was freaking Jimmy Finn for God's sake. He was a rock god as far as some people were concerned, and I was positive he was worth millions.

"Sure, do you want to...?"

He stopped talking when Jimmy jumped from behind me. He was wearing his dinosaur mask and growling at Finn playfully. His fingers were bent as he pretended he had massive claws and he pushed them out toward Finn as if he were about to claw him to death.

"I'm a scary dinosaur. You better run for your life!" He growled cutely.

My heart stopped as I stared down at my son and prayed he didn't take off his mask.

I grabbed his shoulder and turned him around toward the bedroom.

"Sweetie, go back to bed please. I'll be there in just a bit," I said sternly.

His shoulders slumped.

"But, but..." he whined.

"What did I say?" I asked sweetly.

The truth was I was about to lose it. My nerves had hit their breaking point and I was about to snap and slam the door in Finn's face out of fear.

I could feel Finn's eyes burning into the side of my face. Sweat began to gather above my brow and it felt like it was going to drip into my eyes and blind me.

"But, Mommy, I miss you," Jimmy said sweetly.

"I miss you too, baby boy. I'll be in there in just a minute okay?"

I felt like I was going to pass out. This was not happening. No way was this really happening.

"Okay!" Jimmy said happily as he ran back to our room.

A few seconds later, I heard the springs of my mattress when he began to jump up and down on the bed.

Finn looked down at me with hurt-filled blue eyes. His eyebrows pinched down in confusion.

"You have a son." He stated the obvious.

Panic rolled through my body again, and I felt as if my heart was going to beat out of my chest. My throat felt so dry that I couldn't swallow. I had to push out my words.

"I do," I rasped. "He's the only reason I'd ever scrub toilets." I tried to lighten the situation.

It didn't work.

Finn continued to stare back at me like I was a different person. His eyes moved across my face like I was a puzzle he was trying to figure out. The hurt in his eyes burned me and I wanted to look away, but I couldn't. I could see the gears in his head working, and I waited for smoke to come from his ears.

I couldn't take his scrutiny anymore. I needed him gone so I could breathe and have time to think things through. My life was about to take another massive shift, and I didn't know if I could handle that right now.

"We'll talk about it more tomorrow. I really need to get him to bed," I said as I grabbed the knob on the door.

Finn was suspiciously quiet, and I was starting to worry. He opened his mouth to say something but stopped to swallow. Again, he reached out and fingered a piece of my hair.

"You know, I used to dream about having a family with you," he said sadly. My heart broke when a salty tear slid down his cheek. My fingers ached to capture it and smooth it away. "But now I can see that you already have a family of your own.

I'm so happy for you, Faith. I only wish I hadn't been stupid enough to let you go."

I had to tell him. I couldn't do this to him anymore. He needed to know the truth. I opened my mouth to tell him to come in, but his face froze and turned three different colors before settling on a ghostly white. He was staring just beyond my shoulder as if the answers to all of life's great mysteries resided in my living room.

I didn't have to look back to know who he was staring at. I knew and I could only imagine the thoughts that were exploding his mind.

"Mommy, I broke my dinosaur mask," Jimmy said behind me with a sniffle.

When I turned around, he was standing there without his mask, wearing a big frown. His blue eyes popped and in that moment, he'd never look more like his daddy.

I turned back around quickly and looked at Finn. He looked back at me with tears in his eyes.

"Faith? Is there anything you need to tell me?"

And then I broke down in tears. There was no going back. I had to fess up and have faith in Finn.

TABATHA VARGO

TWENTY-EIGHT

FINN

I missed her. It had been weeks since she walked out of my life again, and I wanted her back. I didn't care about anything else. I wanted Faith. I wanted a life with her. Nothing else mattered. I'd be a tied-down puss if it meant having her with me every day the way she should've been years before.

We played three shows and every show I played, all I could think about was getting back to California and talking to Faith. We needed to fix things. I didn't know what she meant when she said, "Something like that," but I needed to know what hell was going on and where we stood.

When I got back to the condo, I wasted no time calling Mrs. Cooper at the temp agency. She'd called and left me a voicemail telling me that we'd have to find a new maid since Faith had quit. I figured she would.

I wasn't sure how I managed it, but somehow I talked Mrs. Cooper into giving me Faith's address. I knew it was weird just popping up at her place unannounced, but a man in love did crazy things.

By the time I could leave, it was already dark out. Once I typed her address into my GPS, I was on my way. As I drove, I slowly made my way into the rough parts of town. It wasn't anything new for me to be in the ghetto, but Faith had no business living in a place like that. If anything, I felt more comfortable in the rough parts. I was raised in the places like that. Faith, not so much.

I pulled up to a broken-down apartment building. Broken blinds hung in windows and dead plants littered the concrete stairs and paths to the apartment doors. Little kids ran around outside in diapers while their moms sat on cell phones and yelled at them from across the yard. It was way past any kids' bedtime. It was crazy to see them running around outside in the dark.

The pool in the center of the courtyard was green with fast food trash and beer cans floating in the center. And the smell was a mix of raw sewage and unwashed ass. The place was a real shithole, and I was angry that Faith was living in such a place. She deserved so much more than this, and if I could, I was going to give her more—so much more.

When I found her apartment number, I tapped on the front door and waited. I heard someone fumbling with the blinds and then nothing. After a minute, I tapped again. It was then that the front door opened. Faith was standing there more beautiful than she'd ever been. Her long hair was wet from her shower and she had on the cutest pink-and-blue pajamas.

She was everything I ever wanted in my life, and I was there to make her mine, but something about her was off. She seemed nervous about something and that made me nervous.

When her son came out in a big blue dinosaur mask, I could hardly believe my eyes. Everything made sense in that moment. The crazy job, the no longer living with her father, everything. My heart broke in that moment as well when I realized that everything I wanted to do with Faith she'd already done with another man.

I wanted her to have my son. I wanted to buy a house together and do the whole domesticated thing. I wanted that more than anything, and my chance was gone. I was never going to get what I wanted, and I wasn't sure how I was going to take it.

My entire life shifted when I saw her son without his mask. The boy looked familiar, like I'd seen him so many times in my dreams, but I was positive this was the first time I'd seen the child. He reached over and grabbed Faith's hand and hid behind her hip. He stared up at me shyly before disappearing behind her completely.

I looked back up at Faith. Her face was covered in shock; her eyes wide as if I'd just caught her doing something wrong. She reached over and sheltered the boy by her side. Again, he peeked around at me and then his eyes caught mine. Baby blue irises stared back at me. Familiar eyes—eyes I'd seen every day for my entire life... my eyes.

"Finn, meet your son," Faith said with tears in her eyes.

TABATHA VARGO

She sounded a million miles away, as if she were speaking through another universe. My mind fumbled over her words as I tried to figure out what she was saying. Nothing was registering. My eyes were glued to the boy who was staring back at me.

He had on thermal pajamas. His caramel-colored hair was a mess, as if he'd been running his fingers through it. He was tiny, so tiny that I could lift him with one hand and hold him in one arm. He was a stranger to me, but he was the most beautiful thing I'd ever seen in my life.

My mind was buzzing and I felt dizzy. I couldn't remember ever feeling so dizzy. I was staring at the woman I loved and my son, and while I knew I should've been angry beyond words that I hadn't been there from the start, I couldn't help but feel so much happiness that my heart burned, about to burst.

"My son?" I squeaked.

I reached out and grabbed the doorframe to keep myself from falling. A piece of jagged wood cut into my palm, but I felt nothing but the love that was filling my heart at a rapid pace.

My son stared up at me and then looked at Faith like he didn't understand what was happening. I longed to pick him up and hold him close to me. I wanted nothing more than to squeeze him and never let him go.

"Yes. I didn't want you to find out this way, but there's no going back now. I'm sorry, Finn. I hope you can forgive me."

I looked at her different now. She wasn't just the girl I loved anymore; she was the mother of my child. Mother, a sainted creature who'd breathed life into the world, who'd breathed life into my son.

I closed my eyes and imagined what she must've looked like during her pregnancy. I envisioned her with a white flowing dress, her stomach protruding and full of life. Her hair catching the wind as she softly caressed her stomach and spoke sweetly to my baby within.

A heated tear leaked out of the corner of my eye and rolled down my cheek. Another followed close behind, and I knew I'd never be able to stop them.

"Jimmy, baby, please go in our room. Mommy will be there in a bit to tuck you in, okay?"

I smiled down at my son as he took off across the living room and down the hallway. His tiny feet smacked against the floor and warmed my heart.

"Finn, I know what you're thinking, but please don't freak out on me. I was going to tell you. I just didn't know how. He's all I have. The only thing I live for. Please don't try to take him away from me."

I stared back at her in confusion. I'd just gotten used to the fact that I had a child. Nothing she said was making it through my thick brain fog. I stared longingly toward the door the boy had run through.

"He's beautiful," I whispered.

She smiled softly and took my hand. It warmed my palm, so I linked our fingers together. When she pulled, I allowed her to guide me into her apartment. The door squeaked closed behind us before clicking into place.

My knees gave up finally from the shock, so I sat on her couch as she locked the front door and put the chain up.

"Of course he's beautiful. He's ours." She smiled over her shoulder at me. I slid over when she took a seat beside me. "So what now?" she asked nervously.

I looked down at her hands and noticed she was wringing them so hard that her fingers were turning purple. Reaching out, I laid my hand on top of hers to make her stop.

"What do you mean what now?"

She looked up and her brown eyes connected with mine. There was so much fear in there that I wanted to pull her into my arms and smooth it away.

"Well, now that you know, we need to get Jimmy used to you. I know you're going to want to see him, but I think we should get him used to the idea of you before we start with any kind of visitation. That is, if you want it." She tucked a strand of hair behind her ear and then sighed. "But most importantly, Finn, there's to be no drinking and drugs around him. Promise me."

My heart sang when she called him Jimmy. I wanted to kiss her for naming my son after me, but at the same time, I didn't comprehend what she was saying. Visitation? Drugs and drinking? None of that mattered to me.

"I'm done with drugs and drinking," I said sternly.

And I was. I had a son—an impressionable son that I wanted to shield from everything bad in the world.

"And as far as visitation goes, that won't be necessary."

Fear filled her eyes again and I could see her breathing change as she started to panic. She twisted her fingers again, making the purple shade return. Again, I laid my hand over her fingers to make her stop.

"Why? Are you going to try to take him?" she asked with wide eyes.

"No. Because once I buy a house, y'all are coming home with me."

And they were. I wouldn't have it any other way. The woman I loved and my son were not going to live in some shitty apartment. He was going to have anything he wanted, and she was never going to scrub another toilet again.

"What? But, Finn, we don't even—"

I stopped her with my finger. Her warm breath tickled my palm, and I smiled down at her.

"You're coming home with me. I love you and I love Jimmy. You're my family and I want to take care of you. Let me take care of you, Faith. It's all I've ever wanted."

A tear slid down her cheek as she shook her head yes, and I captured it with my thumb.

"Yes," she whispered against my finger.

I moved in slowly and replaced my finger with my lips. She threw her arms around my neck and kissed me back. I'd never been so happy. Everything I wanted was in my grasp, and I was determined to never let it slip away again.

I pulled back and rested my forehead against hers. Reaching in my pocket, I pulled out her cross. It warmed my palm as usual, and the blunt tips dug into my skin. I held her hand and opened her fingers. Setting the tiny cross in her palm, I closed her fingers around it and gently squeezed.

"I believe this belongs to you," I said with a smile.

She opened her hand and ran her fingers over the cross.

"You kept it. I can't believe you kept it." She sniffled.

I tilted up her chin so I could look her in the eye. "I used to hold it every day and imagine it was you. I kept it with me everywhere I went. I really do love you, Faith. I always have and always will."

Another tear dripped down her face.

"I love you, too, Finn. Forever."

It's funny how life works. Sometimes you have to jump hurdles to get the things you want. I'd spent my entire life waiting for Faith to come to me. I'd jumped more hurdles than most, but it was worth it in the end.

I wanted something to believe in—something that held me to the earth when I thought I'd fly away into the nothing. I had no idea it would be a woman that made me feel that way, but I found happiness in her smile and peace in her eyes. I found comfort in her arms and joy in her kiss. She was mine. I'd looked for it my entire life, but finally, I'd found faith, and it took me a while to realize that I didn't have faith, Faith had me.

Epilogue

Finn

"Daddy, where do babies come from?" Little Jimmy asked in front of everyone at the table.

He was so smart and he was constantly asking questions that I never knew how to answer.

Having Thanksgiving dinner with the entire band and their families on top of my family and Faith's mom made for a big table full of people. They all looked at me as Jimmy waited for an answer.

Mom smiled to hide the fact that she wanted to laugh at me. She loved Jimmy so much. She'd never been so happy as she was the day I brought him home to meet her. Her and Rick spent a lot of time spoiling the hell out of him, but he loved his Grandma and Pop Pop.

Chet burst into laughter and Tiny smacked him on the arm. I gave them both my *shut the fuck up* face. I looked over to Zeke for a little bit of help, but he and Patience just sat there with their lips glued together to keep from laughing.

"Babies come from their mommy's belly," Faith answered calmly.

I reached down and grabbed her hand. She was always so calm with Jimmy and always had all the answers. She was the perfect mother and wife. I couldn't imagine life without her. Of course, in her profession, she had to be patient. She was a part-time medical assistant until she was done with nursing school. Being a nurse was going to be hard work, and she'd be perfect when it came to dealing with some of the crazy people.

I was happy when she agreed not to work during her pregnancy, but I knew she loved it and more than anything, I wanted her to be happy. The day she walked across the stage and got her high school diploma, her smile had been nothing short of luminous. She never gave up on her dream to graduate and go to college, and I'd never been more proud of her.

She was so strong and independent and I loved that about her, but I also loved that she knew when to let me take care of her because I wanted to for the rest of my life.

I reached down and ran my palm across her protruding stomach. Our first little girl was on her way in two months, and I could hardly wait to meet her. The thought of having a daughter scared the shit out of me. Mostly because I knew there were men like me all over the world. I prayed every night that my little girl never ran into any of them. I had no problem whatsoever choking the life out of anyone who hurt one of my kids.

Little Jimmy dropped the subject of babies and we all ate dinner. The table chatter buzzed as we filled in our families about road life and the different towns we visited.

After dinner, we spent time with everyone in the family room before saying our good-byes. I loved the holidays because it meant spending time with family, but I hated to see them go. I was amazed at the amount of love that surrounded me. As a young boy who grew up with no one, I ended up with some of the best people in my life.

We weren't the conventional family by any means. I'd been adopted by my mom and together we adopted the rest of the band, but we were closer than most families, and they meant the world to me.

Later that night, after everyone had gone home and we finally got Jimmy to bed. I snuggled up to my beautiful wife and held her close to me. I would never get enough of her—never. She looked even more beautiful pregnant, and I couldn't seem to keep my hands off of her.

"I have something for you," she said as she turned in my arms to face me.

Her stomach pressed into mine and I felt the baby kick against me. My heart warmed and I couldn't help but smile.

"Oh, do you?" I flirted back.

"Yep. Do you want it now or do you want to wait?"

I loved it when she was playful.

"I want it now please."

She rolled me onto my back and straddled my lap.

"Are you sure?" she asked.

I reached up and cupped her full breasts. Her entire body had filled out, and I loved occupying my hands with every part of her. She was warm—filled with so much sweetness, covered with lovely soft skin.

"Oh yeah, I'm positive."

She leaned down and kissed me, and I lost my hands in her long, soft hair.

"You can have me on one condition," she said with a devious smile.

"Anything," I said as I nibbled her bottom lip.

"Say something dirty."

I laughed as she used my own words against me, but I wasn't like Faith used to be. I had no problem whatsoever saying something dirty. So I rolled her onto her back and kissed her hard, and then I spent the rest of the night showing my wife exactly how dirty I could be.

Blow Hole Lyrics

Death by Faith

Passionate and fleeting
I live to swim in you
Hold me down, can't stop the bleeding
Devotion breaking through
Worshiping your depths
Your presence lends its heat
Reminding me what's left
Of the man you left in me
Blindly trusting ways
Loyal hands won't hold you high
Convicted by your grace
In a world I can't rely

Chorus:
I wish for you I'd only bled
You took more than I could give
My insides so cold and dead

My wounded eyes no longer live
I tried to run so far away
Since my heart's no longer safe
I can't deny you here today
You murdered me with lack of faith.

Reverence has broken
Exposing breath and bone
Faithless hearts have now spoken
Leaving me to breathe alone
Beliefs unbinding hope
Memories bring sanity
Finding ways to deal and cope
Searching for what's left of me
You taught me how to trust
Then burned me with the lesson
Passion masked by lust
Desire was your weapon
Closed eyes no longer blink
Bliss dies and I'm unsure
The devil in soft pink
In you I found rapture

Chorus

TABATHA VARGO

ACKNOWLEDGMENTS

This is my fifth book and this is still one of the hardest parts for me. If I thanked every single person who has helped me over the course of writing this book, I would be writing another book.

First and foremost, I want to thank my husband Matthew. He has taught me everything I know about love and romance. He's my biggest supporter and always has been. Thank you, baby, from the depths of my soul. I love you.

Melissa Andrea, thank you for listening to me ramble. You're crazy and so am I. Together we make a hell of a woman. You're amazing and I'm so glad we became such great friends. I love you, Mel!

To Julia Hendrix, thank you for everything you've done for me over the last year. You've been entirely too good to me. You've helped me so much and you've kept Matthew sane, as well. I'm so happy to have such an amazing friend on my side. Thank you. Love you, girl!

To Kelly Robinson, for just being awesome and lending me an ear when I need it. You rock and I'm happy to you call you my friend. I love you, chick!

To Paula Kaesberg, aka the speed reader, for being the first person to read Finding Faith and for giving me your honest opinion. Thank you for all of your support over the last year. I really appreciate it.

Regina Wamba... Seriously, do I need to say anything else after that name? I love you, chick. You're amazing at what you do and I'm so glad to call you my cover designer as well as my friend.

Cassie McCown, my sweet and wonderful editor, you're the most patient person alive. Thank you for picking through my garbage and finding the gold that lies beneath. You rock, chick!

To my amazing street team, you guys are freaking amazing. The support you give me blows my mind and I'm so thankful for each and every one of you. If I could, I'd give you all great big squeezing hugs.

To every blogger/page administrator who has posted or shared anything for me since I've started publishing, thank you. I can't stress it enough how much you guys mean to me. You guys supported me from day one and that's more valuable to me than gold. I send you all bear hugs and love.

To all my friends and family who have been supportive of my writing throughout the years. Thank you. I love you.

To my daughter, Ashlynn, who's my inspiration for everything I do. Mommy loves you to the moon and back. You're my life.

And finally to YOU, my wonderful readers, you guys are beyond amazing and supportive. You send me the best feedback and help me to hone my craft and make it the best it can be. Thank you for taking a chance on a new author and turning me into a USA TODAY BESTSELLER. I love you all more than you can imagine. Thank you!

TABATHA VARGO

Printed in Great Britain
by Amazon.co.uk, Ltd.,
Marston Gate.